MORTAL TETHER

CANDICE JARRETT

Identifiers: ISBN 979-8-9891033-0-0 (paperback) | ISBN 979-8-9891033-4-8 (hardcover) | ISBN 979-8-9891033-3-1 (EPUB)

Library of Congress Control Number: 2023917270

First Edition, October 2023

Published by ElectraFox

Las Vegas, Nevada

ElectraFox.com

Description: MORTAL TETHER is YA post-apocalyptic dystopian science fiction with an all-teen cast suitable for ages 13+ up. Its core themes include how fear-driven tribalization disintegrates society, the fight to preserve innocence in the brutal world our parents built, as well as explorations of faith and family from a coming-of-age perspective.

PRAISE FOR MORTAL TETHER

WINNER: TOP PICK 2024 READER READY AWARDS

"MORTAL TETHER is an **electrifyingly original debut** that is paced like an anxious doomsday clock. If you're searching for **a powerful new voice in literature**, just follow Candice Jarrett. She knows the neighborhood."

David Buzan - Author of In the Lair of Legends

"Jarrett has NAILED IT – and has raised the bar for YA science fiction writers everywhere! Once "bitten," you won't be able to put this book down!"

Michael Fletcher - Author of To Hunt a Holy Man

"An unpredictable and perilous journey that redefines the ties that formulate the meaning of family. This compelling novel belongs at the **top of your reading list!"**

Karen Neary Smithson - Author of Death in Disguise

"Not only an entertaining read, but an important one. The fragility of life, insidious way that power corrupts, and **potential of the human spirit to overcome seemingly impossible odds** —these are some of the major takeaways from this fast-moving story."

Elizabeth Hutchison Bernard - Author of Sisters of Castle Leod

For Dolores Valdez
My heart aches you never got to hold
this book in your hands. It's a wound only
soothed by the countless treasured moments we
shared, laughing and dreaming together.
Thank you for believing in me.
"You, I love."

1
5
6
3 2
WELCOME TO COLLINS
1 Amaia's house
2 Food Eagle
3 Golding's Hardware
4 Collins Jr/Sr High School
5 The University
6 St. Mary's
N
W
E
S
4

Don't look.

Mom always said that whenever we passed a nasty car accident on the interstate. She'd warn me that a moment's curiosity could haunt me for a lifetime, that some things were so horrible you'd never unsee them. I didn't need much convincing. I've always been the kind of kid to cover my eyes until the scary part was over anyway.

But not this time.

He loosened his tie. She pushed back her hair. Two sets of pale lips parted, black tar gushing down their chins. For a split second, their faces weren't flesh but stone, screaming gargoyles of skin and concrete. A crack cut its way down the center of the guy's forehead…

I should've listened to my mom.

Instead, I dug my fingernails into the living room carpet as two empty chairs spun like pinwheels behind the news desk. The anchors who'd sat there a moment ago now hovered around the studio lights; their bodies had combusted into clouds of ash. Some of it splattered on the camera lens, making my TV screen look dirty from the inside.

"What's this garbage?" Carlos slapped his meaty palm over my eyes. "You'll get nightmares watching shows like that."

"Get off, *freak*!" I pried his sticky fingers off my face and reached unsuccessfully for the remote he'd swiped. "My only *nightmare* is that you'll bomb your SAT next year, no college will take you, and I'll be stuck with you and your gross-ness til I graduate!"

"Ha. You'll miss me when I'm gone." My brother smirked, sucking Cheeto dust off his thumb. "Better enjoy it while it lasts, *hermanita.*"

I fought the urge to poke him in the eye. It would only end with me getting thrown in a headlock again. Ever since Carlos turned sixteen, my big brother had the power of super strength. Mom keeps reminding us it's *puberty*, and Carlos *hates* that word. So, naturally, I hurl it at him like grenades whenever I really want to do some damage.

With two years and one month between us, hand-to-hand combat with my brother had recently resembled a chipmunk fighting a gorilla. A sharp tongue was the only weapon I had left.

"I'm telling Dad you hit me." I smiled just enough to plant the seed of doubt in his mind I'd actually do it. (I wouldn't… probably.)

"But… I didn't hit you!" Carlos' voice shot up an octave and honked like a bicycle horn. He cleared his throat and forced it lower. "Amaia, it's not cool to make up stuff like that. *Jodóna!*"

A thrill sparkled in my eye. He'd just slipped up. Bad.

"Mom told you not to call me 'jodóna' anymore!" I grinned wickedly. "She said she'd wash your mouth out with soap next time!"

"But you are a *pain in the butt*," Carlos protested. "I'm just calling it like it is. Besides, it's my word against yours, *jodóna!*"

"Hope you like the taste of Tide pods!" I jabbed him in the gut with my elbow.

My brother snaked his biceps around me and lifted my feet clear off the carpet. I squeaked and squirmed to get loose, but I was born with the upper body strength of a hamster. What was Carlitos trying to do, hug me to death?

No. This tough-guy routine couldn't fool me. He was 6-foot-2 and built like Thor, but my brother was shaking like a leaf. He could have simply changed the channel, but he'd shut the whole TV off. Normally, I'd delight in calling him a scaredy cat, but I wasn't in the mood. Every time I blinked, those exploding bodies were stuck on instant replay behind my eyelids. It was freaky seeing those people pretend to die like that, even if it was just special effects.

If this was someone's idea of a joke, it wasn't funny. Halloween was still a week away! What if there were little kids watching? Mom would write a strongly worded letter to the station. The whole thing ticked me off so bad, I might just sign my name too.

For the record, I was totally not scared. But all the news outlets ranting over the past few months about the *'end of the world'* had finally gotten under my skin. My brother's annoying bear hug was actually making me feel the teeniest bit better.

Of course, I'd never tell *him* that.

"Ok, *Carlitos*." I patted his back condescendingly. "Ten more minutes, then we can watch your dumb sports or something, ok? I just want to see if those people come back..."

"YOU'RE NOT WATCHING IT!" Carlos dumped me on my feet and puffed out his chest like a balloon inflated with machismo. "What part of *Mom-and-Dad-left-me-in-charge* don't you get?"

"Fine!" I snapped. "But what do you think *Mom-and-Dad* will say when I show them this bruise I got from you crushing me just now?" I inspected my shoulder, knowing full well there was nothing there. "Dad will probably give you one to match."

Carlos opened his mouth to say something snippy but never got the chance.

Outside, the crash of crunching metal and shattered glass interrupted our fight. Carlos tossed me behind him and bolted to the front door, whipping it open. I draped myself over the back of the sofa and pressed my nose to the living room window to get a peek at the accident. Did tires squeal? Did a car horn blast? Maybe I missed it…

Face smushed against the windowpane, I immediately recognized whose car that was smashed into the front porch of the McGregors' house. Before we knew it, Carlos and I were both racing barefoot across the slick grass of our front lawn and out into the street.

Wooden slats stuck out every which way like a giant's game of pickup sticks, but a beat-up silver Hyundai with a red bumper was wedged underneath the pile. The yellow blinker flashed over and over, an SOS screaming for help.

"*Brit!*" Carlos went from zero to full panic seeing his pretty blonde girlfriend behind the wheel. Boards snapped as he peeled back splintered planks with his bare hands.

Thick red blood oozed from Brit's nostril and trickled past her lips. Her cheerleader's sweater should have been white and crimson, our school colors, but now it was gray and grimy with only the outline of the block letters 'CHS' visible on her chest through a thick coating of ash.

Carlos pried away the last slat and yanked open the driver side door.

"Are you hurt?" He reached over her lap to unbuckle the seatbelt. Brit was shaking and sobbing as tears dotted her pleated mini skirt.

Sad clowns wore happier makeup. Twin rivers of mascara painted two daggers down her cheeks. Highlighter still lit up the tip of her nose, but her over-lined lipstick had been smeared into a frown while splotchy blue shadow ringed her eyes.

Brit's brain was even more screwed up than her face. Her words made zero sense, like my abuela after she'd had way too much wine. For a split second, it almost-kind-of-sort-of sounded like Brit was trying to say, "*Everyone is dead.*"

Carlos didn't respond to her hysterical nonsense but lifted her in his arms and away from the wrecked Hyundai.

Our street was quieter than a graveyard: no cars, no people, not even a stray cat. I know our neighbors are retired old crones who go to sleep at 5pm, but seriously? Why hadn't anyone else come to help? There's no way they didn't hear the accident. The noise was so loud, it could have woken the dead.

I shivered. October was too chilly to be outside with no shoes or jacket. Gray flakes whirled in the breeze, though it wasn't cold enough for snow yet. Those were the ashes people had been so upset about these past few months. Nobody knew where they came from. Weather people said they messed with radar so the source couldn't be tracked. The ashes made everything look dirty, and Dad's been grumbling he's had to waste time and water hosing off our house every day.

"Everyone is dead!" Brit sobbed into Carlos' shoulder.

"Who died?" I asked.

She glared at me as if I'd accused her of something, which I only occasionally did and never to her face.

"Everyone," Brit said. "They're all dead! Didn't you hear me? *Everyone is dead!*"

The shrill pitch of her voice echoed and bounced like a basketball off the houses around us. Mom wouldn't want us hanging out in the street with everything that's been going on.

Brit wiped her bloody nose on her dirty sleeve, leaving a gray smear across her cheek like you'd get on your forehead on Ash Wednesday. Did she lose her contacts? Her eyes blinked funny like she couldn't focus on my brother's face.

"Amaia, call an ambulance," Carlos said. "She hit her head!"

"You're not listening!" Brit shoved him so hard he lumbered three steps back, but the cheerleader couldn't steady herself and collapsed onto the grass in a heap. "We were in the third quarter! Everyone in the stands and even the coach... all the adults... they all... they all just... *exploded*. My parents..." Her voice trailed off. "I got in the car. I didn't know where else to go."

"But you don't even have your learner's permit," I said, not about to be fooled into believing her dumb story. It was probably another trick to make me look stupid again.

"*¡Callate la boca!*" Carlos growled as he ushered me toward the house. "My phone is charging in my room. Call that ambulance now!"

How dare he just tell me to *shut my mouth*?! That was the last straw.

"I'm going to call Mom and Dad," I proclaimed in my bravest voice as I teetered in the doorway.

"I'm so tired." Brit groaned and rolled her head in her hands. Carlos lifted her like a doll into his arms again and carried her over the threshold.

"Does your neck hurt?" he asked as he laid Brit down on the sofa.

Mom said Brit and Carlos couldn't be alone in our house unless I was with them, probably to stop them from kissing. Brit hated me for it. The feeling was mutual. Still, I didn't want to be blamed for not calling help if Brit really was hurt, so I marched up to Carlos' smelly room and snatched the phone charging on his desk.

I dialed 9-1-1.

How many times was it supposed to ring before someone answered? I hung up and dialed again. Now busy? Dialed again. Still busy?!

I dragged my feet across the carpet, stopping at the top of the stairs. Carlos and Brit's voices drifted up from the living room below; so, I tiptoed my way to the middle landing and peeked around the corner to spy.

The cheerleader's knuckles were whiter than the tissue in her trembling fist. My brother held a bag of frozen corn on her head while Brit babbled like an airhead.

"The girls in my cheer squad... the players... even the marching band.... kids were screaming. Somebody said it was a bomb. I went to look for my parents, but I couldn't see. There was too much dust in the air. When I got to the bleachers, there wasn't anyone there, just piles of clothes and shoes and Dad's DSLR. The car keys were in my dad's pants pocket. He was just ashes… He's still on my hands… His ashes are still…"

"Amaia!" Carlos made eye contact immediately. How did he even know I was on the landing? I was perfectly quiet…

"9-1-1 won't answer," I shot back before he could accuse me of anything. "I called a hundred times!"

My brother tossed the frozen corn on the end table.

"I'll drive her to the hospital on Dad's motorcycle," he said. "Amaia, hide up in the attic and stay there 'til I get back."

"You can't take Dad's bike! He doesn't want you to drive it!" I whipped out the phone and tapped Dad's name in Carlos' favorites. My brother shot to his feet and bounded up the stairs in two leaps, but it was already ringing on speaker.

Dad didn't answer.

We both frowned as voicemail picked up.

"That's weird," Carlos muttered, and I forked over his phone.

"Call Mom," I said. Mom always picked up.

His fingers were lightning fast, though his hands shook like crazy.

Mom didn't answer.

My eyes slid over to the sofa. Brit cradled her head in the crook of her elbow with her ponytail flopped over her face.

"No, no, no, no!" Carlos raced down the stairs three at a time and propped her upright. "Don't go to sleep, ok? You need to stay awake."

"I'm so tired," Brit moaned.

Next thing I knew, I was in the kitchen lifting a set of keys off the hook hanging by the garage door. Dad would be so mad. I'd be grounded until I graduated. But Brit really was hurt. She needed help and nobody was coming. I marched back into the living room and dangled the keys in front of Carlos' face as he cradled the girl whose eyes were rolling back in her head.

"There's only room for two," my brother said.

"Just take Brit and get out of here."

He laid the woozy cheerleader back on the sofa and grabbed me by the wrist.

"No way!" I shrieked, but my brother was already dragging me upstairs and yanking on the rope to the attic's trapdoor. "You can't make me go up there, psycho!"

"The hospital's not that far," Carlos said. "I'll drop Brit off then come right back for you. I promise."

"But why can't I just wait downstairs?" I tried to swallow the rising lump in my throat as he prodded me up the ladder.

"You need to hide," Carlos said. "Just in case."

"In case what?"

"You saw those people on TV." He lowered his voice. "What if… what if what Brit said really did… you know… happen?"

"Don't be an *idiot*." I glared down at him through the bright rectangle in the attic floor. "It was only special effects. Besides, you said it yourself: Brit hit her head. That's why she's crazy!"

"You're right." Carlos did his peace-offering smile. "But Mom and Dad will kill me if they find out I left you home alone. I don't have time to argue. Just wait up there until I get back."

"But it's cold up here."

"Ugh, fine." Carlos peeled off his football hoodie and tossed it up to me.

"I don't want your stinky sweatshirt! It smells like B.O." I curled my nose up in disgust and dropped his hoodie to the floor.

"Jodóna!" Carlitos raked his hands through his hair. "You really are a total pain in the butt, Amaia. You know that?"

"Thirty minutes," I said. "Or I'm coming down, and Mom and Dad will make your coach bench you for the rest of the season!"

"Forty-five!" My brother folded up the ladder and snapped the door to the ceiling shut. His muffled voice vibrated through the floor as he added, "In case I hit traffic!"

"In case I hit traffic," I parroted under my breath.

His footsteps faded, and I was alone.

Outside, the temperature did a nosedive.

The blanket I'd found to wrap around my shoulders stank like mothballs, but I was too chicken to go downstairs to snatch the quilt off my bed. Brit's stupid story set my teeth on edge. No way was I stepping one toe out of this attic until Mom and Dad were back from their date night.

Carlos' hoodie laid in a heap on my feet, but I'd rather shove sauerkraut up my nose than let my brother win. My parents would find me frozen solid like one of those arctic cavemen in Siberia. Carlos would be grounded forever.

I grinned like a Cheshire cat in the dark.

Way more than forty-five minutes had passed since my brother zoomed away on Dad's motorcycle with a sleeping cheerleader balanced in front of him, wearing Dad's favorite helmet no less. Brit stole her parents' car without a license, but *I'm* the one who needs a babysitter? I'd be fourteen in six and a half days! I did *not* need to be baby sat, especially by someone with the IQ of a potato. Dad only used me as an excuse to ground Carlos from the game tonight. Why did I have to be punished because my brother's a moron who couldn't do his math homework?

I traced my finger on the freezing windowpane, making shapes in the fog left by my breath. Part of me knew I was being stupid and told me to go downstairs. Still, I waited.

My street was dead quiet until a boy with sandy hair came bolting break-neck speed along the far sidewalk. In the rising moonlight, Liam McGregor raced across his front lawn, scrambled over the wreckage of his porch, and slammed his front door without skipping a beat.

That was weird. He didn't even stop to wonder how his

house got wrecked. Didn't he see the car smashed into the front porch? The stupid blinker was still on!

The windows of the McGregors' house waited in darkness. The boy didn't turn on a single light. It was almost like he didn't want anyone to know he was home.

I slumped down on an old toy box just before the first scream pierced my ears. It wasn't one of those fake screams from people's Halloween decorations meant to scare trick or treaters. No. There was something in this scream that sent goosebumps crawling up the back of my neck like spiders.

I wasn't sure it was human.

Until there was another.

And another.

Closer.

Louder.

Only three kids lived on my street: me, my brother, and the McGregor boy, but there were loads of kids on the street behind us, and they were all screaming at the same time. No attic window on that side meant no way to know what they were freaking out about. Instead, my eyes scanned the distance in hopes a knight on a motorcycle would come to rescue me from my dark tower.

But Carlos still wasn't back yet.

Breaking glass. A car alarm. New screams piled on top of each other and crescendoed to a deafening roar.

I covered my ears and shrank into the corner, rocking myself back and forth.

An expression Dad said a long time ago popped into my head. I'd been throwing a fit at Food Eagle Market when Mom wouldn't buy me chocodoodles at the checkout. My four-year-old fists had pounded the ceramic floor as I kicked my feet and wailed.

Dad said I'd been 'screaming bloody murder.'

With my palms pressed tight on either side of my head

desperate to block out the sound, those words echoed in my mind.

Screaming bloody murder.

Now, I understood exactly what that meant.

An engine revved in the distance, and I scrambled over to the window in time to glimpse a flash of silver, like a bullet cutting down the center of the road. The minivan didn't stop but fishtailed around the corner and out of sight. Five seconds later, a faint crash echoed in the distance.

Chaos erupted on my street as shadows descended over windowsills and through gaping mouths of garage doors left open. Hisses and snarls gathered on the wind as my neighbors quit their houses and fumbled through the darkness. Did they hear those kids' screams? Maybe they were finally going to help?

Mom lingered outside the glow of a yellow streetlight, but I'd recognize her silhouette anywhere. Dad was there too, staggering down the road beside her.

They were finally home!

In that split second before I turned away from the sill to run downstairs and fling myself into their arms, just as they crossed the threshold of our front lawn, the motion light blasted on.

In a flash, I caught the briefest glimpse of my father. The motion light burned his gray flesh like a magnifying glass would an ant. A bloodcurdling screech pealed from his gut before he swiftly melted back into the shadows to soothe his steaming skin in cool darkness.

I screamed my head off.

From behind the hedges, Mom's shoulders stiffened as she cocked her head to one side. I couldn't make out her face, but I could feel her staring a hole right through me. Every hair on my arms stood on end like I'd just stuck my finger in a light socket.

What the heck was wrong with me? I was being crazy. This wasn't a monster. This was my *mom.*

Maybe this was one of those hidden camera shows? An early Halloween prank or something?

Ha, Ha. Very funny guys.

I tried to make myself believe it, but I just couldn't. Something was wrong. I squinted in the shadows. Dark liquid… maybe blood… dribbled from their mouths and down their torsos as my parents moaned and shuffled around on the grass.

An accident! They must've been in an accident!

"I'm coming!" I kicked open the attic ladder and raced downstairs, sliding my bottom down the banister the way Mom always yelled at me not to. I heaved open the front door.

My bare feet skidded to a stop on the welcome mat.

Mom and Dad spread their arms wide to greet me, but once they crossed into the beam cast by the motion light, they dropped flat on their stomachs and twitched like they were being tasered. Inhuman wails of agony with the timbre of my parents' voices ripped across my eardrums. They rolled away, and once back in shadow, spat furious growls through blackened teeth dripping with thick, red blood.

Up close, I barely recognized my parents. Pulsing, black veins bulged beneath cracking gray flesh, like a tangle of tree roots busting through concrete. The bones of their hands had burst through their fingertips ending in dagger-like claws of splintered bone. Their bodies were mostly covered in some kind of bark, a crust that made them resemble living statues from the neck down. I was positive Mom was still glaring at me, though her eyes were crusted shut, overflowing with milky white pus that oozed down her cheeks.

This wasn't a car accident. This was a *disease.*

If these were literally any other people on earth, I would have run screaming and doused myself with hand sanitizer. But I couldn't turn away. How could I? These were my *parents.* And they needed my help.

"Mom?" I was screaming her name, but my voice barely choked out in a whisper. Her image wobbled before me through hot tears storming down my face. "Mom, are you ok? Mom, tell me what to do!"

My mother hissed.

"What's wrong with you guys?"

Maybe they got bit by a raccoon? Of all the useless junk they teach us in school, they could at least have taught us what to do when someone had rabies! What good was knowing how to find a stupid hypotenuse at a time like this? Whatever my parents' problem was, it was way above my grade level.

Dad snarled at me, chittering in the dark.

Where was my idiot brother?! I'd call 9-1-1 again if that meathead hadn't taken his phone. When Carlos finally dragged his butt back home, I was going to kill him!

I TOLD my parents their no-phone-before-sixteen rule was insane. *What if there's an emergency?* I'd said. *Teens-didn't-have-cellphones-in-the-90s-and-we-grew-up-ok* they'd said. Yeah. Fine. That was like a thousand years ago. Now, I bet my parents wished they'd listened.

"Just hang on!" I spun back into the house. Mom and Dad watched me through our living room window like two gray cats eyeing a goldfish. As fast as I wiped away tears, new ones drenched my cheeks. My parents were horribly sick. What if they were *dying*?

How the heck was I going to get them inside and out of the cold? They needed heating pads, blankets, lotion for whatever grayed and cracked their skin… Oh, God, their eyes… their hands…. I shuddered. What they really needed was a doctor, but there was no way for me to take them to the hospital without help. My stupid brother! Carlos should be home by now!

Think, Amaia! Think!

Light must be painful to people with rabies. Yeah, that's it. Raccoons are nocturnal, right? Maybe an umbrella could help shield their skin long enough for me to get them inside the house. I fished one out of the coat rack and burst out the front door, umbrella in hand.

My parents were gone.

"Mom? Dad?" I stepped down onto the walkway and cut

across my front lawn. Frost-bitten blades of grass crunched under my bare toes, but there was no turning back now. The motion light threw my black shadow before me and sliced the empty sidewalk in two.

My parents were sprinting down the street just behind a teenager carrying a gardening rake. More adults, my elderly next-door neighbors, greeted the teen up ahead. He was surrounded.

I couldn't believe my luck! One of them was bound to help get my parents to the emergency room. I waved my arms in the air to get their attention, but they were all fixated on the kid with the rake.

Wait. Wasn't that Mr. Penshaw? I'd never seen him without his walker, but now he was *running* like an Olympic athlete.

I gasped as the teenager swung the rake in a wide arc and nailed the old man in the side of the neck. The wooden handle splintered in two around Mr. P's head, but the guy barely flinched. My mom snapped her jaws open and lunged for the boy's throat. In an instant, the adults were on him like an all-you-can-eat buffet.

Screaming bloody murder.

The umbrella rolled off my fingertips. I spun back toward the house. Blinded by the motion light, I tripped up the porch steps and fumbled for the doorknob.

My parents just… ate someone?

I bolted the lock and thundered back upstairs to the attic. The rope handle burned my palms as I heaved the ladder up behind me.

My parents just ate someone!

I couldn't breathe. The attic walls pressed in on me, squishing the air from my lungs. I blinked hard, and my eyes adjusted to the dark in time to see a shadowy silhouette lurking in the corner. Scrambling backward, my heel caught some old junk, and my body went down hard. My hands shielded my face as I braced myself for the inevitable slash of claws and teeth.

Nothing happened.

The shadow in the corner was only Abuela's old sewing mannequin.

Get a grip, Amaia. None of this is real. It's just special effects…

Blood pounded in my ears as I forced myself over to the window. The kid with the rake had vanished, replaced by only a dark, wet puddle on the pavement. My parents were back on our front lawn, waiting for me. This time they'd brought some new friends.

Whatever they had, it definitely wasn't rabies.

As strings of dark liquid oozed from their teeth, my desperate thoughts turned to the last smile my brother had given me. Carlos was still out there… what if… what if some of that blood dripping from their mouths was *his* blood? What if my brother's never coming back?

I clamped my hand over my mouth and bit down hard to stop from screaming. The floorboards creaked as I tiptoed backward, the shadows of the attic swallowing me whole. Blindly, my fingers fumbled through the darkness and tears to lift the lid off the toy box, and I stuffed myself inside.

CHAPTER
TWO

My brain clawed at the hope the whole thing had been some freakish nightmare, but waking up in the toy box with a kink in my neck brought the hard sting of reality.

How long could I stay in here before I died? Would this toy box be my coffin? The air was sticky and hot with too many recycled breaths, but I couldn't bring myself to open the lid. The image of that creature wearing my mother's face made me want to lock myself in this box and throw away the key.

My stomach growled, but I didn't dare go down to the kitchen for fear I might end up some monster's breakfast burrito. I'd rather starve to death than get eaten myself.

Thump

What was that?

Thump

There it was again.

Thump

Was someone… jumping?

The hinge to the attic door groaned as the ladder sprang open.

Carlos!

I slammed my eyes shut and prayed my brother's name.

Wooden rungs creaked with uncertain steps. What if it wasn't my brother? What if it was one of those *things*? I intertwined my knuckles tight and begged for God to save me.

"Um… hello?"

That's not my brother's voice.

"Amaia, are you still up here?"

Floorboards moaned under a boy's shifting weight.

"It's Liam… from across the street… Are you… I mean… Are you ok?"

A sob escaped my throat. In the span of a few soft footsteps, Liam was lifting the lid off the toy box. When I peeked through my watery eyelashes, a golden-haired boy appeared like an angel hovering over me. A ring of sunlight from the attic window formed a brilliant halo behind his head.

"Good hiding spot." Liam offered his hand to help me up, but I became a human jack-in-the-box instead. My coiled legs sprang, launching me into the air.

Liam yelped as I threw my arms around his shoulders. My body convulsed with the erratic violence of a drowning person clinging to the stranger trying to rescue them, pulling both under.

"It's going to be ok!" Liam shrieked above my screams.

"It's not going to be ok!" I wailed. "They're all dead! *Everyone is dead!*"

Liam hugged me back and said simply, "I know."

Don't get me wrong. Twenty-four hours ago, I never would have let some random boy my own age *hug* me. But now I totally got why scared cats ran up trees even though they hate heights. In this moment, Liam was my tree. He patted my back gently while I sniffled.

Ack, this boy smelled nasty.

Wait. Oh no. OH GOD.

It was *me*.

I'd full-on peed my pants last night. It was half-dried now, but the stench was foul. There was no way he didn't smell it.

Can you die of humiliation? If you could, I would happily crawl back in the toy box and get it over with.

I wrenched away from the boy to compose myself. By that, I mean I wiped my snotty nose on the back of my hand. My knuckles still bore a tender bite mark where I had chomped down to stop myself from screaming. Were Liam and me the last two people on Earth? If so, I wasn't making a very good impression.

"Are your parents…" My voice trailed off because I wasn't sure what word to use. *Alive? Dead? Monsters?* I should have thought it through before I opened my stupid mouth.

Liam's eyes found the floor. He said nothing. He didn't have to. The agony on his face answered my question loud and clear.

I wrung my hands. "Carlos didn't come home last night. He promised he'd come back for me… but he just… he just left me here."

"Amaia…" The corners of Liam's mouth pinched. "There's something I need to tell you…"

"Did you see my brother?" I grabbed a fistful of Liam's shirt. "Those things were *eating* kids… Do you think Carlos… could he be…"

Before the boy could answer, my legs turned as floppy as licorice sticks. I collapsed onto the toy box, sobbing. My brother was dead. My whole family was dead…

"Your brother wasn't one of those kids," Liam blurted out. "I stayed up the whole night, watching out my window. Carlos wasn't one of them. I swear it!"

"Are you sure?"

"Positive!"

His lips forced a smile which shoved me off the cliff. It was the same sort of stupid, fake smile those gossipy ladies give Mom after PTA meetings. You could tell they were holding back some nasty secret.

"Liar!" I shrieked through my tears. "*Mentiroso!*"

"What? I'm not!" he protested. "I swear to God, Amaia! I saw your parents, ok? I saw you with the umbrella, that kid with the rake... I saw everything that happened on our street last night from my window. Your brother wasn't one of those creatures and wasn't being eaten by them either... He... he just wasn't even on our street at all, ok?"

We sat in silence for a long moment, both of us unblinking in an epic staring contest. From the nose up, Liam was telling the truth. His eyes held mine without flinching. If it wasn't for the pucker in his lips, I would have believed him.

But Liam's mouth kept doing this twisty thing I couldn't trust.

Even if he was lying, maybe I didn't want to know the truth. Maybe the truth sucks.

"How did you get over here?" I asked. "Are those things... are they gone?"

Liam wrapped his arms around his stomach.

"When the sun came up, they exploded into dust just like people did yesterday," Liam said. "Now, the ashes are floating around in these kind of foggy blobs... Anyway, there's still animals outside. Dogs and squirrels and things... and the ashes don't react to them at all. So, I made a run for it and came here to find you."

I suddenly had the urge to look out the attic window to see for myself, but the thought of walking in front of Liam with a full view of the pee stain on my leggings was more than I could take.

"Can you look away for a sec?" I asked. "Just don't look at me."

Liam raised an eyebrow but turned his head like I'd asked.

Outside, clouds of ash hung in the air like ghosts. They were all shapeless and faceless, like grey smears left by a giant eraser. The people-turned-monsters I'd seen last night were now nothing more than smudges on a drawing, mistakes that could never be completely rubbed out. Each dusty cloud hovered in place, waiting.

"They're like poltergeists," I murmured.

"What?" Liam turned his head.

"Don't look!" I squealed, squeezing my knees together. My eyes darted to the crimson heap on the floor. I scooped up my brother's hoodie and used it as a shield over my soiled pants. "I've got to take a shower."

"Ok, but hurry. We need to be ready in case those things come back," Liam said.

My feet froze midway down the ladder.

"You think they might come back?"

Through the door in the ceiling, his blue eyes locked on mine.

"I don't know." He hesitated. "But I'm afraid we're gonna find out."

Rain from the shower head mingled with salty tears on my face. I cried the same thing over and over.

"Mom... Dad..."

The last words my parents said to me fuzzed out like static in my head. I'd tuned them out last night, glued to that dumb television. Now, I'd never hear their voices again.

White steam curled like fingers around my bare shoulders, a creepy reminder of the ghosts lurking outside. I freaked out and slapped the air away before turning the cold water on full blast. The mist dissolved, but my lips turned blue.

Teeth chattering, I pulled on a fresh pair of leggings, crisp t-shirt, and my brother's maroon CHS football hoodie which was so huge on me it was basically a dress. The sleeves hung past my wrists and swallowed my hands even after I'd rolled them up.

Carlitos...

My throat went tight. Why hadn't my brother come back for me?

The memory of blood dripping from my parents' teeth

regurgitated in my mind. It was *Carlos'* blood in their mouths. My parents ate my brother. I just knew it.

The hoodie reeked of Carlos' cologne with a hint of old sweat from last practice. I didn't care. I wrapped my arms around my own shoulders, squeezing hard. It was the closest I could get to one of my brother's annoying bear-hugs. Maybe it was the closest I'd ever get.

No. I couldn't think like that. If wimpy kids like me and Liam survived, my linebacker brother must've made it too. Carlos had to be alive. He just had to.

Downstairs, Liam was filling an empty laundry basket with food from the pantry, but Mom hadn't gone grocery shopping yet this week, so our kitchen cabinets were looking pretty bleak. Out of gas, my stomach sputtered, now totally on E. I swiped a fistful of cold *tostones* from the fridge to stuff my face, not waiting for them to come up to room temp.

The last mouthful went down hard as I choked down the knowledge I'd never get to eat Mom's cooking again.

I should've savored it.

¡Estúpida!

"Tonight, we'd better stay in your attic." Liam scratched his arm. "My attic is full of this pink cotton-candy looking stuff that makes you itchy if you touch it. Found out the hard way."

I nodded, relieved about staying at my own house anyway until he added:

"… and we can take turns keeping watch out the window."

I flinched at the memory of pus dripping from my parents' crusted-over eyes.

"We can't," I said. "Last night when I was watching them from my attic… my mom could *see* me… even in the dark."

"What if we put up a curtain or something?"

Rustling curtains every time we peeked out? We might as well hang a neon sign over the window with an arrow that said *Fast Food Open Late.*

"My dad has brown paper for mailing packages," I said. "It

comes in a big roll. We could tape that over the window and maybe cut an eye hole in it?"

"Wow, smart." Liam smiled. "Let's get it done."

Liam hauled the laundry basket of supplies upstairs; he was surprisingly strong for a boy with such bony arms. We made several trips up and down the ladder and piled everything we needed next to the toy box. I'd pulled a knife from the butcher's block on my kitchen counter, but Liam said if the creatures got that close, we'd better just use the knife on ourselves.

There was no way I was doing that.

But I grabbed the knife anyway.

Liam found four long slats of wood in the garage stacked behind Dad's sawhorse. I asked Liam why he needed them; he said he was going to nail the attic door shut from the inside. Then the McGregor boy cut an eye-sized hole in the paper with my knife and kept testing the vantage point until the hole was the right size and he could see all the angles he wanted to.

Who was this kid, some kind of boy scout? Not that I was complaining. If Liam hadn't come along, I'd still be in the toy box.

"What's the bucket for?" he asked.

"In case we…" I bit my lip. "Need to use the bathroom at night."

"Oh…uh… good idea." Liam blushed stop-light red.

I pretended to rearrange our supplies just to avoid the look on his face. After everything was shuffled and re-shuffled, I noticed he'd been awful quiet.

"I need to go out," he said finally.

"No!" The word shot out of my mouth at an involuntary, hysterical pitch. Embarrassed, I immediately added. "We can't leave… it's too dangerous."

"You should stay here." Liam pulled on his jacket. "Don't worry. It's not that far. I'll be back as soon as I can."

Yeah, right. I heard that one before.

Before I could decide whether to follow him or climb back in the toy box, Liam was already halfway downstairs.

"Wait!"

I slid down the ladder like a fireman under a siren.

He was out the door so fast I didn't have time to tie my sneakers as I raced after him. I'd forgotten to lock the door behind me, but Carlos took the spare key anyway. It would be just my luck to accidentally lock myself out.

Four shoelaces whipped my ankles as my feet smashed the pavement over and over. I sidestepped thicker clouds of ash that hung in our path, vaguely aware two of them might be my parents. Loose gray flakes floated down from the desaturated sky like usual, but these clouds at eye level were different. They hovered only a few feet off the ground, like campfire smoke but somehow more liquid, shifty, and flecked with sparkles that glittered like glass. Cold seeped off them in waves the way steam pours from dry ice. They weren't monsters anymore. They were ghosts.

Panting as I ran, I covered my mouth with the sleeve of my hoodie, afraid these evil spirits would somehow get in my lungs and eat me from the inside.

Liam slowed to let me catch up but kept a steady pace.

"Where are we going?" The thickness of the air swallowed my voice.

Liam motioned around the corner.

Running on his heels as we turned onto a new block, I wondered why Liam and I hadn't been friends before this? Sure, he got bussed to the pricey prep academy across town, but why not hang out after school? Our dads often waved at each other from behind their lawnmowers. Our moms traded Christmas cookies. My brother and I always battled over who got the last one of Mrs. McGregor's mouthwatering coconut macaroons. Despite all that, there was an invisible white picket fence between us that wasn't to be crossed.

As if their giant house wasn't a big enough slap in the face, they had the nerve to sell my parents Liam's hand-me-down phone for Carlos' sixteenth birthday three weeks ago. Dad said the McGregors gave him an *incredible deal*. Carlos was over the moon when he unwrapped it.

I was humiliated.

Why did Dad have to scaff up the McGregors' table scraps? Couldn't he have just bought one from a stranger on Craigslist like we did all the time for birthday and Christmas presents? To make things worse, Liam actually tried to say hi to me a few weeks ago. I had pretended I didn't hear him, ran inside, and slammed the door. Kids like us could never *really* be friends.

A distant rumble shook me back to the present. I hesitated.

"What's that noise?"

Liam nearly tripped over his own two feet. "It sounds like... a waterfall?"

We cut through someone's backyard and peered through a fence. The silver minivan I'd seen fishtail out of sight last night had met its untimely end by crashing into a fire hydrant. Its hood was folded around the red post while a geyser spewed water twenty feet in the air and transformed the street into a gorge.

"Come on!" Liam hopped the chain link, and I vaulted myself over behind him.

Our feet splashed through the asphalt riverbed and past the van's driver side door, which dangled open on its hinge. A quick glance told me the driver's seat was soaked.

In blood.

I focused on my feet and seriously regretted scarfing those *tostones*.

At the end of the block, we reached our destination: a ruddy looking house with faded green siding. Liam retrieved a hidden key from under the welcome mat. As I waited impatiently for him to unlock the door, shards of glass twinkled under the shattered bay window beside me.

It had been broken from the inside.

Someone... or *something*... had desperately wanted to get out and didn't use the front door.

"It's my aunt's house." Liam answered the silent question on my face.

"Does your aunt have any kids?" I stepped cautiously inside onto the musty shag carpet. Yuck, this lady really had an unhealthy fascination with the color green.

"My cousin's in college, so he's not here. I sent him a zillion texts last night, but he didn't text back…"

"Oh," I mumbled, wishing I could stuff those prying words back in my mouth. His cousin was probably dead, and I just *had* to bring it up. If I didn't watch my mouth, would Liam get fed up and leave me too? My brother always called me 'jodóna' … now being a *pain in the butt* might just get me kicked to the curb.

We entered a woman's bedroom. The stink of mothballs fluttered in the air as porcelain figurines glared at me from their perch on her dresser. Liam flung open the closet door and began rifling.

"What are you looking for?" I was itching to get out of this dead lady's house. "Let me help."

"My uncle," Liam muttered, ripping open a cardboard box. "Well, the *jerk* that was my uncle anyway… He used to beat my aunt. One time, he knocked out three of her teeth. She and my cousin stayed with us for a few months when I was little. My uncle was livid, so he'd sit outside our house in his car and follow her around whenever she left."

"Why didn't you call the police?"

"The police said they wouldn't do anything unless he tried to kill her." Liam's jaw tightened. "I guess nearly beating her to death all those times didn't count."

"What did she do?" I asked, suddenly wary of the ghost that might be listening to our gossip.

"She bought a gun."

The lightbulb went on in my head, and I knew what Liam was looking for.

He raked his hands through his sandy hair and tossed a

tupper bin of pocketbooks aside in frustration. "My cousin said she keeps it in her closet, but it's not here."

"Let's check her drawers," I offered.

Like two burglars, we ransacked the bedroom, emptying her dresser and pillaging the shoeboxes under her bed.

Nada. Zilch. Zip.

We moved from room to room, closet to closet, but the gun wasn't anywhere to be found.

Liam was gnawing his thumbnail down to the nub.

"We're not gonna find it," I said. "Can we just go now?"

I braced myself for an argument. If my brother had gotten this crazy idea in his head, it'd be like fighting a pitbull for a dirty sock getting him to give up it up.

But Liam simply sighed, put his tail between his legs, and led the way back downstairs.

A blood red streak sliced the horizon over the setting sun. Not a comforting sign. The clouds of ash had clotted and coagulated, much denser than before. They started to look... well... people-shaped.

But the most terrifying thing was the scream. We heard it at the same time, soft but shrill underneath the crash of rushing water from the fire hydrant. Liam's blue eyes went as wide as saucers, reflecting like two giant mirrors the look of horror on my own face.

We followed the cries toward the minivan, splashing through the ankle-deep river as we went. I peered in the passenger side window while Liam threw open the rear sliding door.

There she was, strapped into her gray car seat and kicking her tiny feet in the air. The baby's screams stopped at once, shocked by the strange faces that finally answered her cry.

"*Dios mío*," I whispered.

"Oh my God," Liam echoed.

I tried to unbuckle her. The red button of the car seat clasp was finicky, and the odor of a putrid dirty diaper and the blood-soaked driver's seat that'd been baking in the sun all day threatened to yank my stomach up through my throat. My fingers finally pushed and pull at the right time, and I lifted her away from the minivan. Liam scooped up a baby bag from the floor behind the driver's seat. It'd been hastily stuffed to the brim with baby supplies.

A photo was clipped to the visor.

Two parents, the baby, and a boy about my age.

It was her brother. He died protecting her? I shuddered and pushed the thought out of my head. Liam plucked the picture from the visor and shoved it in the diaper bag.

"Why did you take that?" I demanded. The sight of that photo had somehow unsettled me even more than finding the baby.

Liam zoned out like he didn't even hear my question.

I knew less than squat about babies, but I understood the look on this one's face. She was clutching the sleeve of my brother's hoodie, begging me not to abandon her too.

Some guardian angel must have been looking out for this baby last night. But the sun was setting, and now she was in desperate need of a new protector. If we left her here, she'd die. I crossed my heart and made a silent promise.

I won't leave you like your brother did.

My sneakers pointed in the direction of home, but Liam's scream stopped me in my tracks.

"What?!" I whipped my head around. "What's wrong?"

Liam stood frozen, wide-eyed, and unblinking as he pointed a trembling finger at an ash cloud hovering over the sidewalk. A woman's face formed in the mist, glaring back at us with a snarl pulling at her lips.

"That's... that's... my aunt!" Liam cried.

It was my turn to scream.

"Run!"

CHAPTER
THREE

"The lights are on!" I forced the words out past the runner's cramp in my ribs. Solidifying bodies hovered in my peripheral vision, mere inches from touching ground, but my sights were fixed squarely on my front door. I didn't lock it. What if someone broke in?

"No, it's ok!" Liam panted. "You guys left them on all last night."

He dove through my front door, slammed it behind us, and bolted the lock. All I could think was *the attic. We need to get to the attic!* Liam was two steps ahead of me. We raced upstairs past the bedrooms. I gripped the squirming baby with one arm while I used the other to steady myself up the ladder. On the top rung, I paused and twisted around, eyes desperately scanning the hallway below.

"Carlos?" I cried. "Carlos? Are you home?"

My heart leapt to my throat, anxious for a snarky retort in my brother's annoying bicycle horn voice.

"CARLOS?"

There was no reply except the shrill screams of the infant in my arms. She'd started crying again on the run home, and no matter how much I tried to shush her, the baby would not shut up.

"If we don't keep her quiet, we're dead." Liam chomped on his nails. "I think we're almost out of time."

"Wait! I've got an idea!" I passed the infant off to Liam. Before he could interrogate me on it, I was already half-way down to the garage.

My dad had earmuffs and plugs he used for construction work and lawn mowing. In a flash, I had these things in hand. Part of me worried Liam would've nailed the door shut before I got back, but when I returned, he was standing just where I left him, still holding the screeching baby. The second I was up, Liam thrust her in my arms and set to work raising the ladder. He gripped the rope that normally dangled from the ceiling in the hallway and yanked it up around the lip of the attic door just before it clicked shut.

"What are you doing?" I frowned.

"I'm making it so there's no handle on the outside," he said. "Now, all that's left is to nail the slats over the door to seal it shut, and we should be safe."

Safe. I doubted I'd ever feel *safe* again, but sealing the door shut was a good start.

Liam fumbled with a nail and raised the hammer unsteadily over his shoulder. When the head came smashing down, it nearly took out his thumb and missed the nail entirely.

I cringed.

"You'd better let me do that." I shifted the infant uneasily in my arms.

"Nah, I got it." Liam gritted his teeth and raised the hammer again.

"Stop! You don't need to hit it that hard! If you miss, you're going to break your fingers."

Liam's face turned rosy. "You think you could do it better?"

"I'm pretty good with a hammer." I shrugged. "You look like you've never held one before."

Liam's blush went from pink to crimson. "Fine. You do it then."

I swapped the baby for the hammer and went to work.

My dad had exactly two hobbies: chess and carpentry. Carlos wasn't interested in either, but I loved hanging out with Dad in the garage while he crafted a rocking chair for my abuela. Grandma had said it was the best gift she ever got. Obviously, I wasn't a master carpenter like my dad, but I made quick work of securing the attic door.

The way Liam's mouth pinched betrayed how impressed he was.

"The plugs will probably work best," Liam said as he rifled through the baby bag. "Her head is too small for those earmuffs."

I stood awkwardly as Liam pushed the nipple of a bottle past the baby's lips. She made frantic gasps as she gulped formula, sucking air through her nose in a way that made me worry she'd choke. Liam rocked her and stroked her foot to calm her down. It worked. He may have never held a hammer before, but he'd definitely held a baby. He passed her off to me again so he could keep watch out the window.

She was actually kind of cute now that she wasn't screaming her head off.

Pobrecita! The baby's cheeks were still cold from being outside so long, the *poor little thing*. I rocked her like I'd seen Liam doing, but her full diaper leaked, running liquid poop down her leg. Ugh. What was I thinking? Babies are so not cute.

The packing paper covering the window dimmed from glowing wheat to muddy brown as the last bit of sun outside rotted away like a spoiled orange. I studied the expression on Liam's face for any sign of news.

Stuck in limbo while I sat on the toy box cradling this poopy baby, I remembered how only this morning Liam held me in his arms even though I'd gone to the bathroom on myself. My cheeks burned at the thought.

I studied Liam's posture as he stared out the peephole.

"What's happening out there?" I whispered so low I didn't think he heard me.

Liam raised a finger to his lips and motioned for me to be quiet.

"The geists are back," he said.

I crinkled my forehead, unsure if I'd heard him right. The baby fussed.

Liam tiptoed over and sat beside me, scrounging through the baby bag for anything that would keep her quiet. I silently prayed for a miracle, but if not, that the fresh diaper, wipes, and pacifier would do the trick. Together, I held her still while Liam worked to remove the heavy, warm bag of poo. We made matching faces and tried not to breathe the stench in too deep.

As he peeled off her dirty socks, Liam let out a deep sigh.

"Her name is Sara," he whispered.

"Why Sara?" I frowned. "Maybe we could name her *Angelina*? After the guardian angel who protected her before we came along…"

"Oh." He turned away and set the filthy socks on the diaper. "You think I made it up. I didn't…"

He smoothed out the photo he'd stashed in the diaper bag, tracing his thumb along the crease where it had been clipped to the visor.

"That's Marcus. He's in our grade." Liam winced. "He *was* in our grade. Him and I have been in the same class since kindergarten. Marcus was so excited about getting a baby sister... He even brought the ultrasound picture in for a class project."

"Oh," was all I could manage to say.

With the weight of what he'd said holding down our tongues, we worked silently to finish changing Sara. Her eyelids grew heavy as she teetered on the edge of exhaustion. When I'd eaten a ton at Thanksgiving, I'd always conk out after. Maybe her full belly would keep her sleeping and help us survive the night. Once she was clean and dry, we wrapped the baby in a blanket to keep her warm. Sara mewled softly when Liam gently put the earplugs in, but she let him do it.

The first scream came shortly after.

A little girl's voice far in the distance. There were no words, just a desperate terrified screech that lasted several minutes then was stopped dead. Liam moved closer to me on the toy box and let his warm shoulder press up against mine.

What horrible thing happened to him last night that sent him racing back to his house like that? I knew better than to ask. He was gnawing on his ring fingernail again.

A sudden blast of light illuminated the brown paper, sending Liam scurrying over to the attic window. My breath stopped. I started to shiver, from cold or terror or both, but I fought to keep my muscles still to not wake the baby in my arms.

Liam cupped his hand over his mouth, staring through the peephole with wide eyes. My mind twisted itself into a thousand knots, desperate to know what was happening and at the same time desperate to remain in the dark.

In the dark…

The motion light.

A screeching hiss outside brought back the memory of my parents writhing in agony on our front lawn the night before.

"Geists hate light," Liam murmured, tiptoeing back to me.

"Geists?" My eyebrows raised as he wrapped a blanket around my shoulders. Liam scootched next to me under it to share our body heat.

"That's what you called them this afternoon, isn't it?"

I cast him a sideways glance until it hit me.

Poltergeists.

"I remember…" I muttered. "I said the ash clouds look like poltergeists in the daytime."

"I guess I only half heard you," he confessed. "I was… I mean… I've had a lot on my mind."

"Geists." The word left a bad taste on my tongue because of what those series of letters now meant. The creatures outside were too deformed to be zombies, and they needed a name besides *monsters* or *things*. Mom said identifying a problem was the first step to defeating it.

If geists could even be defeated at all…

I really wished we'd found that gun.

Liam fumbled for something in his back pocket. In the shadows, I couldn't tell what was in his hand until he powered it on. The LED screen bathed his face in soft blue light as he scrolled through his texts. I should have put two and two together! He'd mentioned at his aunt's house that he'd messaged his cousin. Three weeks ago, my parents bought Liam's old phone to give to Carlos for his birthday. Of course, Liam had a phone!

Liam sighed when he didn't find what he'd been hoping for and held his thumb over the power button.

He paused.

"Do you want to call someone?"

"My brother," I gasped before abruptly deflating and blurting out, "*¡Carajo!*"

Liam shot me a look like I'd suddenly grown two heads.

I slapped my hand over my mouth. Mom would have smacked me for cursing, especially in Spanish.

"I haven't memorized Carlos' number yet," I mumbled stupidly. *Why did I have to be such an idiot?*

Liam powered down his phone, setting it on the floorboards beside his sleeping bag.

An animal screamed.

I squeezed my eyes shut, but it was too late. My mind had already conjured the image of the cat's bones breaking through fur as the geist's canine teeth tore through its flesh. They were close. Too close. Close enough to hear cartilage crunching. The slurping of blood. Sounds of the slaughter wafted up from my neighbor's front yard. Even without the power of words, from the timbre of the animal's cry, I knew it was being eaten alive.

"Teach me that thing you just said," Liam whispered.

"What?" I blinked my eyes open.

"Gara - ho?" Liam insisted. "What does it mean?"

"Oh, it's *carajo*." I blushed. "It means like… *damnit*."

"*Carajo*." Liam smiled as the word rolled off his tongue. "It sounds cool."

"Really?" The corners of my mouth twitched. Wait. Did this boy just make me smile in the middle of the apocalypse?

"Does your dad speak Spanish?" Liam asked.

"Only a little. Enough to know when my Mom's pissed at him for forgetting to take out the *basura*."

He twirled his thumbs together. "So… uh… did your parents meet in your Mom's country or something?"

"My Mom's from the Bronx," I said. "Um… you know Puerto Ricans are American right?"

Liam cringed, looking like he wished he could crawl in the toy box and die himself.

"I… uh… I'm sorry. I didn't mean…"

"It's ok." I waved him off. "Actually, a lot of people get confused about us because of our names. Families don't always fit in one box or another. They're all like, 'Why does Carlos have a Spanish first name but not last name?' But it's actually really simple."

Liam frowned. "Is it?"

"Mom said since us kids would have my dad's last name, she should get to pick our first names."

"Huh, I guess that sounds fair."

"Ha! Tell that to my dad. He wanted to call my brother 'Carl' after my grandpa on that side. So, I'm pretty sure Mom compromised anyway."

"That reminds me." Liam's voice softened. "I was trying to remember Sara's middle name earlier. I didn't think Marcus ever mentioned it… or maybe I just forgot."

I frowned, unsure where he was going with this.

"But now that I think of it, I'm pretty sure her middle name might have been *Angelina*." Liam tenderly pushed back a stray hair from the baby's forehead. *"Sara Angelina.* What do you think?"

"Really?" I gaped at him, tears pricking the back of my eyes. "You're sure you remembered it right?"

"Yeah." His mouth did that twisty thing again, but this time I didn't care. This time, it wasn't a lie. It was a gift.

"Sara Angelina," I whispered her name. "It's perfect."

As we both marveled at the newly christened infant, I suddenly realized the animal outside had long since been silenced. Liam's distraction saved me from being tortured along with it. I studied his face in the dark. Something wasn't right. Liam didn't need me. He wasn't my brother. We weren't even really friends. And let's face it, I'd kinda been acting like a total loser since he got here this morning. So, why did he stay?

And worse yet: why did I still feel like he was hiding something?

Suspicions tumbled in my brain like bingo balls, but a wave of exhaustion hit me before I could begin to connect the dots. If I didn't lay down, I'd fall down. My eyelids drooped as I swayed where I sat on the toy box. Liam arranged the blankets and pillows on an area we'd cleared of clutter. He guided me as I laid down on the makeshift bed, still holding Sara Angelina in my arms. She fussed the tiniest bit but stayed sleeping as I set her beside me.

"Take these," he whispered holding out my dad's ear protectors. I hesitated until he said, "I'll keep a listen, and if anything happens, I'll wake you up."

Too sleepy to argue, I let him put the earmuffs over my head and was plunged into silence. The second my cheek hit the pillow I was out cold.

The sun hadn't risen yet, but something stirred me awake. My eyelids flew open. I checked Sara Angelina, who was thankfully still sound asleep. Liam lay in the fetal position, curled up in my brother's old sleeping bag with his back to me. The silhouette of his body trembled like a leaf in a thunderstorm. I held my breath and cautiously slid one earmuff off my ear.

Clutching a pillow over his face, Liam half-sobbed, half-screamed into it. There was something horrifyingly familiar in his muffled cries… I recognized it from spending last night in the toy box.

Terror. He was scared to death.

My mind reeled at the realization my brave protector who'd seemed all tough looking for that gun was now screaming into a pillow and crying for his mommy.

The cool, calm Liam was a total lie. The real Liam was just a scared little kid.

Like me.

My lips opened to comfort him, but I forced them shut instead. What if he was embarrassed that I'd heard him crying? Or angry? Would that make him leave us? Could I end up stuck with a baby *by myself*? I couldn't do this on my own. I just couldn't.

A silent tear plunked down on my pillowcase.

I'm sorry Liam.

I put the muff back over my ear, rolled over, and pretended to sleep.

Just after sun-up, Liam's shuddering breaths turned even. He had cried the whole night. I didn't think he'd ever stop.

Careful not to wake him, I spent the early hours of the morning tending to Sara in every way I could without leaving the safety of the attic. Geists outside had exploded into ashes again at sunrise, but I couldn't stomach the idea of going downstairs without Liam beside me. Even though I now knew he was just a scared, scrawny kid like me, for some reason, Liam made me feel braver. He couldn't protect me anymore than a teddy bear or a blanket could, but I still needed him. Badly.

I cursed myself for not memorizing my brother's stupid phone number in the three weeks since his birthday. Despite racking my brain like it was a math test my life depended on, I could only come up with the area code...

But there were two numbers I knew by heart.

I held my breath as I tip-toed next to a sleeping Liam and lifted his phone from where it rested next to his sleeping bag.

They wouldn't answer, but I was desperate to hear their voices.

You've reached Toni. Please leave a message, and I'll call you back. Have a lovely day!

My mom's voice had a natural melody, almost like she was

singing the words. It was like you could hear her smile when she spoke.

Someone told me once that old people could actually die of a broken heart. Like, emotional pain could hurt so bad that your body can't take it and just gives up. I didn't believe it was possible until this moment, when my own heart felt like it was being ripped apart in my chest.

"Mom," I whispered, holding my hand like a shield over the mouthpiece. "I don't know what to do. *Please*... please be ok. I love you so much. You and Dad gotta fight it. Just fight it ok? Come back. You have to come back..."

I swiped my eyes to soak up the tears and punched in Dad's number next.

Hey there, it's Kevin. I'm out saving the world right now. Leave a message or this phone will self-destruct in 3...2... BEEP.

A smile broke on my face despite my tears when I remembered Mom teasing him about his corny greetings. It was something new every month... a knock knock joke that ended with a beep instead of a punchline. A quote from one of his favorite shows in a silly voice. Sometimes he'd even sing, which unlike Mom, was nails on a chalkboard.

My brother thought it was hysterical, but he'd be too chicken to do something like that himself with his new phone because his football friends might laugh. The way he procrastinates, I doubted he even had his mailbox set up yet anyway...

Carlos...

Maybe he came home yesterday while Liam and I were at his aunt's house searching for that gun? What if I'd missed him?

No way. We hadn't been gone that long. But it was a good lesson; if I had to leave the house again, I'd write a note for Carlos in case he came back, and I wasn't here.

After powering down Liam's phone and returning it, I rifled through my backpack and dug out a notepad and pen.

DEAR CARLOS,
I'M SAFE. NO THANKS TO **YOU,** YOU BIG **JERK!**

My pen stabbed the paper so hard it punctured a hole where the last exclamation point should've been. I tore the sheet from the metal spiral and crumpled it into a ball in my fist. This was a terrible idea. I shoved the wadded-up note in the pocket of my hoodie.

No.

Not my hoodie.

My brother's hoodie.

Carlos literally gave me the shirt off his back to keep me warm.

My idiot brother loved me.

I didn't know what happened to Carlitos two nights ago, but whatever his reason was for breaking his promise and leaving me up in the attic, it wasn't because he didn't care.

Something terrible must have happened. But whatever it was, I just had to believe Carlos was out there, fighting to come home.

I picked up the pen and started over.

> Dear Carlos,
> I'm safe. I'm with Liam McGregor from across the street. We've been hiding in the attic, but if you find this note it means we had to leave the house. Hopefully, we'll be back soon.
> I saw Mom and Dad...

The lines turned watery in my vision, and I could barely make out the words as I scribbled.

Our parents are geists now. Don't go looking for them or they'll eat you. I'm writing this because I still have hope that you'll come home. I know you're alive. You're too stubborn to die.
Ten cuidado.
Love,
Amaia

"Is that a diary?"

Liam propped himself up on one elbow, rubbing sleep from his eye.

"No, it's not. It's something else." I dried my tears on the sleeve of my brother's hoodie. "It's nothing… probably dumb."

Liam wiggled out of his sleeping bag and sat beside me on the toy box.

"It's a note for my brother," I confessed. "If Carlos comes back and we're not here, I don't want him to think that we didn't make it. You think that's stupid? That I still believe my brother's alive?"

Liam took the paper from my hands. For a moment, I was afraid he'd tear it up, shake me by the shoulders, and scream at me to face reality. That's what Carlos would've done. My brother was almost certainly dead. Maybe getting my hopes up would just make things worse. But instead of saying any of that out loud, Liam took the pen from me and scrawled something on the bottom of my note before handing it back. The edges of the paper crinkled in my grasp as I read his words:

PS. Call Liam's phone. (833) 638-8727

"It's not stupid, Amaia," Liam said gently. "It's not stupid at all."

I made quick work of prying up the boards over the door but told Liam we'd need to replace the wooden slats soon. Every time new nails were hammered in then ripped out, the boards would weaken. Eventually, they'd be more breakable than bones… and we both knew geists could easily snap those.

Dad… I caressed the handle of the hammer, imagining thick, powerful hands gripping it instead of my flimsy fingers. My father held this hammer more times than I could count. In a strange way, holding it in my palm made me feel closer to him.

I slipped the hammer into my backpack and crept down the ladder.

Liam shifted uneasily as I taped the note to my brother's bedroom door. He said nothing. That twisty thing he did with his mouth was really starting to grate on my nerves.

Downstairs, we made Sara fresh bottles according to the directions on the back of the formula can from the diaper bag and popped them in the fridge. There was barely any powder left, so Liam suggested we spend the rest of the afternoon on a supply run.

"Every time we go into a new building, we're taking a huge risk," he said. "How do we know these houses aren't crawling with geists? Maybe they've only stayed out of your house because we've kept the lights on…"

I winced.

I'd taken for granted that all geists were harmless ashes during the daytime, but Liam was right. What if some managed to stay solid by hiding in shadows?

Standing in the middle of my street, I imagined myself the lone survivor of a shipwreck, drifting on a life raft, wondering what sharks were lurking unseen in the black water around me.

Liam rubbed his chin as he studied the silver Hyundai with a red bumper wedged under the remains of his parents' porch. The signal was barely blinking; the battery was just about dead. I twisted the key in the ignition. Nope. Wouldn't start.

Liam kicked away a splintered beam with his sneaker. "We're not going anywhere in this."

"What about the van we found Sara in?" I offered before grimacing at the memory of the blood-soaked driver's seat. "Or maybe a different car that's been left in the street?"

"With the keys in it? That's not dead like this one?" Liam raked his fingers through his hair. "No way are we getting that lucky."

Even if I hadn't spied on him crying last night, it was obvious this boy was starting to unravel.

Liam sawed a thumbnail between his lower teeth as he worked up the courage to tell me something big. "My parents and I were at a restaurant when it happened."

"When what…" I stopped myself. "Oh."

Liam looked away. He couldn't meet my eyes as he continued.

"Ever since the ashes started falling, my mom changed. She got totally addicted to the news and wouldn't think or talk about anything else. Mom would snap at us for no reason and was angry all the time. Dad got fed up and said we needed to remind her there was good in the world. So, the day before yesterday, we went to my mom's office just before she got off work. When we walked in to surprise her with a bouquet of roses, it was the first time I'd seem my mom smile in weeks. Then we took her to her favorite restaurant as a treat…"

Liam's lip trembled like he'd burst into tears any moment.

"That's why I'm telling you this. Instead of taking two cars, we left my mom's at her office because all the highways were jammed. Then after the plague hit… *think about it*. People had their feet on the gas pedals, but then suddenly, *poof!* Gone. Cars speeding without drivers. Vehicles smashed into each other, into buildings, sidewalks, you name it. In our neighborhood, you can't tell how bad it is, but the roads a few blocks east of here are a wreck. Even if we did manage to get a car that has a key in it, gas, and the battery isn't dead… a lot of streets will be wall-to-wall cars. We'd need to make a map to plot out what streets are blocked and which ones we can fit through. Otherwise, we could just drive around in circles hitting dead ends."

"Food Eagle isn't too far to just walk it," I said then shut my mouth before I let slip the reason I knew that: a flat tire that couldn't be fixed until Dad's next paycheck.

"I'm pretty sure I know how to get there." Liam hesitated. "I'll go and bring back supplies. You and Sara can wait for me in the attic."

"You can't," I gasped. My heart bungee jumped into the pit of my stomach, buckling my knees and slamming me to the ground with the force of it. "No, no, no…" A lead weight squeezed my chest, compressing the air inside me. Try as I might, I couldn't breathe in.

What was happening to me?

"Amaia!" Liam crouched down beside me. "Amaia, what's wrong?"

I'm gonna die. I'm gonna die like one of those old people whose heart gives out.

"I… I can't…" A feeling of cold dread welled up inside me, flooding my lungs and drowning me from the inside.

Liam's eyes went wide. "It's ok… I'm pretty sure it's a panic attack. My aunt used to get these. Just breathe, Amaia. Focus on breathing. In. Out. Come on, you can do it! In. Out."

Sweat poured down my neck. I grabbed fistfuls of ash-coated grass and ripped them out of the ground in lieu of hair from my own scalp. My thoughts were wild, scratching and clawing the inside of my skull.

"You can't… you can't leave me too."

"It'll be over soon. You're going to be ok."

"Don't leave…" I yanked the sleeve of his jacket so hard he nearly fell over. "Swear! Promise me!"

Liam pulled me in a tight embrace and held my face to his shoulder as I wrapped my trembling arms around him and the baby.

"Breathe like me," Liam said softly. "That's it. You're doing great."

I felt the rise and fall of his chest, closed my eyes, and focused on matching the rhythm of my breathing to his. His free hand traced soothing circles on my back until my pulse began to steady.

"I won't ever leave you, Amaia," he whispered against my cheek. "I promise."

We walked in silence side by side on the three-mile trek to Food Eagle. An hour there, an hour back, plus an hour to gather supplies. Any longer than that would bring us dangerously close to sunset.

Liam was right about some roads being completely blocked, making it only possible to squeeze through on foot. Dead vehicles pressed against each other with shattered windshields and windows, but not from any accident. Their former drivers had quit their cars and were now jay walking through the night. It was probably best we didn't find a usable car anyway. The last kid I knew who drove without a license smashed into a front porch.

Ashes hung in our path the whole way to Food Eagle with certain blocks thicker than others. Come nightfall, those areas would be swarming with geists.

"I have a theory." I shifted the nearly empty backpack on my back. "But it might be stupid, I don't know."

"A theory about what?"

I lowered my voice to a whisper. "About geists…"

"Ok, let's hear it."

"No, it's stupid…"

"Amaia, you can't be afraid to talk to me about stuff," Liam said. "We're in this together. You can tell me anything."

"Yeah, ok…" I lowered my eyes to the sidewalk and

envisioned him crying into his pillow when he thought I couldn't hear. Maybe if I took a chance on trusting him, Liam could take a chance on me, too? "My brother's girlfriend said the coach and adults watching in the stands became ashes, but the football players, cheerleaders, and marching band didn't. And whenever someone's screaming at night, it's always kids' voices. So, I think that only adults became geists."

Liam stopped in his tracks.

"What is it?" I asked. "What's wrong?"

Liam opened his mouth but swiftly snapped it shut. His steps restarted and quickened the pace.

"It's nothing," he said. "You're right. It makes total sense. Only adults became geists. Any other theories?"

"Not really." I grumbled as I shoved my hands in my pockets. Why couldn't Liam have just argued with me and called my theory dumb like Carlos would have? I wished he brought up something, *anything* to prove me wrong… but we both knew I wasn't. Normally, I loved being right. This time, it sucked. This time, it meant every adult I've ever known had been turned into a monster.

"This is a great idea," Liam said. "Let's try to piece together what we know about the geists so far. Did you see the President do that State of the Union thing a few months back?"

"Yeah, my teacher let us during class."

"Mine, too."

President Cotto had urged people not to panic, but what did she expect? Doctors discovered the ashes contained a virus that was showing up in what they called 'the general population.' Carlos told me that meant regular people like our familia. No matter what the president said, that seemed like a real good reason to panic to me. The news was obsessed with it. Adults wouldn't talk about anything else, not even that crazy fire in Australia they used to go on and on about just before the ashes started.

Liam was lost in his thoughts again… and I hated seeing the corners of his mouth turn down the way they were.

"My brother showed us a funny meme of a weatherman at dinner one night," I said. "My dad was laughing so hard, soup shot out his nose."

"Yeah, I saw those ash memes too," Liam scowled. "Nobody was taking it seriously back then."

Yikes. Who spit in his Cheerios? "Hey, it's not like anyone could've known what was going to happen," I shot back.

"Somebody knew." Liam balled up his fists. "I think it was terrorism. Like, some biological weapon or something."

We turned the corner onto a new block.

"It was probably aliens." I cast a glance to the ashes floating down from the dark clouds high above our heads. "There was a scientist on TV who…"

"Oh, God, not you too." Liam rolled his eyes.

"But the scientist said the virus could survive in super hot and cold temperatures! It could've come down on a meteor…"

Liam flashed me a look that said, '*Only idiots believe in aliens.*' I shut my mouth.

"Let's just stick to facts, ok?" he said.

"Fine." I folded my arms around my stomach. I hated this game, but I didn't want Liam to think I was a wimp. So, I decided to keep playing.

Liam adjusted the pacifier in Sara's mouth. "Do you think all the adults exploding has something to do with those sick people in the quarantine camps?"

"Maybe…" I shuddered. "It is a bit weird how they were all bleeding from their eyes and now the geists' eyes are dripping with that… well… you know."

"My dad said it was disrespectful to the victims for the news to parade them around like that for ratings." Liam thrust his chin in the air. "He called it *voyeuristic.*"

I gnawed my lower lip. I'd snuck peeks at the gruesome photos beneath the headlines in my parents' newspapers. Had I really thought about the people in the pictures? They were each somebody… fathers, mothers, sisters, brothers… would they want to be remembered like that? In their most horrible moment? Mom didn't even like her picture taken if she was wearing her glasses…

It was stupid to look anyway. Those pictures gave me nightmares. But I couldn't help it. Other than the ashes falling from the sky, the disease was all anyone would talk about. The news even gave it a name.

The Plague of Ashes.

It was like a giant jigsaw puzzle trying to fit all the pieces together. When you're a kid, no one wants to tell you anything. So, I'd only got bits of it from school gossip, the news, sneaking peeks at the internet, and occasionally snooping on my parents' conversations after they thought I'd been in bed. My mother had been whispering something terrible a few nights ago…

"My mom told my dad it was a bad sign the military was getting involved," I confessed. "She was afraid the government might start killing patients."

"That's crazier than the alien theory! The government would never just go around killing its own citizens."

My teeth clenched. Did he just call my mom a *liar*?

"Don't you think it's weird that all those people were so sick for months, but not a single one of them died? My mom said the hospitals were getting too crowded and eventually the government would do something extreme to try to stop the spread! And not just our government, all of them!"

"Don't you hear how nuts you sound?" Liam quickened his pace. "It's totally psycho. You're as bad as those religious crazies screaming that God was angry and the plague is mankind's punishment."

"God wouldn't do this!"

"Look around us, Amaia! You still think there's a god?!"

I dug my heels into the pavement and came to a dead stop. Liam took several steps before he realized I wasn't following

anymore. We'd been two mountain climbers tethered together…
and the rope between us just snapped. I was in a free fall.

"Take. It. Back." I growled each word through my teeth.

We both stood rigid like two spooked cats. Neither of us
budged. If he did, my claws were ready.

"Come on, Amaia. We don't have time for this."

I spun and stomped away, my feet pounding the sidewalk
like the blows my fists itched to land on his dumb face.

"Wait!" he cried.

That boy must have a death wish.

"Why should I?"

Before he could answer, Sara cooed as she tugged at a shiny
silver button on Liam's jacket and tried to eat it. Our eyes
snapped to her like magnets. Sunlight reflected off the metal and
made tiny stars dance around her face, setting her into a fit of
giggles that filled the chasm between us. That stinky baby might
as well have been tugging on my heartstrings instead of Liam's
coat.

All of a sudden, I did have a reason why.

A promise came back to haunt me.

I won't leave you like your brother did.

How had I gotten myself into this mess? I pursed my lips and
took a step toward them.

For Sara Angelina. I thought.

At least Liam and I agreed on something.

Massive wall-sized windows stretched across the entire length of Food Eagle's storefront, pouring sunlight into the squat, west-facing building on the corner. Inside, several rows of stale fluorescent bulbs lit up the aisles like a hospital cafeteria. A careful glance through the automatic doors told us that while the coast was clear of geists, vultures had already torn Food Eagle to shreds.

Wire shelves behind the cash register, normally crammed with cigarettes in brightly colored boxes, were stripped bare. I frowned at the dollar bills decorating the floor like old party confetti. Now that we could take whatever we wanted, money was only paper. Still, part of me felt like a thief. My empty backpack was suddenly heavier on my shoulders.

Food Eagle was closer to a gas station convenience store than a regular supermarket, but you could count on it for the essentials.

"I found toilet paper." Liam smiled triumphantly. "I guess the geniuses that looted before us were more concerned with emptying the beer cooler."

I hadn't spoken to him for the last few blocks. How could I forgive him after what he'd said?

A sigh leaked from my lips when one of my mom's favorite sayings echoed in my head:

God forgives, and we should too.

It was usually followed by my dad saying:

Now hug your brother or you're both grounded.

My brother…

Barely ten minutes could go by without me thinking about Carlos. That idiot was right. I did miss him now that he was gone.

"See any formula?" I called from behind a rack of cereal boxes and cans of spaghetti loops. My arms were already going numb from Sara's weight, even though I'd only carried her half the trip. Funny how little things seem to weigh a ton when you carry them long enough.

"Not yet," Liam said. "Can't she just have regular milk? There's some in the coolers here. They've got whole milk, two percent, chocolate, strawberry…"

"What is wrong with you? You can't give a baby *regular* milk." I huffed. "They need special milk that either is from their mom or from a formula can."

Liam peeked around the divider. "Why?"

My mouth opened and shut like a carp before I realized… I had no idea why. But I wasn't about to admit it out loud.

"Just find the formula."

"Hey! What about this?" Liam held up a jar of baby food. "It says six months… I think that's the age the baby has to be… not the expiration date… how old do you think she is?"

"How should I know?!"

"Well, you're the expert!"

"Why, just cause I'm a *girl* I'm supposed to know every single freaking thing about babies?!" I kicked a fallen bottle of ketchup down the aisle. "I'M NOT HER MOM! I'M NOT EVEN OLD ENOUGH TO BE A MOM!"

The baby's bottom lip puffed out. Her round face got redder

and redder, like a tomato ripening in a time lapse video. Before I knew it, Sara was wailing.

"Great job, Amaia!" Liam shoved a finger in my face. "You made her cry. You happy now?!"

"Fine." I growled and thrust out the baby to him. "You take her!"

Liam scooped Sara into his arms and bounced her up and down, rocking her sweetly as he hummed a little song. It was magic. Her wide eyes glittered with subsiding tears as a toothless smile spread ear to ear.

Whether he was her big brother or her dad, it didn't matter to Sara. Liam was the guy taking care of her. She trusted him with her life. She had to.

Was it possible for me to feel like more of a total jerk? I wished Liam could soothe the guilty ache inside me the way he'd comforted Sara. To do that, I'd have to tell him I was sorry. Instead I said, "You sing good for a boy."

"Thanks." He blushed and looked up at me guiltily from under his eyelashes. "About before… I shouldn't have said what I said about your mom… and I'm sorry for poking at you about the God thing…"

"Forget it." I turned my face so he wouldn't see the pink on my cheeks, and my gaze landed smack dab on a glass display case. "Over there!"

Ten cans of formula under lock and key. From the price tag, it was easy to guess why.

"I can't believe it's so expensive," I muttered.

Liam laughed and gestured to the fallen cash carpeting the floor. "I think we can afford it."

We crammed our backpacks full of both formula and baby food, in case we ended up figuring out if Sara could eat that gloppy mush or not. Four plastic shopping bags bulged with things for Liam and me: apples and yogurt from the refrigerated display, boxes of cereal and pasta, peanut butter, jelly, chips, and several loaves of bread.

Liam said we should come back for more tomorrow, and I agreed. It was getting late and we'd be slower on the way back, weighed down by all the supplies we'd found. The handles cut into my hands they were so heavy, but the few shopping carts Food Eagle had were equipped with remote locks on the wheels to prevent homeless people from stealing them.

My heart was light somehow, despite everything, as the cans of formula clinked together in my backpack on the walk home.

Liam must have felt it too; I spied an extra spring in his step. Our first supply run had been a success, Liam and I were able to patch up after a nasty fight, and now our friendship felt somehow stronger for it.

Most importantly, my new little familia had a safe place to return every night where we'd be safe from the geists. For the first time, I had hope we might just be ok after all.

I'd just finished hammering the fourth slat down over the attic door when Liam squished two slices of bread together and a drop of strawberry jelly splattered on the floor. I frowned at the red splotch that narrowly missed his sneaker. It reminded me of blood.

"Don't worry." Liam licked his thumb clean then wiped it on his jeans. "We can use toilet paper instead of napkins if we have to."

Yeah, thanks but no thanks. After my epic pants-peeing incident, there was no way I was letting one of the last boys on earth watch me wipe poop-colored peanut butter off my face with TP. I pecked at my sandwich like a sparrow while Liam wolfed down his dinner and crammed his face with chips.

The paper on the window faded from golden to brown to black.

"I brought up a game I found." Liam lit a candle. "We can play if you want to."

"Sure." But my smile sagged into a frown when he set the mahogany box between us.

"Hey, these pieces aren't plastic." Liam rolled an onyx castle between his finger and thumb, studying my father's handiwork in the candlelight.

"My dad carved this set." I cradled a king in the palm of my hand. "He used to go to tournaments and stuff."

"Really?" Liam chuckled. "Kind of strikes me as funny he'd be so into chess, your dad being a construction worker and all."

"Well, he doesn't play anymore, does he?" I snatched the piece from Liam's hand and slammed the board shut.

"Amaia, I…" Liam's voice broke off. "I didn't mean… I'm sorry."

Angry tears stung my eyes. I always knew the rich kid from the big house across the street would look down his nose at us. This is exactly why I never let him be my friend. But if he could hurt me, I could hurt him too.

"What about *your* dad, huh?" My tongue dripped with acid. "What happened at that restaurant with your parents?"

Liam's expression twisted like I stabbed him in the gut. *Good.*

"I can't…" he sputtered.

"I know about last night! I heard you crying like a whiny little baby in your pillow."

"Stop it!" Liam covered his face with his hands and shrunk away from me.

"What happened to you that made you run like that? You better tell or so help me…" I shut my mouth mid-threat. Liam's spine went rigid. A booming racket thundered in the distance, freezing both of us in place. Only, it wasn't screams this time.

Liam nearly tripped over the toy box as he raced to the window.

"What's that sound?" I whispered, thankful Sara already had her earplugs in.

"Gunshots."

A melody approached, and I'd know that song anywhere.

On hot summer days, Carlitos and I would go sprinting in the direction of that music, two dollars in hand, making a game of chasing it down.

The Entertainer.

An ice cream truck.

"What's going on? I can't see!"

"Shhh! Quiet!" Liam said, eye glued to the one peephole cut in the paper. "I don't wanna miss it if it comes by!"

I rummaged through the crate, grabbed the knife, and stabbed a second hole in the paper near the bottom of the sill.

A pair of headlights illuminated the far end of my street, sending geists scurrying like rats. The ice cream truck's new owners had tricked it out so much I barely recognized it. The truck was completely wrapped in red and green Christmas lights with mega bright LED floodlights affixed to it in panels on all sides. A ring of barbed wire formed a fence around the roof where a group of five teenagers sat in chairs that had been bolted down for the ride. Each kid was seated so their backs were toward the center of a circle. The four boys each had an AK47 in his hands. The girl had a shotgun.

Bullets buzzed through the air like biting flies seeking meat. As geists ran, kids shot them in the back, sending monsters sprawling to their bellies. Only, shooting them didn't kill the geists. The creatures scrambled back to their feet, hissing and growling and desperate to get away from the light. As the ice cream truck crawled past my house, kids high-fived and fist-bumped each other whenever a geist got nailed by a bullet.

A familiar silhouette cowered at the edge of my front lawn.

Mom.

My frozen fingertips clutched the windowsill to steady myself. That *thing* wasn't my mother anymore. Deep down I knew it was the truth, but my breath snagged in my windpipe at the sight of her shape anyway. The monster wearing my mother's face lingered only an arm's length from our mailbox. I could make out the soft curve of her shoulders and the sweep of those graceful arms I'd give anything to fall into again.

Run Mom!

It was too late. The pixie-haired girl swung her gun in the geist's direction. A bead of sweat slithered down the back of my neck. My eye darted between the girl and my mom's silhouette as the teen raised the barrel of her shotgun and aimed.

Before I knew what was happening, Liam's body slammed into mine, tackling me to the floor. My elbow smashed on the ground just as the shot rang out.

"It's not her." Liam's hand was plastered over my mouth, muffling my scream. "It's not your mom. It's not!"

My nose struggled to suck in air as he kept his palm clamped over my lips, the smell of peanut butter still on his hands from our sandwiches. Teardrops pounded down my face and wound their way into my ears as I rocked my head back and forth on the floorboards.

"It wasn't your mom!" Liam said through a choking sob. "It was a geist!"

I nodded.

"It wasn't her," he said again, as if saying it a thousand times would make it true. He broke like a dam that had one crack too many. Tears flooded his eyes and rained down onto my cheeks as his face hovered inches over mine. We were exact mirrors of each other, like this broken boy was staring into a bottomless lake and I was his reflection.

In that moment, I really *saw* him. It all made sense. I finally understood why Liam cried out in the night.

He'd watched them die.

I'd seen my parents as geists, but I hadn't been there the moment they died. The people I'd seen become geists on TV were strangers, not the two people I loved most in the whole world. Liam wasn't so lucky. That's why he couldn't talk about it or cry in front of me.

And that's why Liam saved me from being tortured by the

memory of seeing the geist that used to be my mother gunned down. It would have haunted me for the rest of my life.

The chimes of the ice cream truck's melody faded in the distance, and the only sound left was our stifled sobs as we cradled each other in a tangle of arms and tears. The two of us wept for hours, long into the night. When the candle burned out and our eyes were drier than desert sands without a single drop left to give, Liam wiped his face on his sleeve and put a pillow under my head.

As sleep came for me, he was still holding my hand.

CHAPTER
SIX

A beam of sunlight fell across Liam's face like the spotlight of an interrogation room. Whatever secret he was about to confess, he was scared to tell me.

"Right before the plague happened, some people went crazy. Dad said we needed to get out of the restaurant and get home right away. Bad things were happening outside. Cars crashing. People screaming. My mom and I were in the booth waiting for Dad to get back from paying the bill. That's when it happened…"

I reached for his hand. Three days ago, I never would have held hands with the spoiled rich kid from across the street. The end of the world kind of changes things I guess.

"Mom was hugging me and telling me she loved me. I started to say it back… to tell my mom I love her too. But I didn't get the chance. One second Mom was hugging me and the next she was gone. I couldn't hold onto her…I couldn't save her. I couldn't…"

I squeezed his hand tighter.

"Without you, I'd still be in the toy box." I struggled to keep my voice steady, to be strong for him. "And if you didn't try to get your aunt's gun, we never would have found Sara Angelina. You couldn't have saved your mom, but you did save *us*."

"No, I didn't save your life. I ruined it." Liam swatted my hand away. "If you knew what I did, Amaia, you'd never speak to me again."

The sun moved behind a cloud and darkened the attic window. I wrung my hands in my lap as he continued.

"Anyway, the other kids in the restaurant ran out screaming. Not me. I couldn't move. I just sat frozen in the spot I last hugged my mom, staring at her empty pile of clothes and half-eaten chicken parm."

He paused and swallowed hard, like he was seeing it all over again.

"Then something changed. The ashes started to make the shapes of people again, and it stank really bad, like rusty metal and a butcher shop. And I could see her face... my mom... she was floating in the air almost like she was underwater. All I could think was, *I had to get her somewhere safe.* So, I reached up and grabbed her hands, pulling her toward the door. It's kind of half-light, half-dark in that restaurant. *Ambient lighting* my Mom calls it. Thinking back on it, that's probably why the ashes were re-forming so slow. Just before I got to the front entrance, I noticed my dad hovering by the hostess' station. I couldn't drag them both, so my plan was to double back for Dad once I got Mom to the car. But when I got outside, the sun was already down. That's the first time I saw fully-formed geists... and they were hungry."

The hairs on my arms stood on end.

"I ran." Liam slammed his eyes shut. "I dragged my Mom behind me like a kite, but she got heavier and heavier until I couldn't pull her anymore. When I turned my head, she wrapped her hands around my throat. She..."

Liam fell silent and shuddered.

"It's ok, Liam." I put a hand on his trembling shoulder. "You don't have to keep talking about it if you don't want to. I shouldn't have made you... I..."

Liam's head snapped up, fiery blue eyes searing into mine.

"Don't give me an out! I *have* to tell you Amaia." His voice cracked. "This secret is *killing* me, don't you get it? You have to just let me tell you, ok?"

"Ok." I was sure nothing he could say could be worse than what he already told me.

I was wrong.

Liam took a breath like he was about to jump off a twenty-foot diving board.

"Her geist pinned me to the sidewalk. I was kicking and screaming, trying to push it off me. More geists came circling around. I was going to die. Kids all around me were being eaten. But the next thing I knew, I heard a motorcycle engine rev, and when I looked up, Carlos smashed Mom's geist off me with a baseball bat."

My fingers flew to my lips. "My brother?"

Liam nodded. "It happened so fast. Carlos yelled for me to get on the bike, but there was a cheerleader on it too, and the three of us barely fit. I held on for about fifteen minutes before another geist lunged out of nowhere and slammed into us. Carlos lost control of the bike and we skidded. The girl went flying. She was wearing a helmet, so she could have survived it, but she was banged up and all limp like she was sleeping. Your brother and I both rolled away in different directions.

Geists swarmed on the girl. Your brother was fighting them off. He'd lost the bat somewhere, so he was beating them back with his bare hands. I mean, Carlos was literally punching geists in the face like Captain America or something. Carlos turned to me and said, '*My sister's in our attic. Don't let her leave the house!*' Then he threw me this."

From his jacket pocket, Liam pulled out a silver house key with a plastic football dangling from the keychain.

Carlitos' spare key.

My bottom lip quivered so hard I pressed my fist over it to make it stop.

"Your brother wanted me to protect you. That's why he gave

me your house key… but I was so scared I wasn't thinking straight. The next morning, I found you stuffed in that toy box, crying and shaking… and it was all my fault." Liam swiped teardrops from his own cheek. "If I'd just run here to your house instead of going home to mine that night, you wouldn't have been alone… I told myself I'd wait until you stopped crying to tell you about Carlos… but then I just… I couldn't do it."

Sara Angelina blinked up at me in blissful ignorance, and I wished that like her I hadn't been able to understand what Liam's words meant.

But I did.

"You lied to me." My voice came out in a deadly whisper, but Liam heard me loud and clear. "You said you didn't see my brother."

"I didn't lie." His mouth did the twisty thing. "I said I didn't see your brother *on our street.*"

My fists clenched like two bombs ready to explode across his jaw.

"YOU LEFT MY BROTHER TO DIE?!" I shrieked. "Why did you let me write that stupid note and tape it to his door? You already knew he was dead!"

"We don't know that! Maybe he got away?"

"If Carlos got away, he would have come back for me!" I screamed, my spit splattering in Liam's face. "He was coming home, but instead he stopped to help *you*! And now my brother's dead because of it! Because of *you*!"

"I'm sorry…" Liam shrank in on himself. "Maybe your brother is…"

"Get out!" I growled. "LEAVE! I hope the geists rip you to shreds! I hope they tear out your eyes and leave your guts all over the street!"

"You don't mean that." Liam's voice was unsure.

"Get out or I'll kill you myself!" I shoved Liam off the toy box, sending him tumbling onto the slat floor with a *thud*. Liam was dead to me already. As he tried to stand, I pushed him over with my sneaker like kicking aside a pile of trash I didn't want to dirty my hands with.

Red splotches bloomed on Liam's cheeks as tears painted cracks down his porcelain face. He scurried away and clumsily ripped up the boards with the back of the hammer as he choked back sobs. The ladder slammed down hard, and in the breath of a few steps, the boy was gone.

I refused to cry. Sara bawled for over an hour.

I didn't feel like dealing with it, so I turned my back and left her on the quilt to cry it out. She'd better get used to disappointment like the rest of us. Eventually Sara's vocal cords turned hoarse and she fell asleep, her tiny brow wrinkling under a bad dream. Could babies have nightmares? After what she'd lived through already, I didn't see why not. Life was a nightmare.

Liam would have sung to her or made funny faces until she smiled again, but I wasn't about to let that guilt-trip me. We didn't need that jerk anymore. As long as Sara and I had the attic, we were safe. I could go out for supplies during the day and then barricade us up here at night. Maybe I could even teach her things when she got older, like how to read a book and ride a bike. Babies have always struck me as gross, with all that puke and poop. But having a little sister could be kind of cool. If we survived until Sara's old enough to talk, that would be something to look forward to.

Then I realized, without Liam, I wouldn't have anyone to talk to… maybe even for years. When do babies learn how to talk anyway?

It didn't matter. I never wanted to speak to *him* again. He was a liar and a coward. How dare he leave Carlos to die like that?

Something nagged me as I drummed my fingers on the toy box. At first, the question was just a whisper in the back of my mind. But it got louder and louder until it was screaming in the front of my brain.

Would I have left my brother?

If Carlos told me to run and tossed me his key, would I have stayed by his side as the geists closed in around us? Would I have fought the monsters bare-handed, risking my own life to protect his stupid girlfriend? Or would I have raced home in terror, locked the door, and hid myself in a toy box?

I was pretty sure I knew the answer.

And I hated myself for it.

My throat went tight as I wiggled my finger into Sara's sleeping palm. Her tiny hand wrapped reflexively around mine. *How did I get to be such a screw up?*

Carlitos saved Liam and sent him to protect me, knowing full-well he might not make it home alive. My idiot brother was a hero. And I just threw his sacrifice into the trash like an ungrateful brat. Mom always said I had a bad temper, but this was boss-level bad. I could practically hear Carlos' ghost calling me "*jodóna*" from beyond the grave.

I needed to find Liam before it was too late. In one swift motion, I scooped Sara up in my arms and bounded down the ladder. The baby gasped awake and kicked her chubby legs against my stomach with all her might.

"Chill out," I grumbled. "It's not like I'm kidnapping you."

Sara had zero chill. She was full-on freaking out. Maybe she'd never forgive me for turning my back on her? After I'd found out Liam had lied to me about Carlos, I didn't think I could feel any worse. I was wrong. Sara squirmed and screamed, desperate to leap from my arms. She hated me. A *baby* hated me, and I deserved it. My rock bottom hit a new all-time low.

"Shhh," I rubbed her back like I'd seen Liam do. "I'm sorry, ok? I'm gonna fix this."

I hoped Liam hadn't gone far. Across the street to his house? No. It could be crawling with geists. My mind raced. *If I were Liam, where would I have gone to?*

Back to Food Eagle to get more supplies.

I winced.

Somehow, I hadn't been afraid to make that trip when Liam had been by my side. The thought of facing those swirling ashes without him made my knees wobble as I stomped down the stairs.

But if Liam died tonight, that would pretty much make me a murderer. I had to make this right. I had to bring him back.

I closed my eyes and said a silent prayer with my hand on the doorknob.

Please God, let me find Liam.

"Wait! Don't leave," he said.

Startled, I spun back toward the kitchen. Liam lingered in the hallway, wringing his hands.

"I was going to look for you," I stuttered.

Sara was still screaming and thrashing in my arms, so Liam took a cautious step forward and held out his hands for the baby. Tiny fingers grasped at his t-shirt, as if to beg him never to leave her alone with Big Bad Amaia again. He drew the baby into his warm embrace and hummed softly as her cries subsided.

Seeing him cuddling the baby made me want to break into a thousand pieces.

"You stayed," I muttered.

"I promised I'd never leave you." Liam took a trembling breath. "Remember? When you had that panic attack outside my house, I made a promise. I meant it…" His voice broke off. "But if you really want me to go…"

"No. It's ok." I shifted my weight. "You can stay."

Liam moved to wrap his free arm around me, to pull me into his embrace with Sara, but I pressed my back to the door.

"Don't touch me. I'm still mad at you."

"I know." Liam took a step back and bit his lip. "I've been down here this whole time thinking of how I'm going to make it up to you… It's only four blocks from here. We could still make it there and back before dark if you want to see it."

"See what?"

"The place where I left your brother."

Storm clouds swirled overhead, and though I was vaguely aware if the light dimmed too much it might wake the geists early, I worried more that rain might wash away traces of my brother that would prove to me whether he was alive or dead.

I had to know the truth.

I swiped Mom's umbrella from where I'd dropped it on the lawn three days ago. This time, I made Liam use Carlos' spare key to lock up behind us. I was done trusting people.

Four blocks away. Hope fueled my steps, making them light and hurried. I didn't even notice the hovering clouds of ash in my way and plowed right through one, afterward batting it away like a bad smell in the wind. I pressed on.

Three blocks away. My steps grew heavier, knowing each one was one step closer to the truth. The most foolish part of me expected Carlos to be waiting there with a pompous smile plastered across his face. Maybe he'd sprained his ankle and couldn't make the walk home? Maybe he was waiting for *me* to rescue *him*? He'd yell at me for taking so long. My brain instantly conjured a dozen snarky comments I couldn't wait to hurl back in his face. A giddy laugh escaped my lips.

Two blocks away. Despair took me. My brother was dead. Instead of his smirking face, I imagined I would find part of his bloody corpse. A severed limb. Would I know the shape of my brother's hand? Would I be able to identify him by a finger?

One block away. Tears blinded me and I furiously swiped them from my cheeks. Liam reached back to grip my hand, pulling me onward.

And then we arrived.

"Look around, see if you can spot anything," Liam said, casting a wary glance at the darkening sky.

What did we expect to find? A note? A neon sign? A blood splatter on the ground? There was nothing. The sidewalk was one perfect sheet of gray.

"There." Liam pointed. "The cheerleader landed between those two houses, right by the base of those stairs."

"My dad's motorcycle?" I frowned. "It's gone."

"We wiped out pretty hard." Liam scratched his head. "There's the skid marks over there."

"But where's the bike?" I demanded.

Liam shrugged.

"Baseball bat is gone too," he said.

My mind immediately turned to those kids with the ice cream truck.

Scavengers.

Thank goodness we had Carlos' key to lock my front door this time.

On either side of the street, matching brownstones with pointy roofs were crammed in two crooked rows like a set of cruddy, rotting fangs biting into the sky. Chipping concrete stairs lined with rusting metal bannisters lead up to each apartment building, and seeking to improve my vantage point, I climbed to the top of the nearest one.

My inky black shadow spilled down the steps before me, cast by the brightest security light I'd ever seen.

Liam and I stared at each other wide-eyed.

"*Dios mío.*" I crossed myself.

"Oh my God," Liam echoed. "If he stayed on that step…"

"I know!" I clutched the wrought iron railing to steady myself. My brother stood in this very spot. A dried, bloody handprint on the door handle confirmed it. I tested the knob. It was locked.

"It doesn't look like he got into the building," Liam said. "Carlos must have waited under this light until the sun came up."

"Yeah." I frowned. "But then why didn't he come home?"

As I made my way down the stairs, a single drop of rain pelted me on the forehead.

Clouds of ash spun in the changing wind, solidifying more by the second as shadows of monsters began to take shape. A thundercloud blotted out the sun.

"Go! Go! Go!" Liam gripped Sara to his chest and took off like a shot. Mom's umbrella clattered to the pavement. There were worse things to worry about than getting rained on. I pumped my arms and ran for my life.

·······))) ● (((·······

We were soaked to the bone by the time we reached my house. As geists began to touch ground just beyond my front lawn, I silently cursed myself for making Liam lock the door.

Yellow lights shone bright in every window, and mine was the only house on the whole street to still be lit up. Even in the daytime, I'd been scared to turn them off. Maybe superstition was getting the better of me, but what if they didn't come back on? I wasn't about to jinx it.

We were soon safe inside, bolting the door behind us and bounding upstairs. Sara was in hysterics: who knew little lungs could make such a big racket? Liam pulled up the rope handle, and I hammered the boards over the door in record time. We were really getting good at this.

It was still hours from sundown, but one peek out the paper

peephole told me the street below was already crawling with fully formed geists. We'd barely made it.

Each time lightning flashed and lit up the sky, geists collectively shrieked like they'd stuck their fingers in an outlet and got zapped. The short bursts of light weren't enough to make them explode back into dust though, and they meandered on through the storm in search of their next meal.

I wished the rain could've melted geists into puddles of steaming slop like the Wicked Witch of the West, but my own story had no such luck. I did end up getting stuck with Liam the Cowardly Lion though, searching for my brother the Brainless Scarecrow. And I had to admit I'd been the Heartless Tinman to Sara earlier; so maybe none of us was perfect and I just had to accept that.

Thunder clapped so hard the whole house winced like it got smacked upside the head. Sara's fists batted away Liam's clumsy fingers as he struggled to put earplugs in the fussy baby. She spat out her pacifier on the dusty attic floor.

Hungry and cranky was a nasty combination.

Join the club.

Racing upstairs from the geists, I hadn't thought to grab a bottle from the fridge downstairs.

Too late for that now.

Plastic grocery bags crunched and crinkled as I rifled through their contents, tossing boxes of crackers and bags of chips over my shoulder. Finally, I scowled at a container of pumpkin and carrot with a plump-faced baby grinning out at me from the label.

"This goop better work," I muttered. "You changed her, so I guess I can feed her this slop…"

"Nah, I got it." Liam perked up like he actually wanted to do it. Fine by me. He spoon-fed Sara the mushy mixture while I slapped together peanut butter and jelly sandwiches for him and me.

"Vvrrroooom!" Liam twirled the spoon with one hand and

tickled her armpit with the other. "Here comes the airplane! Open the hangar! Nom, nom, nom."

"You're crazy, you know that?" But I couldn't keep myself from smiling.

"What?" Liam shrugged with a goofy look on his face. "She likes it."

Sure enough, Sara's doe eyes were mesmerized as he flew the spoon through the air and landed it in her mouth between giggles. Her tongue moved so much of the orange mush over her toothless gums and down her chin, I doubted she actually swallowed much. But at least she was laughing instead of screaming.

Despite everything, it felt good to smile again. My brother sent Liam to me. The angels sent Sara. No matter what happened, these two were my familia now. And Carlos was alive! He was out there somewhere; I just knew it. It was only a matter of finding him.

And I *would* find him.

I let Liam wear the earmuffs tonight since he hadn't been getting nearly enough sleep. I lay awake listening to the sound of Liam's steady breathing and the baby snoring through her stuffy nose.

Sheets of rain poured in buckets outside, and my worried eyes scanned the ceiling for any sign of a leaky roof. I knotted my fingers and cradled the back of my head as I counted the seconds between the lightning and thunder.

One Mississippi, two Mississi…

Crack.

Barely two Mississippi's away.

One Missi…

Crack.

Every hair on my arms stood on end.

Oh no. No. No. No. No.

I shimmied out of the covers and felt my way to the window, blind in total darkness.

The motion light was off.

The streetlights were off.

I hooked my fingers in and tore the paper peephole bigger to get a better look. Staring straight down, I pressed my nose and forehead against the frosty glass. My house downstairs was pitch black. The green shrubs at the base of the bay window were barely visible in the shadows; the lights from the living room lamps that normally made them glow had switched off.

I didn't realize I was screaming until it was too late.

In another flash of lightning, I caught the briefest glimpse of the horde of geists marching right over my front lawn.

**CHAPTER
EIGHT**

I screamed loud enough to rouse Liam, piercing right through his earmuffs. He fumbled with the flashlight; its beam raced around the room until it found my face.

"Amaia, what's wrong?"

"THE LIGHTS ARE OFF!"

"What do you mean, *the lights are off*?"

"The storm made the power go out."

Liam froze.

A crash downstairs. Shattering glass. I didn't need to see it to know what was happening. Geists were climbing over each other, hurdling the living room couch, and knocking over my mother's lamps and end tables. They could break windows, but could they climb stairs?

Liam raised a finger to his lips and tiptoed to my side.

"Don't make a sound," he whispered so quietly in my ear I barely heard him.

Sara's brow crinkled. I held my breath. She was on the edge of waking up. One wrong move…

Liam double checked the boards were nailed down tight. He took the knife I'd grabbed from the butcher block and sawed off the rope handle he'd pulled around the door casing. Now, there was no way it could slip back through and become a handle for geists to grab.

Instead of cowering with Sara and me in the corner, Liam gripped the knife in his trembling hand, crouched in the attack position, and kept his eyes fixed on the door in the floor. His words from earlier echoed in my head.

If the creatures get that close, we'd better just use the knife on ourselves.

I put a protective arm over Sara.

Watching Liam's silhouette in the glow of the flashlight, I knew now that he'd never be able to go through with it. Those were brave words standing in my kitchen before we met Sara, but now? Part of me wanted to get up and stand by his side, but my legs felt like tembleque.

Just as I thought things couldn't get any worse, Sara decided to wake up.

Her pacifier was in my hand, ready for this moment, but she wouldn't take it. She thrashed her head from side to side and wailed.

Footsteps thundered below, like demons from the underworld rising. I tried shushing the baby, but it was no use. The more I shushed, the louder she cried.

Geists screamed in primal rage, thirsty for the blood of children. They hissed and snarled as they moved from my parents' bedroom to Carlos' to mine, searching for us. Monsters scratched and clawed everything in their path, desperate to sink their teeth into the flesh that cried out like a dinner bell over their heads. The door to the attic rattled as an unseen horror smashed it over and over again from below. Geists were crawling up the walls.

Liam hovered motionless over the door, blade in hand. I thought I caught the faint glint of tears scraping down his cheeks.

It was hopeless. We were all going to die. The wooden boards nailing the door shut creaked and moaned with each blow as geists used their own bodies as battering rams to force their way in. Those planks were leftovers from the sawhorse Dad built. He always said it was better to buy too many supplies than too few. Now, those four extra pieces of wood and a handful of nails were the only things keeping his daughter alive.

Was my dad one of those monsters on the other side of the door? Was Mom with him? I shook my head furiously. Those demons weren't my parents. My real parents would have died protecting me. Mom and Dad wouldn't have cowered in this corner. They would have fought back. Liam said Carlos pummeled geists with nothing but his fists to save his girlfriend. Being a fighter was in my blood.

The geists smashed the floor beneath his feet so hard, Liam let out a squeal of surprise as the knife fell from his hand. It stuck straight up in a floorboard, point down.

Something in me snapped.

I turned my back on the toy box.

My heart beat like a war drum, and for the first time since the Plague of Ashes, I was more furious than I was afraid.

The plague killed my parents. It separated me and my brother. Now, geists dare to break into *my* house to take my new familia from me?

A low, rumbling growl erupted from deep in my chest like the first warning of a volcano ready to melt the world in fire. I wanted to tear a geist's head off with my bare hands, to make them *hurt*. Let them break that door down. I *dare* them. My fingers ripped the knife from the attic door like pulling Excalibur from the stone.

Liam's mouth dropped open as I clutched the weapon in my fist. My face must have been terrifying in the glow from the flashlight, because I got this weird feeling that Liam was just as afraid of me as he was of the geists pounding the slats under our feet.

"We're not dying tonight!" I hissed at the monsters beneath

the floorboards before turning to Liam. "Keep Sara. I've got this."

The assault on the door continued until early dawn when, as quickly as it began, it ceased.

Without heading down the ladder, I knew fierce rays of golden sunlight had already pierced the eastern-facing bedroom windows by this time in the morning. The second floor would be plastered in ash from geists that had exploded back into their ghost-like forms.

Last night, I'd tried to distinguish between various pitches of snarl to gauge how many had gotten inside. The best I could figure was about ten. Would the attic door have held if twenty geists had got in? Or thirty? One look at the jagged cracks splintering the wood told me the answer. These boards were toast.

I was so peeved at myself for not thinking to bring rope up here. Climbing out the second story window and risking a broken leg was way less scary than the alternative.

"Wouldn't it be better to just stay up here in case the lights come back on?" Liam asked. "We can ration the sandwiches. Sara seemed to like that baby food, so…"

"The lights aren't coming back on." I tore the paper from the window in one big swipe. "Why would they? It's not like there's someone from the power company who's going to come fix it."

"Oh. Right." Liam worried his bottom lip with his teeth. "Then we're gonna need battery powered lights. Remember those LED panels on the outside of that ice cream truck?"

"Yeah, I've seen those before at Golding's," I said. "Dad used to drag me there whenever he needed something for his workshop."

"What's Golding's?"

"It's a little shop called Golding's Family Hardware &

Lumber that's only three blocks past Food Eagle, but my dad says barely anyone knows about it anymore since Builder Depot opened up a few years ago and nearly drove them out of business. It's almost always empty, which has been really terrible for Mr. Golding…"

"It was dinner time!" Liam sprang to his feet. "After 6pm, right? It must have been since my mom was already off work…"

"What are you talking about?"

"What time was it? When the adults… when they…"

"Oh," I said. "Yeah, I guess it was after 6. The news was already on."

"What time does that hardware store close?" Liam's voice was urgent. "What if… what if there weren't any customers inside when the plague hit? That would mean there's no geists inside now… except maybe the store owner…"

A smile spread across my face, and I almost laughed out loud I was so giddy.

"Golding's isn't even open on Mondays! I can't tell you how many times Dad forgot, drove all the way there, then was so ticked off!"

"This is perfect!" Liam hesitated. "I hope those scavenger kids haven't thought of it…"

"Not a chance," I said. "Seriously, Golding's sign is so small, you'd drive right by if you didn't know it was there. But they have generators, batteries, solar panels… a whole lighting display! It's the absolute jackpot."

"Cool!" Liam yawned and rubbed his eye.

I felt it too. We hadn't slept since the power outage, and it was probably getting close to eleven by now. The only thing keeping me going were the snacks I'd scarfed down.

"We need to get out of here," I said. "The geists only had a few hours to try to break the door last night before the sun came up, but tonight they'll have the whole night to do it. And what if even more of them get in?"

Liam was spent, purple circles stained the pale skin beneath his eyes. He scanned the room, his gaze lingering on the nails popping up through the boards over the attic door.

"You're right." Liam sighed. "We have to make a run for it."

Liam and I should've rested for an hour to gather our strength before we left, but falling asleep was too risky. While I was positive Golding's would be deserted, we'd need time to fortify the place before nightfall.

I rifled through my old baby things and, in the bottom of a musty dresser, found the treasure I was looking for. I'd only seen it in a photograph: a blue denim carrier that turned a baby into a backpack you wear on your front. Mom never threw away anything sentimental. While Liam adjusted the straps and fastened the baby to his chest, I strained to pry open the attic window before I realized my dad must have nailed it shut.

"What are you doing?" asked Liam.

"I'm going to throw our supplies down onto the front lawn," I said. "We don't know for sure what's on the other side of that door, and I'm going to need my hands free for a weapon just in case. You're in charge of carrying Sara and keeping her quiet. But first, help me bag the stuff that won't break."

"Maybe I should carry the weapon and you should carry the baby?" Liam nibbled his thumbnail.

I shot him a dubious look. "Why? Because I'm a girl and you're a boy?"

"Yeah." Liam's cheeks turned pink.

We sat in silence for a long moment as that word hung between us. It drove me crazy to admit it, but he wasn't wrong. Men protected women. Women protected babies. That's the way the world worked for thousands of years.

If my brother was here, I'd fork the weapon over in a heartbeat. But Liam wasn't Carlos. And if he tried to be... none of us were getting out of here alive.

"Your brother told me to protect you." Liam's eyes found mine. "But what if I'm not strong enough? What if I can't…"

"Stop being an idiot." I poked my finger into his chest to shut him up. "We both know Sara screams when I hold her, and if she cries while there's geists left downstairs, she and I are gonna get ripped to shreds."

Liam's brow creased. "She might not…"

I didn't let him finish. "Who is the faster runner? You or me?"

"I am. But what does that…"

"That's right. You are." I poked his chest again. "I couldn't keep up with you on the run to your aunt's. You're wicked fast!"

"I guess…" He blushed. "I mean, I am the fastest kid on my track team for the 200 meter… Coach even lets me run the Varsity heat at practice…"

"See?" I said triumphantly. "If I needed to sprint out of here, carrying Sara would slow me down and we'd both be geist chow. But you could outrun the geists *and* get the baby to safety… if it comes to that."

"That… makes sense." Liam sighed, though he looked as if a tremendous weight had been shifted off his shoulders. "Ok. I'll take Sara."

And just like that, our plan was in motion. He set to work cramming the last of the bread, cereal, and peanut butter into a grocery bag. Powdered formula was in tins that Liam packed too, but Sara's baby food was in glass jars that wouldn't survive a two-story fall.

Those jars went safely in Liam's backpack along with the flashlight.

I worked at dislodging the nails in the windowsill with the hammer's claw, but it was no use. My dad had driven them all the way down. This was taking forever.

Fed up, I swung the hammer and smashed the window to bits. Shards of shattered glass plunged like falling icicles on the eaves of my porch below.

When I turned, Liam wore a smug smile on his face.

"I'm just glad you're on my side," he said.

I gave him a playful punch on the arm. "Yeah, well, just don't make me mad again and you won't have anything to worry about."

"Deal."

After we tossed the backpack of unbreakables out, I set myself to the task of prying the boards off the door. I didn't have to be a fortune teller to read the cracks and know what our future would have been if we chose to stay. These boards wouldn't have lasted another hour let alone another night. Maybe Sara's guardian angel was still watching over us after all.

The moment the boards were free, Liam threw his arms around me and pulled me tight against his shoulder. I hugged him back as hard as I could.

We might be dead in a few minutes, but this wasn't a goodbye.

In only a few days, despite our quirks and fights, Liam had become the best friend I'd ever had. We'd laughed together. We'd cried together. We'd shared each other's deepest fears and darkest secrets. Now, no matter what happened when we opened that door, we'd face it together.

I made sure Sara Angelina was snugly secured to Liam's chest before I threw on my backpack and said a silent prayer. I hoped Sara's guardian angel wasn't on a lunch break because we could sure use someone to watch our backs this minute.

Would the greasy potato chips we'd scarfed down earlier be our last meal? I'd been so stressed out, I plowed through our whole stash. If I could've picked anything it would have been my mom's *arroz con gandules*.

No.

No way was I going to let *ranch* be the last thing I ever ate.

I clutched my father's hammer in a white-knuckled fist and kicked open the door.

Liam froze at the top of the ladder, so I seized my chance.

This was no time for machismo, and he was out of his mind if he thought I was going to let him go down before me with Sara strapped to his chest in her carrier. We might as well offer the baby up to the geists on a silver platter. Not. Happening. I'd smash those monsters into fish food before I'd let them get their grubby claws on Liam and Sara.

A quick clench of my puny biceps confirmed I was still only hamster-strong. So, why did I feel like I could lift a truck with my bare hands? It's not like I suddenly turned into a pro-wrestler or anything. I didn't get bit by a radioactive spider in the cobwebs of my attic that gave me superpowers. I wasn't one of those princesses whose fairy godmother sprinkled pixie dust over their cradle to crown them the *chosen one*.

I barely got chosen to play dodgeball.

Obviously, there was no way I'd win in a fight against a geist. But at this point, I really wanted to punch one in their stupid face.

They took everything from me. My parents. My brother. My home. My whole world. Those cannibal freaks opened something worse than Pandora's box. The girl in that story got stuck with hope. Hope is for suckers. The only thing the geists left in Amaia's box now burned in my chest.

Rage.

We only had to get out the front door. It was so close. I tiptoed down the ladder, raising the hammer above my shoulder, ready to strike.

The second floor was a minefield of debris that made it impossible to keep our footsteps silent. I scanned bedrooms for any lurking threats and nearly tripped over a chunk of drywall. Holes punched in walls had turned the hallway into a tunnel of swiss cheese, yellow in the golden sunlight. Ragged claw marks scratched from floor to ceiling, some gashes so deep that studs were exposed like wooden bones behind the white flesh of the walls.

I did a quick count of the clouds. Looked like only nine geists had gotten in.

Liam was crowding me. His breath warmed the back of my neck as we inched our way forward, struggling to keep as quiet as the ghosts that hung by our sides.

The door to Carlos' room was the only one left on its hinge, and by some foolish miracle, the note I'd taped up for my brother had survived the night. I doubted he'd ever read it.

On the middle landing, I peeked around the corner to the living room. The last time I'd lingered here, Carlos had been holding a bag of frozen corn on the cheerleader's head as she lay sprawled across the sofa. Now, I barely recognized this place.

A tornado would have done less damage. Mom's lamps were ceramic shrapnel scattered across carpet while her favorite end tables had been reduced to scrap for firewood. The flatscreen I'd spent so many evenings glued to was impaled by a speaker stand. Worst of all, our couch had been flipped on its side, blocking our exit out the front door.

We were trapped.

My tongue turned to cotton in my mouth, but I swallowed

down the panic and focused on my anger instead. Those monsters trashed my house! My mother loved those end tables.

"What's wrong?" Liam whispered over my shoulder.

"Front door's blocked."

Liam's chest heaved as he pressed himself against the wall.

"Don't worry," I said. "We can get out through the kitchen."

I hoped.

"Let's go back up to the attic," he pleaded.

Before last night, I would have been tempted by that offer. But trapping ourselves up there would be a death sentence, and I'd come way too far to let that toy box end up being my coffin after all. My family were fighters. We've always had to struggle to survive, like my great-grandma coming here on a boat from P.R.

Survival was in my blood.

"We've got to keep moving," I said. "Come on." I clutched the bannister and persisted down the stairs before he could try to change my mind.

Liam stood frozen on the landing, torn between his instincts and me. He tensed, tiptoeing and holding his breath as he followed my lead. Each time a stair creaked, Liam winced.

The hall to the kitchen was totally clear of ash. Could all the geists have been drawn upstairs by Sara's screams? Could we have been that lucky? I wouldn't put lunch money on it.

The backdoor waited for us. All we had to do was unbolt the lock, pull open the inside door and push open the screen. After that, we'd rush into daylight and be safe. How many times had I made the trip from the living room to the kitchen to get a snack? A zillion? How many steps were from here to there? I'd never bothered to count. Now, the kitchen floor might as well be a river of lava.

A bead of sweat dripped down Liam's neck, but he kept his cool. Sara's pacifier twitched in her mouth, barely concealing her smile. She looked to be living her best life in her new carrier, snuggling up to literally her favorite person on the planet right now.

Liam crept past a mirror hanging in the hallway, and Sara reached out for her own reflection as if to say, "Look! A baby!"

But we didn't stop.

I poked my head into the kitchen. The back door was on the farthest wall, past the island and next to the refrigerator. I glided my hand around the door casing and felt for the light switch. No good. The power was still out. Behind the sink, venetian blinds did an excellent job of preventing our nosy next-door neighbors from staring at us while we washed dishes. Unfortunately, they also did a great job of making it super dark in my kitchen even during the daytime.

We paused to assess the silence.

No snarls or growls. No monsters demoing walls with bony fists. Nada.

The geists were gone. The ashes floating upstairs really had been the lot of them. We were home free. I turned and gave Liam the thumbs up then made a dash for the back door. With a quick turn of the lock, I swung it open and held the screen for Liam and the baby.

The two of them bounded into the safety of the sunlight, but I paused on the threshold.

The fridge was full of formula. We needed that. Sara needed that. It was so close, right in my grasp. It would only take a sec…

I stuffed the handle of the hammer in the waistband of my leggings.

"Amaia, what are you doing?!"

The cool air of the refrigerator was already on my face. Within two seconds, I cradled an armful of bottles.

My nose crinkled, crushed by a metallic stench like maggoty meat from a dumpster. I nearly puked in my mouth. The fridge still seemed cold enough, despite the power being out. What gives? Did milk really go bad that fast?

Without warning, a million years of evolution slammed into

my body at once, a genetic alarm system passed down from my cavemen ancestors once hunted by bigger, badder carnivores. The warning screamed through every nerve ending in my body that I was about to be something's breakfast. But I couldn't make myself believe it until I turned around.

A stupid mistake.

Mom always scolded me for not closing the door from the kitchen to the garage. She said it let the heat out. Why didn't I shut it when I'd gotten Dad's earmuffs?

In the darkness, a shadow lumbered forward. Milliseconds stretched into eternity as the geist and I, now predator and prey, became frozen statues in the other's gaze.

Then, like pushing off the edge of a waterslide, time was in motion again. Bottles slipped from my arms and shattered on linoleum, soaking my sneakers in baby formula. The geist lunged forward as I spun on the balls of my feet and reached for the screen door. Beyond the wire mesh, Liam screamed my name as the geist grabbed my backpack.

My mind didn't think as my muscles took control. I whipped around with the hammer in my fist and nailed the geist right in its lower jaw, snapping it clean off. Blackened teeth sprayed at the wall and clattered to the floor. In the impact, I'd lost my grip of the hammer. It flew end over end like a runaway boomerang, sliding across the slick tile, out of reach.

I slipped on a puddle of fake milk and broken glass, but the monster's arms waited to catch me. We spun around and slammed into the counter.

I wrenched my arm behind my back, reaching wildly for the kitchen knife I'd stashed in one of the side loops of my pack. My fingers found the hilt! As the geist pulled me toward it, I plunged the blade deep into the monster's chest.

It didn't even flinch.

Instead, the geist lifted me off the ground by my ponytail as if I weighed no more than Sara. I thrashed and punched and kicked, but I couldn't hurt this thing any more than a butterfly.

My scalp was on fire, like it was going to be ripped clean off my head… but my hand found its way to the knife handle, yanking it free. The geist turned and proceeded to drag me by my hair… toward the garage.

I raised the knife over my head and hacked my ponytail off in three swipes.

What was left of my hair tumbled around my face as my body came to a halt, but I couldn't get to my feet fast enough. This time, the geist went for my throat.

My vision darkened as the creature's iron grip choked off my air. The knife slipped from my fingers. I gave a last futile kick the way a suffocating goldfish flicks its tail weakly one last time before it dies. The geist slammed my back flat on the countertop, ready to carve flesh off bones. Having only an upper jaw wouldn't stop the geist from gnawing me to death. It'd only make the process slower and more painful for me, the unlucky snack.

Instead of my life flashing before my eyes, everything just got darker and darker… until there was a beam of light.

The monster squealed and shrank back. I croaked as air gushed back into my lungs, and when my eyes refocused, Liam was trembling in the doorway holding the flashlight.

I rolled off the counter and landed on all fours.

But Liam's flashlight hadn't hurt the geist as much as it had simply ticked it off.

The light wasn't bright enough.

The geist charged Liam and the baby, but I snatched up the hammer and swung in an arc over my body, catching the geist squarely on the back of its knee with the hammer's claw. The creature belly flopped on the linoleum, hitting its head with a sickening *thwack*.

Liam froze in the doorway, slack jawed and paralyzed with terror. His pupils were tiny grains of black sand in clear blue eyes. Sara's cheeks were splattered with tears, but I could barely register her cries.

"Liam, run!" I screeched.

But the boy was stone-still as a marble statue. Why wouldn't he move?!

The geist pushed itself to its knees.

"Run!"

Liam didn't budge.

I slammed myself onto the geist's back, forcing it down on its stomach and pinning the stench of blood and metal under me.

I screamed. Only this time, it wasn't because I was afraid. It was a battle cry.

My foot caught the creature in the center of its back as I took off like a rocket. I smashed into Liam, pushing him and the baby out into the safety of the sunlight.

The geist was faster than I was. It grabbed me again by my backpack, but I was already in motion. My legs pushed with all my might as I thrust my hands forward like Supergirl flying over a city.

As I sailed through the air with arms outstretched, I carried the geist with me. Just before I hit the ground, I gritted my teeth and braced myself for the certain impact of a heavy body smushing me into a pancake. I face-planted in the grass and rolled over, already swinging my hammer.

It caught only air.

Above me, ash swirled and glittered in the sunlight, like a low flying cloud hanging harmlessly over my head. As I stared into it in amazement, I could swear I heard the faint echo of a growl cursing me from beyond.

"What the heck is the matter with you?!" Liam yanked me to my feet. "Why did you go back?"

"Sara needs the formula…"

"The formula?!" Liam's eyes bulged like they'd pop out of the sockets. "Sara doesn't need formula! Sara needs *you. I* need… I mean, you almost killed yourself for nothing! We could've gotten formula somewhere else. That was stupid, Amaia! Stupid!"

I pursed my lips. "We made it didn't we?"

"Are you hurt?" Liam demanded. "Did it bite you?"

I inspected my arms. The geist probably would have tried to bite me a lot sooner if I hadn't smashed off its lower jaw. My throat ached like it had gotten crushed by a truck, and I expected there'd probably be a hand-shaped bruise around my neck. Other than that, it wasn't much worse than losing a wrestling match with my brother.

"I'm fine." The corners of my mouth twisted into a grin. "I told you I was good with a hammer."

Liam scowled at my joke as he rubbed circles on Sara's back to soothe her. I couldn't believe he was actually blaming me for the baby's bad mood again. Didn't she realize I nearly died trying to get her food? Dad was right; kids are so ungrateful.

We both stood in seething silence for a long moment until the tension shifted. He turned to me with a strange look on his face.

"Your hair…" he reached for my face then pulled his hand back as though he thought better of it.

"Oh." I felt heat rising in my cheeks. My own fingers brushed the uneven ends that now stopped just below my chin. My heart sunk at the thought of my poor ponytail lying somewhere on my kitchen floor in a puddle of glass and fake milk. For some stupid reason, my eyes filled with tears. "I guess a bad haircut is the least of our problems."

"It's not…" Liam cleared his throat and turned his face away. The way his neck turned pink made me think he might be blushing too. "It… it actually looks really good like that."

"Liar." I smiled.

"Mentiro-something right?" Liam grinned.

A laugh escaped my lips. "Yeah, something like that."

We circled around to the front of the house and picked up the supplies we'd tossed out the attic window. Hard to believe that was only, what? Like ten minutes ago?

I gazed up at the empty darkness of that room and imagined my own face staring back at me through the shattered window.

That first night, I'd been standing right in that very spot: alone, terrified, and waiting for my brother to come rescue me. Grownups were always saying that you never know what you got 'til it's gone. Boy was that the truth. I'd been so mad when Carlos had made me hide in our attic. Now, I'd give anything to have that dusty room - and my idiot brother - back again.

My steps were uncertain as I stepped off my front lawn and onto the sidewalk. This was the street I grew up on, but I'd never been more lost. For the first time in my life, I was homeless.

Neither of us brought up what happened in my kitchen again, and I spent the walk to Golding's massaging my tender throat and trying to forget the whole thing. I led the way this time because, as I'd told Liam in the attic, the hardware store was easy to miss. Unlike those fancy big-chain stores, old Mr. Golding had been too frail to get up on a ladder to dust the ashes off his sign every day.

"That's weird," I muttered. "Wasn't this street blocked yesterday?"

Liam picked at a hangnail that had started to bleed as he surveyed the cars rolled haphazardly toward sidewalks, making a winding path large enough for a truck to snake through.

"Guess someone must have cleared it," he said.

Someone? Looks like it would have taken a small army…

Since Food Eagle was on the way to the hardware store anyway, we couldn't resist making a quick pitstop for more supplies. I hoped for more peanut butter and bread, if it wasn't already scaffed up.

The automatic doors wouldn't open. I waved my arms in front of the sensor like I was doing a set of jumping jacks without the jumping. No such luck. The doors were sealed shut like the gateway to a crypt.

"Ugh. It's broke."

"No, look," Liam said. "The power's out here too."

I pressed my face to the glass. Sure enough, though sunlight still poured in the large storefront windows lining either side of the market, the fluorescent lights overhead were a dull, lifeless gray.

I began to wrestle the hammer from my pack, but gunshots stopped me in my tracks.

"It's probably those kids," Liam said. "The ones with the ice cream truck."

"Should we try to talk to them?" I flinched as another shot rang out. Liam held Sara tighter to his chest. "On second thought… maybe we should hide."

"Come on!" Liam pulled me behind the dumpster in the alley between Food Eagle and the barber shop next door.

The white truck swerved around the corner. Five kids still sat perched behind barbed wire ringing the roof, but the mega bright LEDs, red and green Christmas lights, and music were all switched off in the daylight. After the truck came to a screeching halt, the pixie-haired girl with a shotgun blasted a hole in the "O" of a stop sign.

"Ha! Too bad you can't hit anything while we're moving," a boy sneered.

"I still got top score," the girl snapped.

"Knock it off you two. We're here." A teenage boy with a face full of braces hopped out the passenger side door. "A-ten-HUT!"

The kids stood, snapped their heels, and gave a salute.

A girl – must have been the driver - sauntered around the front of the truck, gripping a battery-operated LED panel in one fist.

She was maybe sixteen or seventeen and absolutely gorgeous with rich, dark brown skin and a waterfall of ebony braids that cascaded all the way down to her waist. The softness of her face and features was in stark contrast to the sharpness of her gaze, which took in every minute detail of her surroundings. She stuffed the car keys into the back pocket of her camouflage pants and motioned with two fingers for the kid with braces to follow her onto the sidewalk.

He obeyed without question while the others waited at attention.

"At ease," the driver said. "Nate, stand guard. No one else moves until I say it's clear, got it?"

"Yes, Captain!" They replied as one.

The captain widened her stance and shot them a glare.

"I'm not losing anyone else on my watch," she hissed. "You get me?"

"Yes, Captain!"

Satisfied, she switched on the light in her hand. The kid she called Nate helped her wrestle open the automatic doors with a crowbar, and she disappeared inside.

A few moments later she was back wearing a relieved smile.

"Clear! Let's get it done."

The five teenagers threw empty duffles off the roof and swung a ladder down over the side. The lot of them practically skipped into Food Eagle like it was a field trip to an amusement park.

"*Let me out!*" a muffled voice called from the back of the truck. "I know you jerks can hear me!"

Liam and I frowned at each other as someone's fist relentlessly pounded on metal.

"When I get outta here, I'll knock your heads off!"

"It can't be…" I stood to peer over the dumpster, but Liam yanked me back down.

"Shhh!" he whispered furiously. "You wanna get caught?"

Two kids sauntered out of the market slinging bulging bags over their shoulders. They opened the ice cream truck's back double doors and tossed their bounty inside.

"You can't keep me in here!" the voice bellowed.

"It's your own fault," Nate snapped. "Captain says it's not safe to let you out."

The prisoner protested with a string of profanities as the two kids disappeared once again into Food Eagle, leaving the back doors of the truck open and unguarded.

"Stay here," I said to Liam as I darted out from our hiding place.

"Wait!" He tried to grab me, but I shrugged him off. There was no time to explain. Those kids would be back any second and nothing and no one was gonna keep me from that truck.

I knew I recognized that voice.

"Jay!" I gaped at my brother's best friend: a muscly quarterback locked in a wire cage wedged between the driver's cab and the ice cream freezers.

"Amaia?" Jayden gasped. "Amaia! You're alive!"

My fingers reached through gaps in the wire and intertwined with his. The cage was secured with the same kind of padlock I had on my locker at school.

"Is Carlos with you?" Jayden lowered his voice. "Go get your brother. He's got to help me get out of here…"

"He isn't." My throat tightened. "I was hoping you might have seen him…"

Jayden let his fingers slip from mine as tears flooded his eyes. "Carlos… is dead?"

"He's not. He's just… lost." I cut him off and cast a careful glance to the storefront. "Where's the key?"

Jayden shook his head. "Their leader, she's got it. Listen to me. These kids are dangerous. They call themselves *Gamerz*. Kept me locked in here all last night, parked under a streetlight surrounded by those… those… *things*. The captain won't let me out no matter what I say. You need to get out of here right now! Run!"

Not a chance. I didn't run from a geist. No way was I running from a group of stupid kids that called themselves *Gamerz*. With the initial shock of finding my brother's BFF wearing off, I finally noticed the dried blood caking the corners of Jayden's face.

"Are you hurt?" I demanded. "Did they do that to you?"

"No." Jayden turned his neck to the side to reveal overlapping circles of red teeth marks. "I got separated from the other scouts yesterday during that thunderstorm and those *things* cornered me. Gamerz picked me up, which don't get me wrong, I owe them for that... but their leader freaked when she found out I got bit, so she won't let me out of this cage! She thinks I'm going to infect her crew or something..."

"A geist bit you?"

"Geist?" Jayden crinkled his brow.

"Because they're like poltergeists in the daytime. So, we've been calling them *geists*."

"*Geists*," Jayden murmured, but quickly shook the image out of his head. "Amaia, you gotta get to Unity before sundown... Tell President Denny what happened to me."

"President? Unity? What are you talking about?"

"Just get to the school," Jayden said. "You'll be safe there."

Approaching voices startled me so bad I nearly fell backward out of the truck. I scurried onto the street and ducked behind a rear wheel. Kids lumbered out with more duffle bags and threw them in the back of the truck beside Jayden's cage.

"Zelda says three more loads should do it." One of them wiped his hands on his jeans. "Then we gotta get to that house."

"Better not let the captain hear you call her by her name," the other sneered. "She'll put you on toilet duty." The two hurried back into the store without noticing the girl in the red hoodie hiding under their truck.

"Amaia! You still there?" Jayden whisper-yelled to me as I shimmied out from my place behind the tire.

"The captain's name is Zelda," I muttered. "I'll talk to her. I'll make her let you out!"

"You can't trust Gamerz!" Jayden shot me a stern look. "I heard someone say I'm not the first kid they locked up. If they catch you, they might throw you in here with me. If you want to help me, get to the school quick as you can. Tell Denny the

Gamerz need diesel. They want it real bad. He can trade it for me."

"Diesel. Got it." I nodded. "Don't worry Jay. I'll get you out. I promise."

I turned to dash back to the dumpster, but he called me back.

"Wait!" Jayden's voice trembled, sounding half-strangled in his throat. "Carlos could've made it. Your brother's the toughest kid I know."

"Second-toughest." I winked.

Jayden grinned in spite of the wetness in his eyes. "Guess it runs in the family."

The moment the ice cream truck drove out of earshot, words tumbled out of my mouth as I gushed to Liam all about my conversation with Jayden. I expected him to light up at the news about kids surviving at the school, but Liam was so furious that all he could say to me was: *"What's wrong with you?"*

"You should be happy!" I snapped. "I just found us a new home!"

"We *have* a new home. We have a plan, remember?"

"Oh, *please*." I rolled my eyes. "I only suggested the hardware store because I thought we had no other choice."

"You don't know anything about those Unity kids!" Liam put a protective hand over Sara. "What if they're as bad as the Gamerz? Or worse?"

"What do you want me to do? Leave Jay locked in that cage?"

"Yes!" Liam struggled to keep himself from screaming. "We've got our own problems! Let those Unity kids and the Gamerz figure it out. We shouldn't get involved."

"Fine. Be a *coward*." I stamped my foot. "Go hide at Golding's if you want. But good luck finding it without me. I'm going to the school. Either help me gather supplies and come with me or get out of my way."

Liam's bottom lip quivered. I was only calling his bluff about abandoning him and Sara, but it totally worked. He rose to his feet and marched into Food Eagle without a word.

The vultures had picked the market's bones clean. There was almost nothing left.

Was God punishing me? Why did the only bag of chips left in the whole store have to be *ranch*? Of all the disgusting, nasty flavors… maybe mankind deserved to be wiped out after all.

Cans of tomato sauce sulked unloved and unwanted on the bottom shelf, but since they didn't expire for over a year, I stuffed them into my bag.

"Hold her." Liam unhooked the carrier and set Sara in my arms. Being bossed around always made my teeth grind.

Liam laid flat on his stomach in aisle after aisle and shined the flashlight under the shelves to check if anything had fallen. I groaned inwardly. What was he going to find under there other than dust bunnies and old chewing gum?

But when Liam stood up and dusted himself off, he didn't do it empty handed. He'd scored. Was there a greater treasure in the entire world than a perfectly wrapped chocolate bar? Saliva flooded my mouth, and I wondered if Liam was still mad enough at me not to share it.

But what other choice did I have? I couldn't just sit by and let them lock Jayden in a cage like an animal. Besides, how do the Gamerz figure getting bitten will turn someone into a geist anyway? All the people who died in The Plague of Ashes had just exploded. There was no warning. No bites. Just death and the hunger that came after.

Despite the fact I was certain the Gamerz were being overly paranoid, I was secretly relieved the geist in my kitchen hadn't had the chance to use me as its chew toy this morning. Because, what if it was true? What if one bite would crust my own eyes shut, turn my skin to stone, and make me crazed for the blood of children?

"Your brother's friend said the school is safe?" Liam asked.

"Totally," I said. "Safest place we could be."

It was *probably* true… but even if Jay had said CHS was infested with deadly scorpions, I'd still head there for one reason and one reason alone.

Kids were meeting at the school… and that meant Carlos might be one of them.

Collins Jr./Sr. High School was no fancy prep academy like Liam was used to. CHS reeked of rotting cabbage, fish stick farts, and teenagers who hadn't discovered deodorant. I'd rather have gone to the dentist every weekday instead, and my visits there were always bloodbaths.

Today was a different story. Today, my feet couldn't get me to those sprawling brick buildings fast enough.

The football field to the left of the main campus lurked in my peripheral vision, but I didn't make eye contact. My brain was imagining Brit's recap of Monday night's game. A hundred pairs of empty adult-sized shoes now lay to rest under heaps of pants, sweaters, and shirts. Baseball caps tumbled in the breeze, in search of the lost heads they used to sit on... No doubt all these things would still be littering the bleachers now that their former owners had risen from the dead and wandered off in search of other entertainment. Brit's parents' clothes were among them. I shuddered and kept my eyes glued to the building ahead.

My feet had blisters on blisters, but Liam and I sprinted up to the entrance anyway, only to find it locked. A piece of construction paper greeted us, taped to the inside of the glass double doors. Written in kid's handwriting with rainbow-colored markers in bubble letter font was scrawled the following warning:

NO TRESPASSING!!!!!!!!

A yellow smiley face drawn below it happily told us to scram.

"Hey! Anybody in there?" Liam banged his fist on the glass.

No reply.

Lights illuminated the hallway as far as we could see, a promising sign that outweighed the rude one meant to scare us off.

We stalked the perimeter of the high school's main building, standing on our tip toes and peering into classroom after classroom hoping to find someone to let us in.

"This was a mistake." Liam said. "If we head back now, we can still make it to the hardware store, right?"

"Or I could break a window with my hammer."

Liam squished his lips at me. "These kids don't want us here. You think busting up a window is the way to change their minds?"

Ok. He had a point. I left my hammer zipped up in my backpack... *for now.*

We were halfway around the building when voices rang out through an open window high on the second floor. The chaos of laughter and kids jabbering over each other all at once was sweet music to my ears.

Liam and I flicked pebbles up at the window to get their attention and shouted at the top of our lungs, "Hey! Let us in!"

A girl with beige blonde pigtails popped her head out.

"More survivors!" Her over-lined lips burst into a toothy grin. "Hold on a sec. Aren't you Brit's boyfriend's little sister? O-M-G! Is Brit with you guys?!"

This was going to be awkward...

"Brit smashed her parents' car, so my brother took her to the hospital," I called up. "That was four nights ago. I was hoping maybe they were here?"

An uneasy silence filled the space between us.

"Go around front. I'll meet you there," Pigtails said.

She didn't have to tell me twice.

As we jogged back to the entrance, I picked at my brain to remember Pigtail's actual name. She was one of Brit's cheerleading besties for sure, but those girls were basic, identical copies of each other. They dressed the same, did their makeup the same, even talked with the same nasally scratch in their voices. Mom said many girls believe in order to be *beautiful* they all need to paint on the same pouty lips, thick eyebrows, and non-existent noses. It turned them into clones, and I had no idea what this one's name was. Not that it mattered, since Pigtails hadn't bothered to learn mine either beyond *Brit's boyfriend's little sister*.

Only one person needed to show up to let us in, so naturally, an entourage of thirty kids arrived to get the job done. None of them were Carlos. I shrank in on myself as sixty eyeballs stared at me, like fresh meat on my first day of Middle School all over again. What made it even worse was that these teenagers all seemed way older than Liam and me. There wasn't a single face I remotely recognized other than Pigtails. Teenagers pushed in shoulder to shoulder in a tight circle, crowding us like we were a campfire on a cold night.

A boy with fiery-orange hair and a constellation of freckles across his cheeks sauntered through the throng of teens who all parted to let him through whispering *"Make way for the president"*. His soft brown eyes glittered when he smiled at me, and I was mortified when thirty upperclassmen saw me blush.

This was the president?

Gosh, he was cute. He definitely had my vote.

Play it cool, Amaia.

"Glad you two aren't dead." President Denny put a warm hand on my shoulder.

"Actually, there are three of us," Liam said as he turned to give the kids a better view of the baby in her carrier. "I'm Liam, and that's Amaia. This little one here is Sara Angelina."

"We're glad we're not dead too," I chimed in quickly. My joke made the red-headed boy smile at me again, which set my heart fluttering and my mouth in motion. "We've been hiding in my attic, but the geists got in my house last night because of the power outage. So, now we really need a new place to stay."

"Geists?" the kids murmured all at once.

Blood rushed to color my cheeks even darker. I must have looked like a strawberry by now.

"Oh, uh, that's what we've been calling them. *Geists*. Because they look like poltergeists during the day… but at night… well, you guys know… they're something different."

"Geists." The freckled boy tested out the word on his petal-pink lips. "We've been debating on what to call them, and that's the best name yet. You came up with that yourself, Amaia?"

"I did," I beamed proudly. Liam gave me the stink eye but didn't rain on my parade. I couldn't put my finger on it, but for some reason, I really wanted this red-haired boy to like me. His eyes were the color of my dad's coffee: a dark rich brown that was almost black. From his dazzling smile to his expensive-looking sweater and designer jeans, he was head-to-toe perfection like he was Photoshopped in real life, more flawless than those models on the cover of Teen Vogue.

"Are you gonna let us in, Denny?" Liam asked. "Or are you gonna make us wait out here all day?"

Wow. I'd never seen Liam this cranky.

Sara buried her face in his chest, clearly unsettled by being the center of attention. I shifted on my sore feet, remembering despite my excitement, how much I ached to take my shoes off and stretch my toes.

"What have you got to pay the entrance fee?" Denny asked.

With that, the mood around us altered like a cold front sweeping in. Kids crowded us even tighter, eager to see what treasure we had to offer.

"We've got food." Liam jiggled the grocery bag brimming with canned goods. "We're happy to share it."

The president threw back his head and laughed.

"We have a whole cafeteria," he said. "What else you got?"

Liam's expression darkened. Was Denny really going to turn us away? Didn't he realize we'd be killed if he didn't let us in?

No, Denny wouldn't do that. He seemed so cute and nice. But right now, his warm hand wasn't on my shoulder anymore… and under his orange hair, his fiery grin turned as menacing as a jack-o-lantern's.

"We have information," said Liam. "About the Gamerz."

Denny's smile extinguished.

"What information?"

"Let us in and we'll tell you," Liam insisted.

"Pay up first," Denny said. "If your info is good, I'll let you in. You think we can just let anyone in who shows up at our door? We're an exclusive club. That means a membership fee."

"Jayden sent us," I blurted out. Liam shot me a hard glare, but I didn't care if I was ruining his negotiation tactics. I was desperate to get in the school.

Totally ironic, but still.

My brother could be in there, and it was already getting late. They just *had* to let us in.

"The Gamerz are keeping Jay prisoner," I said. "He's locked up in the back of their ice cream truck."

That revelation ruffled some feathers. Everyone started twittering at once in a full-on freak-out fest. Kids skittered about like flustered chickens while the girl with the pigtails lashed out, grabbing and shaking anyone within reach.

"We've got to help Jay!" Pigtails crowed. "Denny, we can't just let them take one of us. We can't!"

"We'll make 'em pay for this!" a muscly boy in a gray t-shirt said. "I say we go there right now and bust some heads!"

"Wait!" I yelled above the clamor. "Jay said they need diesel!"

"Everyone, quiet!" Denny pulled me closer. "Say that again?"

"The Gamerz need diesel," I said. "They'll trade Jayden for it. That way, nobody gets hurt."

Denny smiled at me and nodded his approval. "Listen up everyone!" He wrapped an arm around Pigtails to comfort her. "No one messes with one of ours. We're going to get Jay back, but we've got to be smart about it."

A few groans of disappointment were drowned out by others shushing them.

"Thank you Amaia for trusting us enough to share that," Denny said loud enough for everyone to hear. "Unity is Community. Communities are built on trust." Denny turned to place a hand on the muscly boy's shoulder. "We can't leave the school undefended. That's just what the Gamerz want us to do. Are you gonna fall into their trap?"

"No, Mr. President." The boy nodded solemnly.

"Good. What do you say everyone?" Denny swept his arm out in a grand flourish. "Who votes to let Liam and Amaia in?"

No one raised their hand until Denny did, but once his arm was high in the air, every other kid shot theirs up too.

It was unanimous.

"Finally." Liam groaned as he took a step toward the door.

"Not so fast," Denny jabbed a finger into Liam's shoulder. "That info was good for two membership fees. You're one short."

Liam's face scrunched like he was ready to punch Denny square in the nose, but instead he reached in his pocket and pulled out the chocolate bar he'd found at Food Eagle. The president's eyes got super wide; the bar of chocolate might as well have been a bar of solid gold. Liam slapped the candy squarely in Denny's hand.

"Welcome to Unity, Sara Angelina." Denny moved to pat the baby's head, but Liam leaned his body out of reach. Denny laughed it off and embraced the crowd instead by saying, "Unity is Community."

"Unity is Community," thirty voices echoed in unison. Smiles pressed in on us, slapping me on the back and pulling me by both elbows as three of us were herded inside.

My old neighborhood crawling with demons had become a living hell, but inside the sanctuary of the school, the gym was absolute heaven.

Pastel purple and yellow streamers fluttered down from ceiling rafters, dotted with flowery paper mâché decorations normally used for Spring Fling. A blow-up pool overflowed with jelly beans, and kids dove in and out, spraying a fountain of rainbow colored candies in the air. On each end of the gymnasium, hoops with plexiglass backboards hovered mid-air, but instead of basketballs, giddy boys were slam dunking watermelons from the cafeteria.

Pink juicy flesh exploded as the melons smashed down, spurting black seeds all over the waxy floor. In a flash, those black seeds transformed before my eyes into a geist's blackened teeth spraying against my kitchen wall. My eyelids clamped shut, and I shook my head like an etch-a-sketch to erase the mental picture. If Liam and Sara hadn't stood beside me safe and sound, I might've run out screaming. Was this my life now? Triggered by a melon? Doomed to live in constant fear something innocent could drag me back into my nightmares while everyone around me laughed?

"Pretty amazing, right?" Pigtails smiled. "And this is only the beginning."

"What are those for?" Liam asked. Kitty-corner across from each other, and as far away as space allowed in the massive room, huddled two separate clusters of dome-shaped camping tents.

"We stay in the gym at night for safety," Pigtails informed us. "Girls sleep on the right in the red tents, boys over on the left in the blue. It was the president's first act when he was elected."

She beamed up at him proudly. Denny rewarded her with a handsome smile before he took command of the tour.

"The gym doors are heavy steel," Denny said. "We double lock them from the inside with chains and padlocks, so even if those things - what did you call them? Geists?"

I nodded.

"Ok, so even if *geists* were to breach our defenses, they wouldn't be able to get at us in here. It's just an extra precaution of course. Those things hate light, and we've got an unlimited supply of that. So you're free to roam the school any time before curfew. It's perfectly safe."

I shifted uneasily.

"Um, Denny?" I clumsily raised my hand for permission to talk.

"Yes, Amaia?"

"Last night, my house lost power because of that storm," I said. "The geists almost got us. If the school's lights go out... what if the doors don't hold them? What if..."

Denny squeezed my shoulder and steered me toward the hall.

"Let me show you something."

The custodial wing had been off-limits to students, and I paused briefly to read the bold letters on an obnoxious red door that warned **Roof Access: Authorized Personnel Only**. We breezed past it. Apparently, our fearless leader had some other destination in mind.

After a maze of unused-classrooms-turned-supply closets, we came to an emergency exit that dumped us outside. Denny kicked a wooden wedge under the door to prop it open and motioned for me to follow. I emerged like a cautious turtle, uncertain if I wanted to be on this field trip.

The back of the school stood guard over rolling hills and an ominous patch of forest that bordered the city park. Everybody knew ditching seniors would sneak out and hide among those trees to smoke during lunch. Were geists lurking under those shadowy branches, trampling some teenager's discarded cigarette butts? Could I make it back inside the school faster than a geist could get up that hill? I didn't want to have to find out.

"This way." Denny led the expedition with Pigtails hot on his heels. Liam and I shuffled behind, casting worried glances over our shoulders. Purple and orange clouds ringed the rosy sun in the distance. Four days ago, I would have thought it was pretty. Now, sunset was a warning plastered across the sky.

"Do you know what that is?" Denny asked, diverting my gaze from the horizon to a fence enclosure housing a gigantic gray metal box twice my height. Yellow pipes poked out the bottom and burrowed into the cement pad underneath. I'd seen one before. My dad let me watch him operate the crane that lifted it into place when Mom and I brought him lunch one afternoon.

"It's a generator!"

Before I knew it, I was shaking Liam by the shoulder, accidentally startling Sara and setting off a chain reaction of pouts and fusses again. I couldn't help it. Forget the sunset, that dingy gray box was the most gorgeous thing I'd ever seen in my life!

"Do you know what this means, Liam?" I said. "This means, even if the whole city lost power, the school wouldn't! The lights would stay on!"

"It gets even better. Look there." Denny pointed. "See those yellow pipes? This generator is hooked right into the city supply of natural gas. It'll basically never run out."

Tears flowed from my eyes. Jayden was right: the school really was safe.

And I suddenly understood why the Gamerz needed diesel so bad. They didn't have a natural gas generator. Theirs needed diesel, which meant they'd have to refill it over and over. *Of course* they'd trade Jayden for it. It was a matter of life and death.

"You don't have to be afraid anymore, Amaia." Denny's breath was hot against my cheek. "Now that you're with me, nothing can hurt you."

Denny wrapped one arm around me, warming me like a winter coat. My heart was doing Double Dutch until the look on Liam's face tripped it up. His blue eyes were clouded with something I couldn't quite recognize before he lowered his gaze to the floor.

CHAPTER
TWELVE

Not-sleeping last night, narrowly escaping geists and Gamerz, then walking miles and miles for our lives had me whipped. Each step felt like I was wearing sneakers made of lead. All I wanted to do was drag myself back to the gym, curl up in the nearest tent, and conk out.

"Later, I can show you my locker, Liam." I yawned without covering my mouth. "I've got some stuff in there we could use: an extra coat, my gym clothes. I think there's fruit snacks leftover…"

Denny skidded to a stop.

"What grade are you in?" he asked.

"Eighth."

He spun and pointed a finger right in my face.

"The junior high is a dead-zone. Forbidden, got it?"

"Why?"

The president quickened his pace. "A bunch of kids must've thought turning *off* the lights would be the best way to hide. It wasn't." He sighed. "If the smell wasn't bad enough to begin with, the kids that found them the next day left behind enough puke to do the job."

I gulped.

Liam made that mistake. That first night, he didn't turn on a single light in his house and just hid in the dark. I hadn't realized how lucky we'd been. What if Carlos had turned our lights off before he left the house with Brit? When I'd screamed in my attic, the geists would've come for me.

And I'd be dead. Liam and I never would have found Sara…

"Don't worry about any of that." Denny shrugged on a smile. "The high school is big enough for all of us. Come on, I'll give you the grand tour."

I'd already been to the high school's main gym to cheer on my brother during wrestling matches. An extra credit assignment last month sent me to the auditorium to watch the older kids in a play, but that was a total snooze fest. Other than that, the rest of the high school building with its three floors and zigzagging hallways was new territory for me.

First stop was biology lab. A handful of science-whiz honor roll students in lab coats played tug of war with microscope slides while others scribbled formulas on a whiteboard. Apparently, the end of the world hadn't meant the end of homework.

"We've got new recruits." Denny's announcement turned all eyes on us. Several faces greeted me with annoyance at the interruption, and I felt less like a new recruit and more like a losing science fair experiment. "Amaia, Liam, this is our biology team. They're working to find a cure."

"A cure for what?" asked Liam.

Denny ignored his question. "Right now, they're starting small: only experimenting on airborne samples collected in daylight. We hope to be able to do more advanced trials, but all in good time."

"You're bringing ashes *inside?!*" Liam screeched. "Are you insane?!"

"It's perfectly safe." Denny exaggerated each word, like he

was talking to someone who didn't speak his same language. "They're only allowed to take a pinch at a time. You probably tracked more ashes in here on your clothes."

That made sense to me, but Liam sulked and stared at a girl poking a red-hot wire loop into a flaming bunsen burner. The loose tendrils that framed her face nearly caught fire, but just as I opened my mouth to warn her, another kid yanked her back before she became a human candlestick. Denny ushered us out, politely waving to the kids in lab coats and thanking them for their hard work in trying to bring our parents back from the dead.

"Do you really think they'll find a cure?" I gushed to Liam, caught off guard at the excitement rising in my own voice. What if they could bring my parents back? And Liam's too?

"What? No way!" Liam nudged me with his elbow and whispered behind Denny's back. "Those aren't *scientists*. They're kids in costumes!"

"Shh! Are you trying to get us kicked out ten minutes after we got here?" My eyes darted to the back of Denny's head, but he just kept walking.

Liam grumbled.

My mood soured. Liam was right. How were a bunch of teenagers going to figure out a cure for the Plague of Ashes when real grown-up scientists with PhDs couldn't? Then again, if Denny was confident his biology team would find a cure, maybe there really was a chance… They had to at least try, right? I'd give anything to hug my mom and dad again…

"And here's where you can blow off some creative steam," Denny said. "No graffiti in the gym, but everywhere else is fair game."

We poked our heads into the art room where kids played slip n' slide with watercolor paints. Stacks of blank white canvases sat unloved and ignored while handprints and brush strokes decorated the ceiling, walls, and windows in every shade imaginable. It was an odd mural: wild doodles roamed every surface with no clear style or picture. Where rainbows collided, dazzling colors bled into gray.

Gray.

Gray like ashes falling from the sky.

Gray like the stinking flesh of a geist's hand crushing my throat…

"Amaia, you ok?" Liam touched my back with his fingertips.

I gasped in a lungful of air.

When had I stopped breathing?

"Yeah, I'm fine," I said . "Just not much of an art lover, I guess."

I shrank back and hid behind an easel when I should have been jumping for joy. I mean, it was amazing Denny took us in. I was even still a teeny bit optimistic about those kids finding a cure, despite Liam's bad attitude. And believe me, that generator downstairs was a straight up miracle. But how could these art-room kids just pretend we're all at summer camp instead of facing the end of the world? Were Liam and I the only ones who even cared our parents had turned into soulless cannibal monsters?

Everyone was celebrating. No one else was crying or getting triggered or having panic attacks. What was wrong with *me*?

Faces shielded behind welding masks, kids in the shop room blowtorched some metal monstrosity behind a stack of heavy rubber tires. I spied four huge sheets of plexiglass lined up against the far wall and looked to Denny for an explanation like he gave in the biology lab, but he was tight-lipped until we passed.

Instead, our next stop on the grand tour was the computer lab. It had none of the excitement of the other rooms and was deserted except for a team of two. The boy and girl clacked away at keyboards; their eyes super glued to monitors so they didn't even glance up when we came in.

"This used to be journalism club, but now it's our outreach

team," the president said. "These two are messaging kids from all over the world to learn as much as we can about geists."

"Geists?" The boy glanced over his shoulder, pushing a pair of thick glasses up the bridge of his nose. He recoiled for the briefest second when he set eyes on Sara. Glasses wouldn't be the first boy to be freaked out by a baby, but it made me realize how lucky I was to have Liam.

"Yeah, geists. That's what we're calling them now," Denny said. "Spread it around. Make sure everyone uses it."

"Yes, Mr. President." The boy whirled back to his laptop with supercharged fingers.

A girl with a face full of braces scooted off her swivel chair and scurried over to us.

"Newcomers!" She clapped her hands. "Let's do an interview. I need to know if you know anything about the creatures we don't yet, ok?"

"Call them geists," Denny corrected her.

"Geists," Brace Face said without missing a beat. "One: we know geists hate light. Two: we know the sickness only affected adults over the age of twenty. Anyone who is still a teenager or younger appears to be immune. Look! You even have a baby! This is great information to tell the others. You should have the doctor examine her."

Gosh, does this girl breathe between sentences?

"Doctor?" Liam frowned. "I thought you said no adults survived?"

She cocked her head to the side like a confused chicken. "Who says only adults can be doctors?"

I laughed, which turned her ruddy cheeks purple. Liam's *kids in costumes* comment popped in my head, and as always, my mouth couldn't resist blurting out something to get me in trouble.

"A kid can't just throw on a stethoscope to be a doctor," I said. "That's like dressing up on Halloween and saying it's real."

"You can be anything you want!" Braces balled up her fists, ready for a fight.

"Ok, cool. Then I'm an astronaut!"

Denny leaned in the doorway, content to sit back and watch us duke it out. Liam's eyes widened as the girl drew her arm back.

"Thanks for the offer," Liam said. "But the baby is perfectly healthy. See? You can check her out yourself."

Brace Face glared down her long nose at Sara, who cringed away from the witch. The girl was so ugly, Sara was probably worried she was a geist.

"I'd better document this." Glasses sighed and marched over reluctantly, phone in hand. "From the look of her, she's five, six months old tops."

Liam and I exchanged looks. Neither of us had been able to guess Sara's age… For a boy that hated babies, Glasses seemed to know something about them. But just as I was warming up to the kid, he had to go and do something that really ticked me off. The flash from his dumb phone set Sara screaming in hysterics.

"This infant might be the youngest person on earth," Glasses muttered, barely looking at the baby in front of him because his face was buried in a screen. "Before her, the youngest documented so far was a 1-year-old in Taiwan… and… sent!"

His phone whooshed.

"What happens if a teenager turns twenty?" I asked, eager to divert attention away from Sara as Liam calmed the baby down.

"There are some rumors, but no proof yet." Glasses looked to Denny before he continued. "In Paris there's a nineteen-year-old with a birthday tomorrow. The team there is locking him up tonight and keeping him under observation. We'll know something in a few hours."

The image of Jayden trapped in that cage flashed in my mind, and my temper flared again. "They can't just lock people up like criminals when they haven't even done anything wrong!"

"Relax." Brace Face faked interest in her chipping nail polish. "You don't even know that kid. God, you freak out over the tiniest thing."

"There's air-holes. It's perfectly safe," Glasses added, glare shielding his eyes behind his spectacles. "They even sent prototype schematics in case we need to build an observation box here. That's why it's important we all share information as fast as we can while the internet's still working. We're talking about the survival of the human race here!"

My blood boiled in my veins, but Liam gave me a slight shake of the head, warning me to cool my temper. He was right. I'd already made my first enemy arguing with Brace Face. Better not add Glasses to that list.

"The box will be surrounded by lights on all sides," Glasses said. "So, if he does explode on his twentieth birthday, the ashes won't be able to solidify."

"I shined a flashlight at a geist," Liam said, "and it didn't do anything other than make it mad."

"The Mumbai kids figured that one out." Glasses straightened. "Only a certain brightness sustained for a period of several seconds will actually trigger the mechanism where geists explode into dust. The stronger the light, the faster the change. A dim light or a bright flash mostly just makes them mad. Our scientists have been conducting experiments from the roof, and I've been reporting our findings to the global teams."

"That lines up with what we saw watching geists from Amaia's attic," Liam said. "A motion light burned their skin, but they didn't stand under it long enough to make them explode. Also, we know bullets don't hurt geists."

All necks snapped to Liam's direction.

"Bullets!" Braces screwed up her mouth. "You've got a *gun*?! You brought a gun *here*?"

"What? No way!" Liam turned out his empty palms.

They pressed in on us.

"He said no, ok?" I shrugged off my backpack and tossed it

at their feet. "We don't have a gun. Go ahead, search us if you want!"

"Waldo. Violet. Check it out." Denny nodded the command, and Glasses and Braces set to work fumbling through our backpacks. They probably would have loved sharing a juicy story about two kids who snuck a gun into Unity when it's clearly forbidden. Obviously, Waldo and Violet didn't find what they were looking for, and the only thing they got to write was the disappointment written all over their faces.

"See? I knew they had nothing to hide." Denny nudged his knuckles playfully against my cheek.

"Then who?" demanded Braces.

"The Gamerz were shooting…" The last word got caught in my throat. I'd wanted to say they were shooting *geists*, that should have been easy-peasy, right?

Except one of those geists used to be my mother. Was my mom in there somewhere? Her memories? The geist still wore her face. Could any of her be left in there at all? Did she feel the bullet?

Beads of sweat burst on my forehead.

Don't fall apart, Amaia. Don't fall apart.

"*Gamerz*, ugh, that explains it." Violet rolled her eyes until they were only white balls in her head. "Those religious freaks are the reason I had to post the *No Trespassing* sign on the front door. But are you sure bullets don't work? Even a headshot?"

A headshot? I felt like I was going to be sick.

"They're not zombies," Liam muttered. "Our lives would've been a whole lot easier if they were."

"Better spread this news." Waldo swiveled back to his laptop screen with fingertips lashing the keys like whips. "Gamerz… have been… shooting… geists. Bullets… have… no effect… and send!"

"*Religious freaks*?" Liam asked. "Why'd you call them that?"

"Because they're a total cult!" Braces twirled a lock of hair around a knobby finger. "I'm writing a story to expose those mutants. It's so juicy it's insane. Denny knows their leader, the girl they call 'the captain'. What a dumb name. I heard she wasn't even elected. Anyway, Denny told me that she…"

"Violet, you're not running a gossip column, are you?" Denny scolded her with a smile. "Right now, top priority is to finish the tour and get these two initiated."

"Three." Liam patted Sara's back.

Violet deflated like a punctured balloon. She tucked a lock of frizz behind her ear and waved goodbye, her gaze lingering on Liam as we were rushed out the door.

"We'll hit up the cafeteria then circle back to the gym," Denny said.

"Great!" I grinned, though my stomach grumbled, empty and angry. I'd give my left arm for one of the cafeteria lady's infamous Sloppy Joe surprises. Carlos told me the *surprise* was mayonnaise with the expiration date scratched off the label.

My nose sniffed the air as we got close but smelled only the usual funk of high school hallways. As I stepped into the lunchroom, broken glass from a smashed vending machine crunched like fresh snow under my sneakers. The entire dining area was empty save for two boys in matching hairnets and aprons who sat back on their chairs, muddy sneakers propped up on the table.

"Dish duty done already?" Denny boomed. "Or are you failing to contribute *again*?"

"No, Mr. President! I mean, almost done sir!" A round-faced boy gave a salute and raced into the kitchen.

The second dishwasher, a pale kid with bad acne, shot Denny a defiant glare over his shoulder and dragged his feet. He grumbled something about it being too much work for two people before he vanished.

"Some people never learn." Denny smiled at us apologetically. "Wait here. Two seconds. I promise." He stranded us in the cafeteria doorway, his footsteps quickly fading down the hall back toward the gym.

Liam placated Sara with a pacifier, which wouldn't work for long. She was starving. We all were.

"Oh, so that's why Denny let Sara in," I muttered to the empty vending machine.

"Wait, why?" asked Liam. I could tell his mind had been somewhere else, and he was only half listening to me again.

I pointed toward the rows of empty metal coils robbed of the candy bars they once held. Two halves of a chocodoodles wrapper were the only thing left, ripped apart by the kids that fought over it. This must have been what happened before Denny took charge. Chaos.

"Hey, I need to talk to you." Liam leaned in close even though we were already alone. "There's something I need to tell you about Denny. He went to my school, but last month he got kicked out… not like suspended. Like *expelled.*"

From down the hall where Denny had vanished, four boys in matching gray t-shirts marched toward us, closed fists swinging at their sides. Liam zipped his lips. I recognized two of the kids from the football team with Carlos and Jayden, but they didn't stop to say hello to me. Instead, they barged past us, stomped across the cafeteria, and punched through the swinging doors to the kitchen, disappearing out of sight.

Liam and I both yelped when the girl with the pigtails snuck up behind us and tapped us each on the shoulder.

"Denny got busy," she said. "He's the president, so a lot depends on him, obvi."

"How did Denny get to be president?" Liam asked. "He doesn't even go here."

"We voted, silly! It was totally unanimous. Well, two people voted against him at first…" Her eyes flickered toward the kitchen, but her mouth didn't miss a beat. "They came around, and *then* it was unanimous! Community is Unity." She paused, clearly expecting us to say something. "Well?"

"Oh right," I straightened. "Community is Unity."

Liam grumbled something that must've sounded close enough because she let it drop.

Behind the kitchen doors, pots and pans clanged to the floor over the sounds of a scuffle. Deep thuds were punctuated by a boy's yelps that reminded me of the time my old next-door neighbor kicked his dog. My parents called the cops, and the man was arrested. That story had a happy ending though: one of the police officers found the dog a forever home in the country where she'd be safe. Why couldn't the cops have done that much for Liam's aunt?

The boy behind the door cried out again.

If my brother was here, he would have stopped it.

I took a step forward, but Liam grabbed my arm.

"What?" I snapped.

"Don't" Liam whispered. He flicked his eyes to Sara and back to me. I bit my lip. Was Liam implying we'd get thrown out into the street if I interfered?

I frowned at the baby. Liam may have been the one to grab my arm, but Sara was the one holding me back. The kitchen went quiet. It was over anyway.

I wasn't strong enough to protect everybody. Maybe I'd never be.

Pigtails flashed a sheepish grin as she escorted us back out to the hall. She introduced herself as 'Peggy' to Liam, which was lucky for me because she probably wouldn't have liked me calling her 'Pigtails' to her face. On our way back to the gym, Peggy was explaining the meal ticket system. Every day, people get three tickets good for breakfast, lunch, and dinner. Each person had to contribute to Unity daily in some way to earn their meal tickets.

Peggy blathered on and on about this and that, but it was hard to focus on what she was saying. All I could see was the misery on Liam's face. Instead of getting into an exclusive VIP club, you'd swear he'd just been handed a life sentence in prison.

"So, what will you contribute?"

I blinked hard.

"Um, what?"

Peg's giant painted-on eyebrows nearly touched over her scowl. "You weren't listening to a word I said!"

"Yes, I was!" I shot back. "You were talking about our initiation and meal tickets… and other stuff."

"Yeah, and how will you *earn* your meal tickets?"

"Engineering," Liam blurted out. "Amaia should be in engineering. Her dad taught her stuff about construction and carpentry… and she knows about generators!"

"We both can be engineers!" I nudged a playful elbow into his ribs. "But I'll have to teach you what a wrench looks like first."

No one laughed at my joke.

Peggy and Liam exchanged an uneasy glance like they knew some secret I didn't. Maybe I should've been paying attention after all.

"Like, we don't need a zillion engineers, *obvi*." Peg rolled her eyes. "But we do need people to go out and get supplies. Liam will probably end up being a scout."

A scout?

Jayden was a scout. That's how he got bitten by a geist then locked in a cage. I cringed at the image my mind conjured of geists surrounding Liam, snarling and snapping their bloody teeth, yanking him into darkness…

"NO!" I shrieked. "You can't make him go out there! You can't!"

Peg tossed a pigtail over her shoulder and started away from me. "O-M-G dramatic much?"

I whipped out the hammer from my backpack. If Peg wanted drama, I'd give her *drama*.

"Hey!" I grabbed Peggy's shoulder with my free hand and spun her back around. She was several inches taller than me, so I yanked her shirt and pulled her down to my level.

"This morning, I smashed off a geist's jaw with *this*

hammer!" I held it up an inch from her contoured nose. "I nailed it right in the face and knocked it's teeth out! *I* should get to be a scout, *me*, not him."

"Stop it!" Liam tried to get between us, but I held firm. "Please! Amaia doesn't mean it. She's just tired and…"

"Liam froze! Did he tell you that?" I spat the words, knowing they'd shock Liam into silence. I had to shut him up for his own good. "When a geist attacked us, he froze like a deer in headlights. Liam can't be a scout. He'd be dead the first day."

Peg's eyes slid from my face to the hammer and back again until I lowered my weapon and released her collar from my grip. She straightened her t-shirt and cautiously backed away from me as if I was a rabid dog foaming at the mouth.

Liam's jaw was slack, eyes bulging in disbelief at the crazy person I'd become.

I didn't care.

"Look, it's not my call. It's up to Denny." Peg paused outside the gymnasium. "But if you, like, so much as put a wrinkle on my shirt again, and I'll report you to security. You heard what happened to the kitchen boy. Keep it up and it's you next. You got me, little girl?"

I threw my shoulders back and lifted my chin the way I'd seen Carlos do a million times when he was mouthing off to Dad.

"O-M-G, I like totally got you," I parroted, mocking her singsong voice before my words turned gravelly and low. "But if you let Denny make Liam a scout, you'd better run outside to take your chances with the geists… they'll be gentler on you than I will."

Peg's cheeks burned as she threw open the door and stomped her way into the gym.

"Tell her you were joking." Liam grabbed my arm, but I yanked it away.

Yeah. Ok. Fine. Maybe I had a screw loose in the head, but I wasn't about to take back what I did. If Unity wanted to force Liam to be a scout, they'd have to do it over my dead body.

I hoped it wouldn't come to that.

My empty stomach played jump rope with my throat, and I had to choke the acid back down. Was *this* what Mom was complaining about every time she was stressed out?

Maybe threatening that girl wasn't my smartest move. How many enemies had I made so far today? I was beginning to lose count…

I lingered in the doorway to the gym. Over two thousand kids had gone to CHS, but now there were a little more than a hundred.

Liam cradled the baby and seemed to shrink in on himself, looking like he wished he could turn invisible. I couldn't say I blamed him. Big things always ate small things. Sara was a minnow, and Liam and I were middle-school guppies, fresher meat than freshman.

Despite what Peg said earlier about Carlos not being here,

my eyes scanned the gym searching for my brother anyway. I knew it was stupid. But I couldn't stop myself from hoping.

"I don't believe it," I muttered. "Yvette!"

Her back was to me, but that neon pink hair made her impossible to miss. She whirled around at the sound of her name.

"Amaia!" Yvette rolled up in her silver wheelchair and spread her arms so wide it looked like she could fly. "You're alive!"

I bent over to hug her but lost my balance and crash landed in her lap. I jerked back, worried I'd crushed her, but she wrapped her arms around my shoulders, squeezing as tight as she could.

"You made it," she said, her voice trembling.

"Barely." I faked a laugh to stop myself from crying.

"I never thought I'd ever see another kid from our class again," she confessed.

I stood up awkwardly and pushed a smile onto my lips. My fingers knotted together behind my back so she wouldn't see my hands shaking as I asked the question I was dying to know the answer to.

"Is my brother here?"

Her face fell. Yvette turned away as she pretended to adjust the brake of her chair. "Carlos isn't here," she said, still not meeting my gaze.

Liam steadied me with a gentle hand on my elbow and came to my rescue by changing the subject.

"I'm Liam McGregor." He gave a timid wave. "And this is Sara Angelina."

"Yvette Lin." Her perfectly manicured fingers tucked a lock of magenta curls behind her triple studded ear. Yvette wore black leggings with strappy high heels and a rock and roll t-shirt peeking out from under her vegan leather jacket. She was a fashionista, style always on fleek and the polar opposite of someone like me who'd wear her brother's dirty, oversized hoodie in public.

"Have we met before?" Liam asked.

The corners of Yvette's mouth curled like a ribbon. Gosh she was pretty.

"I've got a familiar face," she teased.

"Yvette has a million followers on her beauty channel," I gushed. "She's famous."

I didn't admit I'd only seen one video. It was a sore subject with me since Mom wouldn't let me wear makeup yet.

"I don't think Liam watches my tutorials." Yvette smirked as her almond eyes shimmered under soft blue eyeshadow. "Actually, I recognize you too. Our mothers work together. You were at their office on Monday. I think you were with your father? He came in carrying flowers..."

Their smiles melted as they locked eyes. The agony of an innocent-memory-turned-tragic passed between the two of them like static electricity.

The last time they'd seen each other, the world hadn't ended. Now it had.

I sawed my teeth across my lower lip.

Yvette had said their moms 'work' together instead of 'worked'. Maybe talking about her mom in the past tense would be like admitting she was really gone.

"So, what's up with this initiation I heard about?" Liam asked.

Yvette rolled her eyes and rocked back on her wheels.

"Denny likes to make a big deal out of everything," she said. "All you have to do is promise to follow the rules then say what you are going to contribute to Unity. Then you're in."

"What did you contribute?" I asked.

"Decoration committee." Yvette gestured to the Spring Fling decor complete with paper mâché flowers hanging over our heads. "Some of the kids wanted Halloween decorations since it's only a few days away… but I thought everyone needed a brighter theme instead…"

"It's perfect," I said.

Her hands fidgeted in her lap. "There aren't any more spots on the committee, otherwise I'd invite you both to join…"

Liam shifted his weight, obviously thinking about the hammer incident in the hallway.

"Then we'll have a big party for you guys!" Yvette chirped. "That part will be super fun. We had a big celebration the second day when a few more kids joined, and I overhead Denny say we'll have another for you."

A party? For us? My fingers inspected the jagged edges of my geist-inflicted haircut.

"I don't really have anything to wear to a party," I said.

"MAKEOVER!" Yvette shrieked at top volume so everybody in the gym turned to stare at us. "Can I do your hair and makeup? Please, please, please?"

I clapped my hands over my smile and nodded. If a silly makeover made Yvette happy, why not? There wasn't enough happy things in the world anymore. Though, Mom wouldn't have approved…

Liam was frowning again, but I wasn't about to let him ruin this for me. If we had to be stuck here anyway, might as well make the best of it.

"What's this I hear about you smashing a geist's jaw off with a hammer?" Denny's face hovered over my left shoulder.

Liam wedged himself in front of me like a barricade.

"Amaia's dad did carpentry and construction, and he taught her stuff," Liam said. "She should be in the engineering group."

"Maybe." Denny rubbed his chin. "Seems she's got brains and guts. Powerful combo. We should let her decide what she wants to do. How do you want to contribute to Unity, Amaia? Engineer or scout?"

Liam pinched my elbow in a vice-like grip and yanked me out of earshot of the others.

"Ouch! Quit it!" I said. "Stop embarrassing me!"

"We can't both be scouts," Liam growled in my ear. "One of us needs to stay with Sara Angelina."

"But Sara hates me!"

"She doesn't hate you…" He shoved the baby into my arms to prove his point, and like the traitor she was, Sara smiled at me.

"Yeah, well… she likes you better." I handed her back.

"Why do you want to go back out there so bad?" Liam demanded. "Why can't you just stay in the school where it's safe?"

His brow creased over watery eyes. Desperate. Pleading. We both knew Unity needed another scout now that Jayden had been captured… and Liam was planning on sacrificing himself to save me.

Not. Happening.

"If I listened to you on the stairs when you begged me to run back up to the attic, we'd both be dead right now." I poked a finger into his shoulder, forcing him back. "Then when you were face to face with the geist in my kitchen, what did you do? You froze. You didn't fight. You didn't run. You just stood there to let yourself get eaten."

Liam winced. "Amaia, don't. Peggy said they're only going to force one of us to be a scout. We both don't have to die."

"You're right. Neither of us do."

Honestly, I hated the idea of being a scout. The thought of being close enough to smell a geist's breath again made me want to hurl. But I couldn't shake the picture in my head of Liam paralyzed in my kitchen doorway with a geist lunging for his throat and Sara Angelina strapped to his chest. I refused to lose anyone else I cared about to those monsters.

"Scout!" I sidestepped Liam and locked eyes with Denny.

"Now, this is equality!" Denny grinned. "We've finally got our first girl scout!"

The kids around us snickered, but I wasn't laughing.

"Me, too." Liam's voice squeaked. "Scout!"

"Nah-ah," I said. "Liam's a scaredy cat that will just slow me down. Better send him up to the computer lab with the rest of the nerds."

The kids laughed again, and this time I joined them.

"I… I'm not! I can be a scout!" Liam stammered. "Denny? Denny, please!"

The president clapped a hand on my back and smiled down on me.

"Have it your way, Girl Scout."

Balancing Sara on one arm, Liam turned away from us and put his face toward the wall, pretending to rifle through his backpack with the other. I knew better. I could tell by the quivering of his shoulders that he was crying again.

Sweat soaked my palms and my heart beat like it was trying to punch its way out of my chest, but I kept telling myself I made the right decision.

I'd survived three days and four nights without the safety of the school, that was more than any of these clowns could say. Besides, Carlos could still be out there. I'd never find my brother if I spent all my days locked in here swimming in a kiddie pool full of jellybeans.

Who knew a makeover was the perfect distraction to take a girl's mind off her impending doom? Yvette's makeup case was bigger than my dad's toolbox. "*Makeover*" must be the French word for "*torture*" because holy moly did it hurt. The first thing she did was rip out brows I never knew I had. Why even bother? After she was done, she drew my eyebrows back on bigger and darker than before. But after buffing, concealing, contouring, and something called baking, my makeup was finished. She even trimmed my hair so it was mostly even.

Her eyeshadow palette had a huge mirror, and at first, I didn't recognize myself. I actually felt… kind of pretty.

Pretty and *starving*, so I snuck a lick of the cherry gloss on my lips.

"I'm a genius." Yvette rolled back to admire her masterpiece. "Wait! What color are you wearing under that hoodie?"

"Um…" I peeked at my t- shirt hoping I hadn't chosen something totally humiliating. "It's blue."

"Perfect!" Yvette rifled through her oversized purse and flung out a gorgeous turquoise and silver scarf. I peeled off my brother's dusty, ash covered hoodie, and Yvette draped the sparkly fabric around my hips, fashioning a skirt over my leggings.

"The scarf is beautiful, but…" I clutched Carlos' hoodie in my hands. "This is my brother's… it's the last thing he gave me…"

"Relax, nobody's going to steal your dirty sweatshirt. It'll be safe in my tent." Yvette gave me a wink. "Listen, let's just have fun tonight, ok?"

I gave her a small smile. "I'll try."

The initiation ceremony was straight up weird.

Someone dug out a golden toga and laurels from an old school production of Julius Caesar, and Denny was all too happy to play the lead role. They made Liam and me stand center court then dimmed the lights overhead, which really freaked me out. A junior with a buzz cut and an eyebrow ring beat the bass drum from the band room while kids in matching togas held flashlights under their chins and chanted, marching around us in a tight circle. Sara was not amused.

Brace Face, the witch, had left her computer lab cave, and despite the fact this was supposed to be a party for us, was bent on making herself the center of everyone's attention. Her megaphone squealed at a pitch that made my teeth sting.

"Silence!" The amplification of Violet's already shrill voice made the entire gymnasium cringe. "Now we recite the sacred laws. Repeat after me. Rule number one: don't turn off the lights."

I frowned and squinted at the dimmed ceiling. Hadn't they already broken this rule? Hypocrites. But, whatever, I just really wanted to get this over with.

"Don't turn off the lights," one hundred voices said in unison.

The bass drum beat wildly.

"Rule number two," Violet proclaimed. "Obey or be punished."

What did I need to obey? I guess it didn't matter. Anything was better than being tossed out on the street with geists, so I decided to roll with it.

"Obey or be punished."

The drumbeat pounded in my chest.

"Rule number three!" Brace Face paused for dramatic effect. "We are family. Community is Unity!"

"We are family." This one was easy. Standing next to Liam and Sara Angelina, I really meant it. "Community is Unity!"

The drum stopped dead.

"Initiates step forward to proclaim your contributions!" Denny unrolled a comically long scroll. Probably another prop from the theater department… and almost certainly blank.

"Liam, your position requires organization and intelligence. You will hereby serve Unity in the computer lab!" Denny decreed. "Outreach team!" Thunderous applause erupted from the audience, and the president gave me a sly wink. Waldo and Violet leapt forward and gave their new teammate congratulatory pats on the back. Liam hung his head in resignation.

"And the moment we've all been waiting for!" Denny's eyes

locked on mine. "Amaia, you will serve our community in a position that demands bravery and honor…. Unity, I present your newest scout!"

All at once, it felt like two hundred hands were on me. Patting me on the back. Trying to give me a high fives. Older kids had always made fun of me or pretended I didn't exist. I'd been an invisible gnat. But now… now I was a chosen one! I was *somebody*.

"And finally," Denny shouted over the clamoring crowd. "We have little Sara Angelina."

My neck swiveled so fast I almost gave myself whiplash. What job could he possibly give Sara? She was just a baby…

"Sara will serve Unity as a beacon of hope for the next generation! She will bring laughter to our halls. We will build a new world for her!"

"Sara! Sara! Sara!" Chanting voices beat to the rhythm of the drum that started up again with a vengeance. A few kids tried to pry the baby from Liam's arms, probably to hoist her in the air, but Liam doubled over and shielded Sara like a bodyguard.

Then the music started.

I was swept away in a flood of bodies as the urge to dance became a primal, tangible thing. My feet pounded the floor and transported me in my mind deep into the heart of a darkened jungle soaked in humidity and sweat. Strobe lights pulsed and made my arms move like animated characters from a flip book. The rhythm was intoxicating. Dancers spun and twirled me around until I was too dizzy to stand and laughing too hard to breathe.

It was miraculous.

So, this is what being popular felt like. A party in my honor? I could get used to this. We danced until my feet throbbed, but I stubbornly refused to stop. I never wanted tonight to end.

Denny sat on his golden throne and raised a goblet in the air. He certainly had a flare for the dramatic. Maybe we both did. He nodded at me and put the drink to his lips, toasting me from afar and letting me know that I was the most special girl in the room. My heart fluttered in my chest. Wow. I finally understood what they meant when they say you get *butterflies*.

Boys in gray t-shirts surrounded Liam and hoisted him over their shoulders, forcing him to crowd surf with the baby still strapped to his chest. Before I knew what was happening, hands reached out from all around and lifted me up too. My body floated above the masses, every nerve ending whirring with electricity as music reverberated through my bones. The terrors outside melted into nothing. When had I ever been this *happy*? Maybe the world hadn't ended at all. Maybe it was just beginning.

It was the most perfect moment of my life.

But buried under the roaring cheers and pulsing beat, I could swear I heard the faint sound of Sara screaming.

At the close of the ceremony, the gymnasium lights blasted back on. We all groaned and shielded our faces from the glaring brightness, the way geists hiss and cringe away from streetlights.

Cafeteria workers wearing matching hairnets and aprons wheeled carts stacked high with styrofoam containers. "Cheeseburgers and fries!" A boy in a chef's hat banged a pot with a ladle. "Line 'em up!"

I recognized him as the round-faced kid from the cafeteria. I scanned the faces of the other workers, but the boy with the acne was nowhere to be seen.

I wondered if he was ok. A boy in a gray t-shirt handed me a paper ticket to redeem my first meal here.

Kids stampeded over each other, but I elbowed my way to the front of the line. The savory smell of meat and grease made my mouth water. No one, and I mean *no one*, was getting in between me and my dinner. Yvette and Liam were being slow pokes, lounging by her tent and talking quietly as Liam mixed a scoop of powdered formula into a bottle of water.

"Can I get two extra burgers for my friends?" I asked the kid in the chef's hat.

"One per ticket," he said. "Tell 'em to get in line."

The president glided up beside me.

"Make an exception," Denny commanded with a smile.

"Yes, Mr. President! Of course, sir."

I was on top of the world as I strutted toward Yvette's tent with my bounty, but my friends weren't impressed with my newfound VIP status.

Yvette picked out the meat and tossed it to the side like hot garbage ruining a perfectly good sesame seed bun. *Ugh.* How was I supposed to remember she was vegetarian?

Liam's cheeseburger got cold as he tended to Sara's needs first. Not mine. I scarfed each juicy bite and let grease drip down my chin, not caring if it ruined the makeup Yvette had caked on my face. This was my first hot meal in days, no way was I going to miss one single delicious bite for a snotty, cranky baby.

Liam was punishing me with the silent treatment again. How dare he be mad that I volunteered for scout duty? He should be on his knees thanking me! I just saved his life!

"Boys are crazy," I grumbled to myself through a mouth full of french fries.

$$\cdots\cdots) \;) \; \mathbf{)} \; \bullet \; \mathbf{(} \; (\; (\cdots\cdots$$

A beefy kid rolled a giant trash can around the gym to collect our empty styrofoam.

"Boys over in the blue tents," he barked at Liam. "It's curfew."

"I know, I'll just be a sec." Liam said. Sara was nestled comfortably in his arms, already doing that slow blink she liked to do just before she fell asleep.

The boy scowled darkly.

"I said, move it."

"But she'll be out in a minute," Liam protested. "Just let me sit here and hold her until then."

The boy's bushy black eyebrows pinched together so tight, they looked like someone took a permanent marker and drew a horizontal line across his forehead as a practical joke.

"Morning." Denny's voice was bright and cheerful. "Sleep ok?"

"Yeah," I lied.

"Good. I'll introduce you to Xander when he wakes up. He'll be your scout leader."

I'd just opened my mouth to ask how scouting missions work when we were rudely interrupted. Glasses from the computer lab, Waldo, tumbled as he tripped over the blue flaps of his tent and rolled onto the gym floor. He darted toward Denny waving his phone in the air like he was in the middle of a relay race and ready to do the handoff.

Denny sighed. "What is it now?"

Waldo's glasses magnified the terror in his eyes.

"Mr. President!" He panted. "Paris… birthday… LOOK!"

Denny's and my faces both hovered over the kid's phone, staring at a video of a plexiglass box. It looked something like an ancient phone booth or one of those clear cages that divers swim in that gets sharks riled up.

Only, there wasn't a person in the box… just a swirling cloud of gray ash. Silver duct tape had been hastily applied over what I figured used to be air holes.

Denny clutched the phone in his fist like he wished it was a soda can he could crush. This was bad. This was really, really bad.

"You sure this is legit?" the president asked.

"No doubt." Waldo was shaking. "Sunset on his twentieth birthday. Just like those rumors said. Their team is freaking out. They don't know what to do…"

"Have you shown this to anyone else?"

"No, Sir. Not yet…"

"Good. Let's keep it that way." With a few swipes of Denny's finger, the video and texts were wiped out of existence. "The last thing we need is a panic on our hands, understand?"

"No panic, right, got it." Glasses nodded, beads of sweat

pouring down his neck into the collar of his speech and debate t-shirt.

Denny turned to me.

"Amaia, listen up." He took my face in both of his hands, and the rest of his words went fuzzy. He wasn't going to kiss me, was he? I've never kissed a boy. Oh no, I hadn't brushed my teeth. I tried to pull away, but he tilted my face up to look at him squarely in the eyes as he said, "Amaia, are you listening to me? This is important."

"Um, yes?" I cleared my throat. "I mean, yes. I'm listening."

"Waldo needs time to get more intel on what happened in Paris. Keep this news to yourself until we know for sure what's going on. When the time is right, I'll let everyone know myself. Is that clear?"

"Crystal."

He moved his hands from my cheeks to my shoulders and gave them both a firm squeeze.

"Especially not to Liam," Denny warned. "That kid's way too *sensitive*. Not everyone is strong like you and me. We need to protect the weaker ones, you get it?"

"I get it." Wow, Denny really was a great leader. It's almost like he was born to be president. He really knew how to take charge.

"There's my girl." He flashed me his most dazzling smile. "I'm trusting to you to keep it top secret. Can I count on you, Amaia?"

"I won't let you down." I sealed the promise with three fingers up in the air. "Scout's honor."

I sprawled my legs across the long backseat I had all to myself, wishing the cutest boy in Unity who'd been smiling at me so much lately was seat-belted in next to me. To make things worse, Denny hadn't even said goodbye when we left.

A longing sigh escaped my lips.

I'd been hoping Denny would see how brave I could be on my first scouting mission, but the president had more important things to do than forage for toilet paper.

Liam watched me through the glass double doors as we drove away, holding Sara in his arms and waving goodbye like he was terrified he'd never see me again. He reminded me of the puppy Carlos and I used to have. It would climb in the window and pout whenever we left for school. Mom lost her job, and we couldn't afford to keep it anymore.

I kept my word and didn't mention anything to anyone about that guy in Paris exploding on his twentieth birthday. The secret was eating me alive, and I was *desperate* to talk to my best friend about it. It's not like Liam couldn't keep a secret. He hadn't told anyone about me peeing my pants that first night in the toy box. If Denny found out… well, it would ruin my chances of being his girlfriend for sure.

I'd never had a boyfriend before, but I'd be fourteen in a few days. How old was Denny? Maybe fifteen or sixteen? That would be the first math problem Mom would smack me upside the head for.

We were given a list of items to gather on this scouting mission, and I frowned at the chicken scratch on the paper.

"Whose handwriting is this?" I complained. "It's just squiggles."

"It's called *cursive*," Xander hissed. "Idiot."

Guess that answered my question.

My cranky scout leader gripped the steering wheel like he wanted to wring its neck. Xander didn't bother trying to hide the fact he resented a pesky girl coming along for the ride. He took a hairpin turn and swerved around a dead car in the road.

Tyrell sat in the passenger seat of the truck, resting his arm out the window like it was a summer day. I shivered in the backseat, sure I was going to freeze to death.

Outside, vacant buildings whipped by so fast they streaked together in one gray blur. I took a deep breath, letting the crisp autumn air fill me to the brim.

My brother's out here, I thought to myself. *And I'm going to find him.*

······))) ● (((·······

We stopped at a gas station for diesel, but it was a total fail. Xander found a lady's pocketbook by the cash register and fished out credit cards to swipe, but no matter what we tried, we couldn't get the fuel pump to work. It kept asking us for a zip code, and we punched numbers only to get declined.

Xander cursed at the pump and smashed the nozzle against the keypad until it bent. When our scout leader was done throwing his tantrum, the three of us stood in awkward silence until Tyrell rerouted our attention back to the list and suggested we move on to something else. The lights were on in the convenience store, and the gas pump had power, so I figured only certain blocks had outages from that storm. My house just happened to be on an unlucky street.

After that rocky start, the rest of the mission was child's play. I spied a delivery truck parked right outside the SuperMart loading dock.

Jackpot.

SuperMart wasn't just a grocery store but a mega shopping metropolis that had everything from cough syrup to flip flops to tennis rackets. Tyrell worked on the back of the delivery truck with a long crowbar until the lock finally snapped open and clattered onto the metal lift gate. Wooden pallets stacked floor to ceiling boasted a trove of treasures that even Aladdin's genie couldn't have conjured better.

"Wow! Look at all this stuff!" I grinned at packages peeking out from behind shrink wrap. Xander scowled and tossed a pocket knife my way.

I fumbled to catch it, but my clumsy fingers let it slip to the floor.

"Ty, I thought you said her brother was quarterback?" Xander jeered. "Girl Scout can't catch."

"Linebacker." Tyrell snickered as he ripped packaging off a crate of paper products. "Her brother can't catch either."

I flicked the blade open and stabbed the box at my feet.

"Girl's got his attitude though." Ty laughed and gave me an approving nod. "What's in that one?"

"Electronics." I held up a package of walkie talkies.

"Put it in the take pile." Xander barked the order at me, but I stood tall as I obeyed. If my big brother taught me anything, it was that easy targets get hit first. If people think you're weak, they'll hurt you just because they can.

Except Liam.

Liam knew the weakness in me better than anyone, even my own family, but he'd never use it to hurt me. These boys were different. Unless I earned the other scouts' respect and became a real member of their crew, they might use me for geist bait. Maybe that's what happened to Jayden…

My instincts were silently screaming Xander couldn't be trusted. Tyrell was harder to read. I had to keep my guard up.

It took the whole morning to sort through what was valuable and what wasn't in the SuperMart truck. I snagged a few first-aid kits, but our fearless leader ordered me to leave them behind. Xander said the nurse's station at the school would have more than enough antibiotic ointment and bandages.

With the way I'd seen kids messing around in the gym yesterday, I highly doubted that. Whoever the teenager was playing doctor-dress-up, he better get real good at fixing people up with duct tape.

"Just found the mother lode." Xander gloated over about a zillion rolls of toilet paper.

"Dude, no way is that all gonna fit in the truck," Ty said.

Xander flashed a wolfish grin. "Just pile it on Girl Scout for the ride back."

Oh, goody.

I scowled but was suddenly glad Denny wasn't here after all to see me stacked in TP.

"Hey, Girl Scout. Check this out!" Ty waved me over, and I had to climb a mountain of boxes to reach him. "That baby of yours could probably use some of this stuff, right?"

A miracle. It was a gosh-darn miracle.

An entire pallet of baby things.

"Ty, you rock!" I squealed like the giddy schoolgirl I was, forgetting to keep my emotional armor on. We grabbed packages indiscriminately like it was a Black Friday shopping spree, piling up diapers, a car seat, play mat, and something called a *travel bassinet* that looked suspiciously like an extremely small, very portable crib.

"We don't have room for that crap! Put it back." Xander snapped.

Ty frowned and dropped a stuffed bunny he'd been holding.

"Please, I can make it fit," I begged. "I'll put it on my lap."

"Nah, you hold the toilet paper. Shut up about it and get back to work."

"But the baby needs these things. It's dangerous for her to sleep without…"

"Leave it! That's an order."

"No."

"What do you mean, *no*?"

Xander cocked back his fist, ready to strike. He lunged for me, but Tyrell hooked a meaty arm across his chest to keep him back.

"She's just a little girl," Ty said. "You seriously gonna beat up a baby girl?"

I wasn't a baby, but I also wasn't about to argue that point.

My hand ached from how tight I clutched the pocketknife.

"Just leave her be." Tyrell lowered his voice. "You wanna lose two scouts under your watch in one week? Huh? What's Denny gonna say about that?"

"She'd better learn quick to watch that mouth." Xander threw off Ty's biceps and stomped away from us, calling over his shoulder, "Load up and we out."

Xander retreated to the truck, either because he was a sulking coward or because he was strategically punishing Ty and me by making just us two pack the entire truck by ourselves. Probably a little of both.

The weight of the boxes set my arms and legs on fire, and I lost count of how many times I climbed up onto the pickup truck bed, slid boxes to the back with my whole body weight, then stacked them as high as they could go.

"Last one." Ty wiped his brow before he handed me a huge brown box that wasn't nearly as heavy as the others, despite its size. "Careful with that one, Girl Scout. It's fragile."

"Fragile?" I frowned. I hadn't remembered anything breakable in the take pile, but *whatever*. I had more pressing things on my mind. Sweat soaked my armpits making two smelly stains. Would Denny be meeting us at the entrance? Or would I have time to clean myself up before he saw me?

"I'll put the fragile one right on top," I said. "We're done, right?"

"I'm done, you're not done!" Ty handed me a rubber hose and a bucket. "Siphon the diesel we need to get Jay back from the Gamerz. Hop to it Girl Scout."

"Hey! Where do you think you're going?"

"Gonna kick back in the truck." Ty stretched. "Perks of seniority."

Fine. I see how it is.

My muscles throbbed, and I wanted so bad to flop myself in the backseat to take a nap, but I'd promised Jayden I'd help free him. I had to make good on that.

It took me fifteen minutes to figure out how to open the fuel door from the driver's cab. Once I did, I threaded the rubber hose through the opening and took a step back. Nothing happened. The loose end sat limply in the bucket, dry as the Sahara. I resisted the urge to bash my head against the truck and kicked the tire instead.

"You giving yourself a manicure Girl Scout? What's taking so long?" Tyrell asked.

"The tank is empty. Nothing's coming out."

Ty stared into the bucket and sighed. "You know how to get it going, right?"

I shrugged.

Tyrell threw a careful glance over his shoulder. Xander was blaring metal music in the truck, but half looking like he was taking a nap.

"Listen, kid," Ty whispered. "You shouldn't be out here. It's not safe for you."

"The world ain't safe for me," I shot back.

"True." Ty put the tube to his lips and sucked in. He slapped his thumb over the end and released it over the bucket just as diesel came pouring out. "I can't decide if you've got guts or if you're just a special brand of crazy."

I grinned. "Probably about 50/50."

We stood in silence for a few moments, watching the stream of fuel filling the bucket slow as molasses. I thought this would have been faster…

"How much diesel you think we'll need to get Jay back?" I asked.

"Depends on Denny." Tyrell shrugged. "If it was any another kid, maybe he'd just let the Gamerz have him. But scouts are important. No kids in the school wanted to do this gig. Heck, I didn't want to do it. You'd have to be out of your mind to actually *want* to be a scout."

"So why did you?"

"Xander." Ty's jaw tensed. "You think I'm gonna leave the survival of me and everyone else at the school up to *him*?"

I glanced back toward where Xander waited in the truck. Ty had a point.

"What's your excuse?" Ty prodded me. "The way I hear it, you volunteered to protect your boyfriend."

"He's not my boyfriend!"

Tyrell raised an eyebrow.

I coiled the hose around my arm and stomped on the lid to close the bucket. "Why I volunteered is none of your beeswax!"

A smirk spread over Ty's face. "Beeswax?"

Ugh, how could I have let that slip out? Ty was looking at me less like a tough girl and more like an adorable talking gerbil… until the smile suddenly melted off his face.

"It's your brother, isn't it?" Ty's eyes widened with understanding. "That's why you volunteered. You're leaving the school hoping to run into Carlos."

His words hit me like a slap. Tears sprang to my eyes, and I cursed myself for it. "How did you guess?"

"Carlos said that *beeswax* thing once when we were JV." Ty smiled sadly. "The team never let him forget it. We'd snap towels at him in the locker room and say 'bet that *stings.*' He got us back too, though. Your brother was alright."

"My mom says *none of your beeswax* all the time." I wiped my cheeks. "That's where we both got it."

"Amaia..." Ty pressed his lips together to stop himself. I knew what he was thinking. He was going to tell me looking for my brother was useless because Carlos was almost certainly dead, eaten by my parents. Scouts didn't cry, so I should shut my mouth and stop whining...

But Tyrell didn't say any of those things. Instead, he blinked back tears of his own before turning his face away from me and clearing his throat.

"You're alright, Girl Scout," he said. "You're alright."

We strapped everything down to the truck bed with colorful bungee cords, though one came back and whipped my arm so hard it left a welt. Being a scout sucked. My forearm throbbed as I scooted into the backseat, collapsed in exhaustion, and grumbled while Ty buried me in rolls of toilet paper.

Xander gloated in the rear view.

Tyrell grabbed a heavy lock and chain from the floor of the passenger side seat. That's when I knew for sure we'd be back to get more supplies from this abandoned truck. Ty mumbled something about this truck being complicated to drive and too big to fit through most of jammed up roads, otherwise we definitely would have brought it to the school.

I should have been happy we were coming back, but I wasn't hopeful Xander would ever allow me to grab Sara's baby things, even on our next trip.

What kind of coward holds a grudge against a girl and a

baby? I seethed at Xander's stupid smirk and knew I'd just answered my own question.

As we weaved through the streets, I scanned the distance and wondered, wherever he was, if Carlos was looking up at the gray clouds carpeting the sky and thinking about me too.

Even though our scouting mission was a success, I wanted to stamp my own forehead with a big fat "F" for failure. Sara Angelina still didn't have a safe place to sleep tonight, and I was no closer to finding my brother than I'd been when today started.

Xander backed the truck up to the mouth of the school's main entrance so we could unload boxes to the waiting crowd in assembly line fashion. Between the toilet paper and pit-stains, I was relieved Denny was busy off somewhere else but also found myself strangely annoyed Liam hadn't bothered to show up to ask how my day went. He was probably stuck in the computer lab or something…

Ty tossed the fragile box discreetly over the far side of the truck bed, out of view of the other kids. I didn't rat him out. If he wanted to get some side action from our hustle today, it was no skin off my back. Besides, Tyrell had risked his neck stopping that psycho Xander from pummeling me. I'd made a ton of enemies at Unity in my first 24 hours, but maybe – just maybe – I'd made a new friend too.

The way kids caught things in the air and rushed off to tear open the packages, I felt like one of Santa's elves tossing presents off the back of his sleigh. It would have truly been like Christmas Day except for the fact that instead of fluffy white snowflakes, dark gray ashes swirled around me in the frosty air. And also… there was no gift for little Sara.

We hopped down from the truck and were barely clear of the

rear wheels when Xander peeled out and raced off to the parking lot. Safely alone, Ty turned to me wearing a mischievous grin.

"Don't snitch or you'll get me in trouble." Tyrell tore open the fragile box he'd kept apart from the others.

"Oh! You *didn't*!" The travel bassinet and car seat looked up at me, nestled in a heap of fluffy diapers. I felt like doing a cartwheel.

"Shh! This was the only stuff I could grab under the radar," Ty said. "But maybe next time …"

"No, this is perfect… I don't even know what to say… I seriously owe you, Ty."

"You don't owe me, Girl Scout." Tyrell scooped up the box as I held the door for him. "My mom raised me right, rest her soul. No baby's gonna sleep on a cold gym floor on my watch. And no bully's gonna go around beating up little girls either."

My sneakers practically sprouted wings the way I flew upstairs to the computer lab. If I had to keep this good news secret for one second longer, I was going to burst.

Liam's nose was inches from a computer monitor while Violet leaned over him and prattled on about something. Her unruly brown locks tumbled dangerously close to brushing his cheek.

The room was ripe with the stench of roses and vanilla. I crinkled my nose in disgust.

Was Violet wearing *perfume*?!

My good mood evaporated.

"Where's Sara?" I marched in like the Spanish Inquisition, ready to bust some heads.

"Yvette has her." Liam shrugged innocently. "I didn't expect you'd be back so early, or I would've gone down to meet you."

"We got lucky with a supply truck." I eyed Violet who was puffing out her lips like a duck taking a selfie. "Liam, I need to talk to you. *In private.*"

Before I could blink, Liam leapt out of the swivel chair and threw both arms around my shoulders. Violet's face turned a witchy shade of green.

"I knew it!" He squeezed me so tight I could barely breathe. "Violet said you wouldn't, but I didn't doubt you for a second!"

Brace Face practically had smoke pouring from her ears as she stomped out, muttering something about using the girls' bathroom.

"I probably only got part of the story," Liam said. "So, maybe between the two of us, we can piece it all together. Tell me everything!"

What the heck was he talking about? My thumbs twirled around each other as words tumbled out of my mouth. "Ok… well… Yvette told me it's dangerous for Sara to sleep next to us because babies can suffocate to death in blankets. I was going to try to get a crib, but we found a SuperMart truck that had a car seat and this thingy called a *travel bassinet* which is like a mini crib that folds up into a backpack. Cool, right? Anyway, I thought Sara could sleep in either one of those two things, but the car seat box has a warning that says babies and toddlers can't sleep in car seats without being watched because they could slip down and get their airway blocked. Car seats are safe for travelling in cars, but we can't use it as a crib. Not even for a little nap. It was really lucky Sara was ok when we found her in the minivan. I'm not even talking about the geists. She could've died from just sleeping in the car seat unsupervised!" I shuddered at the thought. "This is serious. It's only safe for Sara to sleep in a crib or a bassinet without any blankets or pillows or anything, got it?"

God, babies were complicated.

Liam's mouth gaped open. "*That's* what you wanted to tell me?"

I suddenly felt like I was failing a geometry test again, missing the answer even though it was right in front of my face. "Um… the there is something else… you can't tell anyone."

Liam perked up. "Go on."

I lowered my voice. "Xander told us not to take the baby

stuff, and Tyrell could get in trouble for disobeying our scout leader. So, it's a secret, ok?"

Liam's jaw tightened.

"Aren't there any *other* secrets you want to tell me?"

"Not really." I shrugged. "What's with you anyway?"

Liam's right eye twitched.

"There's no secret Denny forbid you from telling me? Like the one where you and I are probably going to explode and turn into flesh-eating monsters six years from now?"

Oh. That secret.

I wished the floor would open up and swallow me whole.

"How did you find out…?"

"One of the Paris kids texted Violet the video," Liam huffed. "She bullied Waldo into spilling his guts. He told Violet Denny told you not to tell me."

"But why would Violet tell you?"

"The real question is, why wouldn't *you* tell me?"

"Because Denny…" My mind fumbled over itself to come up with an excuse that didn't sound bad.

"You have a crush on him!" Liam crossed his arms like a shield over his heart.

"I… I don't…" The hurt in his eyes forced me to look away. "Denny doesn't like me like that. And I don't… I mean.." Why was it so hard to tell Liam the truth? We both saw the way other girls looked at Denny too. It's not like I was the only one who thought the president was cute.

Liam's accusation hung like a guillotine in the silence between us. He said nothing as he let me squirm under his gaze. My mind wandered to the ticking of the clock above the doorway, the computer hard drives whirring on the racks behind him, and the lingering stink of Violet's perfume in the air.

"I can't believe you of all people fell for the popular jerk." Liam threw up his hands. "You think Denny cares what happens to you? If you didn't come back from one of your scouting missions, you think he would go out to rescue you?"

"He might," I shot back.

"He wouldn't!" Liam's voice cracked. "Denny's a coward and a bully! You'd see that if you stopped drooling over him for five seconds!"

"Oh yeah?" I wavered on my feet. "Like you'd run out there at sunset to come save me? You'd run away again just like you did with my brother!"

As soon as I said the words, I wished I hadn't.

Carlos' voice echoed in my head. *How does that foot taste in your mouth, Jodóna?*

"I didn't mean it." My throat stuck shut like I'd swallowed a fistful of cotton balls.

"Yeah, you did." Liam's cheeks turned red and splotchy. "Don't lie."

"I'm not…"

A waterline filled Liam's eyes halfway, turning each blue iris into a cold moon behind a horizon of tears.

"What was the word you called me in the attic?" Liam gritted his teeth. "*Mentiroso?*"

I drew in a sharp breath. "I'm a girl… so… it's *mentirosa.*"

He didn't repeat the word back to me. He didn't have to. I'd just admitted it for the both of us. I was a liar. Maybe not as good of one as I thought.

Violet's high heels came clacking back down the hall as quick as castanets. The stench of flowers and sweets wafted in, a fart in the breeze. How long had she been snooping out there? How much had she heard? Instead of letting the frizzy-haired troll gloat, I took what was left of my pride and bolted.

Kids were in the midst of a paint-filled balloon fight in the art room. Their squeals and giggles echoed off the metal lockers lining the hallway as my sneakers squeaked on the waxy floor.

I didn't stop running.

Past the biology lab, kids in white lab coats and nitrile gloves were in in a fist fight over a textbook. Had they heard about that kid in Paris? I quickly decided I didn't care.

My feet carried me into the stairwell.

There was no way I was going downstairs to waste the afternoon watching kids swimming in a tub of jellybeans or playing watermelon basketball. I hated the idea of running into Denny with his perfect hair and sparkling smile telling me what I great job I did getting the toilet paper today.

So, I went to the one place in a school full of kids I figured I was sure to be alone.

The library was completely dead like every author who'd written every single book on these dusty shelves. Liam hadn't run after me. I hadn't expected him to. So, why did that hurt so bad?

My eyes drifted over random words on the spines of each novel, hoping a clever phrase would jump out at me like a sign from God to tell me what to do. I came up blank.

Sara hated me. Liam hated me. I hated me.

I'd thought we'd be safe in the school, but now I was in danger of losing everything I cared about. I fell to my knees and clasped my hands together.

Dear God,

I know You're there, but I feel so alone right now. I wish we never left the attic. I wish the geists would all stay dead. I wish... I wish...

I doubled over with my hands twisted around my stomach as hot tears scorched my face. With no one around to hear, I bawled like a baby.

I wish Carlos was here. God, please help me find my brother.

The memory of Mom's voice whispered sweetly in my ear.

Let it all out, mija.

I could almost feel the pressure of her hand patting my hair. That made me wail even harder. How was it even possible for a heart to hurt this bad and not kill a person? I missed my family so bad every part of me ached. Exhaustion came and went. When I wiped my nose on the sleeve of my brother's hoodie two thoughts crossed my mind.

First, I needed a shower.

Second, I needed to tell Liam the truth.

But how could I face him? I'd been acting like a jerk since before we even left the attic. Why should he forgive me now? My fingers knotted themselves deeper in prayer. I bowed my head.

"Amaia!" Liam called frantically from the entrance to the library.

"I'm over here!"

Liam darted in so fast he skidded right past the bookshelf I was leaning on and doubled back for me.

"I've been looking for you everywhere!"

Ok. Here goes nothing.

"Liam, I'm sorry. I was stupid for not telling you. You deserved to know. Heck, everyone deserves to know about what happened in Paris. You might not be able to forgive me, but I promise…"

"What? No. Amaia, this isn't about that."

"*Dios mío!*" I gasped. "Is Sara ok? What happened? Where is she?"

Liam waved me off.

"Sara's fine! It's Carlos… Someone sent me a text."

"My brother texted you?"

"No… someone else." Liam unlocked his phone with his thumb and handed it to me.

"He's alive…" My trembling fingertips grazed my lower lip.

"This might be some kind of prank," Liam said. "Do you think some stranger could've got my number? Maybe they saw the note we left in your house…"

"God answered my prayer." I murmured.

"Amaia." Liam winced. "God isn't… I mean… Listen, even if God *is* real, this still might just be someone's idea of a sick joke."

I read the text over and over, letting my eyes rest on the one word I knew could only have come from my idiot brother's lips.

Jodóna

The phone was already ringing in my hand as I leaned my back against a bookshelf for support.

"I already tried calling," Liam said as an automatic voice sang out, *'We're sorry. The user has a mailbox that has not been set up yet.'*

"Why aren't they answering?"

"Maybe we should listen to their text." Liam frowned. "There's probably a good reason your brother doesn't want you to find him."

"Or maybe he's just being a moron like usual." I dialed again. Automated message. I wanted to slap my brother through this phone.

"We'll find him," Liam said as he scooted closer to me.

"Wait, what do you mean 'we'?"

Liam's eyes drifted up to the ceiling.

"When you left this morning, I was terrified I'd never see you again." He pounded his fist on his knee. "I never should have let you go on that scouting mission without me."

"*Let* me?! I only signed up as a scout to protect you and Sara!"

"That should've been my job, not yours," Liam said.

"Why, 'cause I'm a girl?" I was two seconds from throwing this boy in a headlock.

Liam's cheeks went scarlet.

"Stop saying that!" He shoved a finger in my face. "This isn't about boys and girls. It's about you and me. I'm not like Denny. I *would* run out there at sunset for you. You think I'm a coward? Well, I'll show you. I'm gonna prove it..."

"I never said..." I bit my cheek. Yep. I'd said it. I'd called him a coward. "Liam, you're not a coward, ok?"

He wasn't convinced.

"I can't watch you leave again. What if next time you don't come back?" His voice got real soft. "Sara cried for hours after you left."

Ugh. Not this again.

"I told you, Sara hates me!"

"No. She loves you."

Liam's gaze was so intense I had to look away. I squirmed as we both shifted in uneasy silence.

"I thought it over." Liam was doing that twisty thing with his mouth that made me want to shake him. "I'm pretty sure it will be ok to leave the baby with Yvette while we're gone."

"Gone?" I had a bad feeling I wasn't going to like his answer. "Gone where?"

Liam bit his thumbnail again. I smacked his hand away from his mouth.

"YOU VOLUNTEERED TO BE A SCOUT?!" I screeched.

He nodded.

"You... you... *idiot!*" I shoved him so hard he spilled onto the floor. "You can't! If we run into a geist and you freeze again, you'll die!"

"I already talked to Denny. With all this Paris stuff, I knew he'd be happy to have one less person in the computer lab." Liam lifted his chin defiantly. "It's done."

I wanted to pummel him. I wanted to rip every book off the

bookshelf and chuck it at his dumb head. Why were boys so *infuriating*? My tongue moved in my mouth with the taste of salt. I hadn't even noticed that tears had been scraping their way down my cheeks and onto my lips. "Why, Liam?"

He took a step toward me.

"Because we both know you need to find your brother… " His voice softened. "But you don't need to do it alone."

A sob broke through my lips. How could he be so stupid? Now neither of us was safe.

Liam dried my tears with his sleeve, and I went limp into his arms again just like I had the first morning he came to find me in the attic. His shirt smelled sweet like orange slices and peanut butter. He squeezed me so tight he was shaking. This hadn't been easy for him. Behind his brave face, he was terrified again.

Liam was right. I did need his help… and I hated the part of myself that was relieved he'd be with me on my next scouting mission.

Because if Liam died out there, I'd never forgive myself. I should've prevented this. I should've…

"Achem." A voice startled us from the doorway. My nostrils flared. Could Violet have picked a more rancid perfume? I pulled away from Liam, but she'd already seen us hugging. The vein in the side of the troll's neck pulsed like her head might explode any second.

"I've been looking everywhere for you guys," Braces sneered. "Denny's called an emergency assembly."

Denny sat cross-legged on the golden throne. Although he wasn't dressed as Julius Caesar this time, his flaming red hair was spiky with gel in a new hairstyle he wore like a copper crown.

A line of muscly henchmen advanced through the gym, marching around wearing matching uniforms of gray t-shirts and jeans. Denny's foot soldiers rounded kids up while Xander howled at everyone to sit their butts down on the basketball court. One by one, thugs ripped open the boys' tents in search of stragglers.

Violet bumped me purposefully with her shoulder as she shoved past and melted into the crowd. Whatever was going on, it wasn't going to be a dance party.

Yvette's wheelchair was parked outside her tent. Liam and I made a beeline for it, unzipped the flap, and stuffed ourselves inside. Sara Angelina was asleep in the bassinet, sucking a pacifier with a sleepy grin plastered on her face that told me her babysitter had worn her out with peek-a-boo and playtime all afternoon. Yvette wasn't smiling. Her mascara, though obviously waterproof, had barely held up under a barrage of tears.

"Yvette, are you ok?" Liam demanded. "What's going on?"

She glanced up in a daze. "You two haven't seen the videos?"

Liam and I stole a look at one another.

She pressed play on her tablet and a boy about our age stared up at me from the screen, shouting in Spanish at the top of his lungs. Behind him, kids were screaming so loud it was hard to hear him above the chaos. His voice kept cutting in and out, but I got his meaning loud and clear.

"He says he's in Caguas, it's a place in Puerto Rico," I told Liam. "He says his cousin exploded into ashes at sunset on her birthday. She was turning twenty."

"Every kid left alive must be on the internet." Yvette tapped the screen. "Look how many views this one has. It's gone mega viral! There are hundreds and hundreds more videos just like this one about teenagers turning twenty and…" She made an exploding gesture with her fist.

"Is this what Denny's assembly is about?" I asked. "He needs this video translated?"

Yvette's pink hair flew about her shoulders as she shook her head.

"No. It's because of the comments under the video." Yvette leaned in and whispered. "Denny says people are spreading lies on the internet, and he's got some plan to stop it…"

Liam tensed. He whipped out his phone from his back pocket, powered it down, and slid it in Sara's travel bassinet, snug in one of the hidden pockets underneath.

"There's more. Check this out." Yvette swiped at her tablet a few times and flipped it toward us again. "That's a meteor crater in Australia. They're saying this is proof the plague is some kind of alien virus. Remember when the news was reporting on that crazy earthquake a while back? And then all those fires?"

I nodded. Those headlines screaming *mass evacuations* echoed in my mind. My science teacher said the Australian earthquake and wildfires that followed were the greatest series of natural disasters since the dinosaurs. But once the plague started, everyone kinda forgot about the planet and looked to their own.

"They started the fires," I gasped. "They must have been trying to stop the plague from spreading."

"Who?" Liam flashed me a disbelieving look. Ugh. I *told* him it was *aliens* and the world governments were working together to cover it up! But last time we had this fight, the two of us stopped speaking. I couldn't take that now.

"It doesn't matter." I let out a deep sigh.

The video on Yvette's tablet showed an unending column of ash blasting up into the sky from a gaping hole in the earth. It looked like photos I'd seen in my history book of an atom bomb where the entire sky was the mushroom top. This must have been the biggest global coverup in history… only there were no adults left alive to keep it classified anymore.

"Ok, let's just say that thing was sent by *aliens*." He shot me a sideways glance. "Where are they? Why drop this thing out of the sky and then not show up?"

"There's like a zillion theories in the comments." Yvette motioned toward her tablet. "Most people agree it's some kind of bioweapon that was programmed to know when a human's body has circled our sun exactly twenty times before it sets off. That could explain why it effects people only on their birthdays."

"It can't be a weapon. I mean… if they wanted to kill us all, I'm pretty sure they'd have done it already," I said. "Maybe it's an experiment and they're just watching us all to see what we'll do…"

Liam was only half listening, still scrolling through the comments. "A hive mind?" he mumbled. "This person's saying the virus waited until everyone on the planet was infected before forcing the transformation of people into geists. They say that's why all the adults exploded at the same time…"

Made sense to me. Liam's brow creased, unconvinced.

The shadow of a meaty hand slapped the top of the tent over our heads, forcing the plastic poles to buckle and spring under the weight. "Yo, Yvette! Out of the tent!"

Yvette put a finger over her lips and motioned for us to be quiet. She swiped her tablet from Liam, shoved it in her shoulder bag, and used her arms to slide herself out of the tent.

"Chill," Yvette called up to the unseen thug. "I'm coming."

"Anyone else in there?" the boy's voice boomed.

She zipped the door shut behind herself before he could peek in.

"Just a sleeping baby," Yvette said nonchalantly. "But if you wake her up, Denny's gonna make *you* change the diaper!"

"Ack, nasty." The boy's footsteps faded as he moved on to rustle the next tent.

Liam and I held our breaths for fifteen seconds before scrambling out of our hiding place to join the others. Not knowing what to expect, we left Sara behind in the tent, sleeping safely in her bassinet.

Waldo slumped on the floor like a heap of dirty laundry tossed at the foot of Denny's chair. Dark spots stained the armpits of his speech and debate t-shirt, and a sheen of fog misted his glasses from the heat of his sweat. His wrists weren't bound, so I had no reason to suspect he was some tortured prisoner, yet the look on his face said otherwise.

A discord of anxious whispers ricocheted off the gymnasium walls as one hundred kids were herded onto the court.

"Quiet!" Xander stomped an army boot. We obeyed.

Our leader rose from his throne. In the sunlight, the ornate carvings on the president's chair were exposed as just spray painted styrofoam instead of solid gold. It didn't matter. Denny made it real.

I wrinkled my forehead. Did presidents sit in thrones? I tried to remember if I'd seen a picture of George Washington in a fancy chair or not.

"Unity is the safest place on Earth." Denny proclaimed as he clasped his hands behind his back. "But you don't feel safe anymore, do you?"

Murmurs spread through the crowd as people looked to one

another before deciding what their answer would be. Denny paced like a lion in a field full of lemmings.

"And why are you all so afraid? Well, I'll tell you. It's because of this." Denny freed his phone from his sweater pocket and held it high over his head. "We all saw what the media did to our parents, didn't we? How adults used to argue over nothing? How easily lies were spread?"

Assent rippled through the crowd as several kids nodded their heads in agreement. Liam slid his hand across the floor and entwined his fingers in mine.

Both of our palms were sweaty.

"Our parents listened to those lies!" Denny shouted. "And now they're all dead!"

A boy let out a wail of anguish as a dozen kids burst into tears at once.

"Now the same thing is happening to us!" Denny said. "People on the *outside* are saying things to scare us. Fear is how they manipulate you. They want to control your minds! But you elected me - your president - to protect you, and so I'll do whatever it takes to make sure Unity stays safe... now and forever!"

Denny motioned for the henchmen in gray t-shirts to step forward, each one of them holding an empty garbage bag in his fist.

"Outsiders are trying to divide us because *they* want what *we* have: they want our school! Are we going to let them take it without a fight?"

"No!" Peggy screamed.

Anxiety was so thick in the air, I could cut with a knife. I cast a worried glance at Yvette's tent. Sara had started crying, but I didn't dare go to her. Best not to draw too much attention to ourselves.

"First, one of our own was taken prisoner," the president continued. "Now, they attack each and every one of us with their filthy lies. You know what I say? We shut out their noise until the geists shut them all up once and for all!"

A henchman opened his trash bag and Denny slam dunked his phone inside.

"We are safe here in these walls as long as we don't let outsiders drive us apart from each other. No one divides Unity! Who is with me?!"

"No one divides Unity!" Peggy leapt to her feet and chucked her phone in the trash with Denny's. Shouts erupted from the captive audience, echoing the phrase over and over while the president's eyes sparkled in triumph. Phones and tablets disappeared, devoured into the gaping mouths of black plastic bags. Several kids smashed screens on the ground and stomped them underfoot, roaring with delight.

Yvette clutched her tablet in white knuckled hands, but when one of Denny's thugs came by, she tossed hers in with the rest. Just before it disappeared, I caught a glimpse of her lock screen; it was a photo of Yvette and her parents pulling silly faces at the camera on a bright summer day. My heart twisted in my chest. That device probably held hundreds of pics of her family and friends, and without it, she'd never see their faces again. As Yvette watched the garbage bag make off with her greatest treasure, a tear raced from her eye to chase after it. Yvette herself didn't move a muscle.

It wasn't fair. What right did Denny have to rob her of that keepsake? Because of some stupid comments on the internet?

Xander's black army boots stopped right in front of me.

"Girl Scout, give up your phone," he hissed.

"My parents said I can't have one until I turn sixteen," I said.

Xander scrutinized my face for any trace of a lie, but of course, I was telling the truth. His eyes drifted to the floor where Liam's hand was still in mine. We let go and scooted away from each other.

"This the new scout?" Xander appraised Liam with disdain, like dog poop on his shoe.

Liam scrambled to attention and gave a sloppy salute.

Xander held out the trash bag.

"I don't have a phone either," Liam said, his mouth twisting.

"I'm not buying it," Xander said.

"I don't have one, I swear!"

"Oh, you've got a phone alright." Xander raised a fist in the air and summoned two more henchmen to his side. "Latest model. I'm betting mommy and daddy are filthy rich, aren't they? Look at those sneaks."

One of the boys in gray whistled. "I'd kill for a pair of those."

A smile spread up the side of Xander's face as he gave the order:

"Frisk him."

"No wait!" Liam struggled as the boys held his arms and legs. They tore his shirt off and tossed it like a flag at a football game. Liam struggled and screamed and kicked his legs as they ripped both shoes from his feet. Standing barefoot and half naked, Liam wrapped his skinny arms around his torso as girls around us snickered.

"No phone," one of the boys said. "Thanks for the sneaks though."

"Search his tent," Xander ordered. "The girl scout's too. Find it."

I held Xander's gaze without flinching, but in the corner of my eye, Yvette spun in her wheelchair to intercept the boy heading toward our tent.

My hands clenched into fists. Xander grinned.

"You hiding the phone for your little boyfriend, Girl Scout?" he said. "Maybe I should frisk you myself."

"I'll kill you if you touch her." Liam's posture changed. Suddenly he didn't seem to care about having been stripped of his shirt. He drew his skinny arm back, but before Liam could land a punch, Xander jabbed him right in the nose with a sickening *crunch*. Liam's blood splattered across the floor like red paint flicked off a brush. He cried in agony and clutched his face with both hands, laid flat out on his back.

"They'll make anyone a scout." Xander laughed.

As much as I wanted to deck him, I knew I wouldn't win against Xander in a fist fight. I'd have to be smart and bide my time. If this psycho thought he was going to get away with hurting Liam without feeling the wrath of my revenge, he really was as stupid as he looked.

This wasn't over.

"Xander!" a deep voice cut through the chaos. "Denny wants to see you."

Tyrell lumbered toward us, a thick bag heavy with electronics draped over one shoulder. Xander eyed me with suspicion, but turned on his heels to heed his master's call. Just beyond him, Yvette was being led away from our tent, flanked by henchmen on all sides. Sara Angelina wasn't with them.

I had already fallen to my knees beside Liam. Black and purple bruises sprouted under both his eyes.

"His nose is busted up pretty good," Ty said. "There's ice packs at the nurse's station, but Denny's not gonna let you two leave until this is over. Just keep pressure on it and have him tip his head back like this until the bleeding stops."

"It hurts so bad," Liam moaned as blood poured over his top lip.

"Hold still, let me take a look." Tyrell lifted Liam's chin and tilted it to the light. Ty let out a deep sigh. "That's what I thought. Hold still. This is gonna hurt."

Ty gripped Liam by the back of the hair with one fist and snapped his nose back into place with the other. Liam shrieked.

"I said it was gonna hurt," Ty said, though his tone was sympathetic. "You're ok, kid. Gonna be a bump now in the bridge, but I've had worse."

Wow. Unity should've made Tyrell the doctor.

"You broke your nose before, Ty?" I wondered out loud, noticing the bump in his bridge for the first time.

"*I* didn't break my nose. My stepdad broke it for me." Ty tapped his nostril twice and smiled. "Don't you worry Girl Scout, if I ever see his geist out there, I'm gonna pay him back for it real good. He's gonna wish he stayed dead."

"Everyone shut it!" Xander silenced the room. Just the sight of him made my blood boil again.

"Last announcement. As you all know, we have a star in our midst." Denny lounged back on his throne and gestured toward Yvette who sat uncomfortably at his side. She tugged at a lock of her pink hair so hard, I was afraid she might pull some out.

She scanned the audience as though looking for help, and at first I was sure her eyes landed on me. But no. Her gaze was fixed just over my shoulder. At Tyrell? It was hard to tell…

"If the enemy wants to put out videos, we'll fight fire with fire!" Denny said. "Yvette's an influencer, but this time instead of making mindless beauty videos, she will deliver a new message! Our message! A message of hope and love. A message that Unity will never be divided and anyone who tries will face our wrath!"

Wild whoops and hollers rose up around us as kids began to chant our school fight song. Denny didn't sing along. After all, he didn't even go here. Still, he smiled and bobbed his head to the melody. Once it was done, Xander sounded the airhorn that was used at our football games, whipping everyone into a frenzy. Music blared over the loudspeakers and kids leapt to their feet and danced like it was prom.

I swiveled my head around, but Ty had vanished.

Denny singled me out in the crowd. As he closed the distance between us, kids parted to let him through.

"Xander can get carried away." The president put a hand on my shoulder. "I'll talk to him."

Carried away? I wanted to scream. I wanted to rip Denny's spiky hair out of his stupid scalp. Instead, I put on my best puppy-dog eyes and batted my eyelashes at him.

"May we be excused to the nurse's office?" I asked.

Denny leaned forward, his cheek hovering next to mine. I

recoiled, but he gripped my shoulder to keep me close.

"I know it wasn't you who betrayed me," Denny whispered in my ear. "You'll be rewarded for your loyalty. Those who don't deserve my trust… well, they'll be punished appropriately of course."

He flicked his head to the right, and my eyes followed suit. Practically everyone else around us was celebrating, but Waldo hadn't moved from his spot on the floor by Denny's throne. Was he in some kind of time-out or something?

As a gesture of good-will, Denny helped Liam stand and handed him his tattered shirt that several dirty shoes had trampled on already. I ducked my head under Liam's arm to help steady him.

"I can have my guys carry him to the nurse's room, would you like that, Amaia?" Denny asked.

"No, I can manage." I flashed what I hoped was a genuine looking smile.

"Tough cookie." Denny brushed the hair away from my cheek. "I'll send the doctor to take a look at him."

"The doctor?"

Denny jerked his thumb to my left where a bunch of kids were laughing themselves silly as they smashed beer bottles against the wall. I didn't know which one the 'doctor' was, but it didn't matter.

"Nah," I said. "Liam's just a big baby. It's not as bad as it looks."

"We've got two babies in the gym then." Denny laughed at his own joke. "Hurry back or you'll miss the party."

"Denny?" I called after him. "One more thing?"

"Sure." There was that dazzling smile of his again. It didn't have the same effect on me as before. His actions had vaccinated me against it.

"There's been a misunderstanding. Liam's not going to be a scout," I said. "So, he'll just keep working at the computer lab, ok?"

Liam jerked his head up to protest, but the sudden movement was too much for him. His legs buckled, nearly toppling us both.

"I see the problem. Can't be a scout barefoot, now can he?" Denny winked at me. "I'll have new sneakers in his tent before curfew. What size is he?"

"9," Liam moaned, still holding his nose.

"Got it." With that, the president disappeared into the crowd. I was tempted to scold Liam for ruining my shot at getting him out of scout duty, but he was already suffering enough.

"Sara…" Liam wobbled on his feet like he was standing on a waterbed.

"With what extra hand am I going to carry her? I've already got you to deal with!" I said. "You're gonna fall over if I let go."

"I'll help," Yvette rolled up behind us and came to our rescue. "Set Liam on my lap. I can carry him. You get the baby, we can't leave her here…"

"On it!" By the time I had Sara in hand, Yvette had already wheeled herself and Liam halfway down the hall. I rushed to catch up, though I had to fight my way around a mass of dancing teenagers who started a mosh pit.

·······))) ● (((·······

"It's not just our parents we have to save now," a girl's voice sounded from the cafeteria. "If we don't find a cure, we're all going to die!"

"Shhh! Do you want someone to hear you?" another kid said.

"Stop it you guys! Focus. We need one of those boxes like the one from Paris if we're going to do proper experiments on fully-formed geists."

"The engineering team's already on it."

Yvette and I exchanged glances as Liam kept his head tilted back.

The nurse's station was still a little way away, but the

heated argument erupting in the lunchroom detoured us. I peered around the broken vending machines to get a better look.

Eight skittish kids in white lab coats huddled around a table, looking like a group of jackals ready to tear each other apart.

"We can't do this!" A freckled kid punched the table with his fist. "I only got a B minus in biology! It's hopeless. You all get that right? Real scientists couldn't figure it out, you think any of us stand a chance?"

"We've got friends online," a lanky girl blurted out. "The Tokyo team has already isolated the virus. That's the first step, isn't it?"

"Hannah's right," another girl chimed in. "They have an optical fluorescence microscope, which you need to see something as small as a virus. And we'd have to use dye... this is like, college level stuff."

"And now the internet is banned." Hannah sighed. "How are we supposed to look anything up?"

"Maybe we can get some textbooks?"

"From where? The library upstairs? I checked. It's got zilch on virology."

A boy who'd been silent until now leaned forward over the table and grinned.

"That's why Denny had me call you all here, you're all getting your phones back," he said.

"What?"

"Seriously?"

"We have special privileges," the boy beamed. "The eight of us can keep communicating with the global teams, we just can't tell the other kids in Unity about it. Finding a cure is the president's top priority. He says he'll order the scouts to get us anything we need."

"We *need* an optical fluorescence microscope..."

"And there's something else." The boy leaned in conspiratorially. "The Melbourne team found something. Meteor fragments with black veins running through them that look like… well… they look like *them.*"

I stifled a gasp and leaned further in the doorway.

"So… what the heck does that mean?" the freckled kid demanded. "It's an alien virus after all?"

The boy nodded. "When we get our phones back, I'll show you the video. Even the little rocks are shedding ash like crazy. That's where it's all coming from. With global travel shut down, there's no way we can get a hold of one of those samples, so the best we can do is to isolate the virus here and share our findings. Who knows if it's already mutated and how many variants there might be…"

Sara Angelina spat out her pacifier and let out a wail because we'd stopped paying attention to her for two seconds. That was our cue to bail. The biology kids snapped their heads in our direction, but we didn't waste time getting caught. We swerved around the corner and into the nurse's office, bolting the door behind us.

· · · · · · ·))) ● (((· · · · · ·

Alternating fresh cold packs onto Liam's face for several hours helped the swelling come down, but the bruises had spilled down his cheeks and onto his jaw. Yvette rifled through the nurse's cabinets and found children's Tylenol for the pain.

At least one of us was thinking clearly.

The only thing I could think about was wrapping my fingers around Xander's throat and wringing it like a wet towel. That kid was gonna get what was coming to him sooner or later. Hopefully sooner.

Liam finally fell asleep on the examination table, and we decided to let him rest until it was time to head back to the gym for the night. Yvette and I didn't talk about what we'd overheard from the biology kids in the cafeteria, but from the sour looks on both our faces, I knew it was bothering her too. Those alien-conspiracy crackpots on TV were right after all, but I didn't rub Liam's face in it. His face had gone through enough trauma for one day.

"Liam's phone's still in there." Yvette nodded to Sara's bassinet, hastily folded up into its backpack form. "No one messed with it. You'd have thought the baby was kryptonite the way she puts the fear in some boys." Her smile faded. "They tore the rest of my tent apart though. Broke my favorite compact when they spilled out my makeup case. Our sleeping bags are inside out too…"

"Sorry about that." I grimaced. "Thanks for not ratting us out."

Yvette sighed. "You know you can't keep the phone, right? They'll catch you eventually."

"Don't worry, I'll get rid of it," I lied.

Right now, that stranger's text was the only clue I had to finding my brother. What if Carlos tried to contact me, but Liam's phone was lost forever in the bottom of one of Denny's trash bags? I couldn't let that happen.

"Did you hear what the science team said?" Yvette whispered even though we were alone. "They can't really plan to do experiments on geists… wouldn't that mean… bringing one inside the school?"

I shuddered. "Yvette, do you know who the oldest kid here is?"

"Xander. I'm pretty sure he's eighteen."

"What about Denny?"

"Sixteen… I think… why?"

I scratched my scalp, caking a bit of white grime under my fingernails. I wiped it on my pants.

"But that doesn't make any sense. If no one is having a birthday where they turn twenty, how do those kids think they're going to get a geist into a plexiglass box?"

"I don't know." She shook her head. "But I don't think I want to find out."

"What are you going to do about the videos Denny wants you to make?"

"I'm going to say whatever he wants me to, obviously." Yvette pinched the bridge of her nose like she had a headache. "He said he'll have my first script ready tomorrow morning."

"But… what if he makes you lie?"

Yvette snapped her eyes open, anger flashing over her face.

"If I don't go along with it, Denny will make my life miserable," she said. "You don't get it. I'm off the decorating committee. Denny said I've been *promoted*… But he could just as easily demote me if I say no. You think I'm going to spend one second on toilet duty? Have you caught a whiff of the boys' bathrooms?"

"What if you ran against him in the next election?" I asked. "People like you. You're popular! I'd vote for you…"

Yvette turned away from me, unbolted the door, and smashed her fist into the button to automatically open it.

"I'm going to pretend I didn't hear that." Yvette wheeled herself into the hallway. "Listen, I want to keep helping you guys, but just… don't make me regret it, ok?"

"I won't," I said, hoping it wasn't a lie this time.

"And get rid of that phone!"

I forced a smile and nodded. "Ok."

"You and Liam need to watch your backs with Denny." She wedged her chair in the door and kept her fist on the automatic button to keep it propped open. "The biggest egos are the most fragile."

"What the heck is that supposed to mean?"

"It means, just do whatever he says, even if it's stupid. Make him look good, or he's going to make your life hell. Keep your head down like the rest of us, and we'll all get through this, ok?"

I pinched my lips and said nothing. She sighed.

"One more thing. About the next election…" Yvette hesitated just before the door snapped shut. "I doubt there's going to be one."

That night, tucked away in Yvette's tent, dreams haunted my sleep again.

Cartoon orcas chased each other around the edge of the plastic kiddie pool, only I wasn't in my backyard this time. Now, the pool was a life raft floating in a gray ocean.

And I wasn't alone.

Liam curled up across from me, cradling Sara in his arms and counterbalancing my weight in the flimsy craft. One sudden, jerky move could tip us over to our deaths, but Liam didn't look like he'd be flailing any time soon. His skin was the color of frozen milk, but if I could've reach out to feel his forehead without flipping our boat, I suspected it would have been boiling to the touch. Liam was sick. His head bobbed with the waves as though he wasn't strong enough to hold it up on his own. There was no land in sight. No safety to bring him to.

I was about to reach my hands in the water and start paddling when the flash of a rainbow-colored mermaid tail caught the fading light. Yvette's head poked out of the ocean and she blinked up at me though glittering lashes, a crown of sparkling seashells adorning the pink hair that floated about her shoulders.

"You've got to choose," Yvette said, nodding toward the horizon.

A steely battle cruiser roamed in the distance. Though I couldn't see his face, I somehow knew it was under Denny's command.

"It's not safe," came a tiny voice.

"Sara?" I blinked at the baby. "Sara, did you say something?"

Liam shrugged indifferently, but a trickle of blood leaked from his nostril.

"Liam!" I shouted. "Tip your head back!"

"Choose," Yvette gurgled as she disappeared underwater.

"No, wait! Come with us!" I plunged my fist into the icy ocean seeking her wrist but grabbed nothing. Dozens of shark fins rose in concentric circles, closing in on us, and I jerked my hand back into our raft. A shadow blocked out the sun, and when I raised my eyes to the sky, a skull and crossbones grinned down at me.

A pirate ship.

The plastic pool melted way to wooden boards that creaked beneath my feet, but Liam and Sara had vanished. I cried out their names in a panic, roaming the ship's deck in vain as I searched for my familia. The world went silent save for the black sails ruffling overhead in the breeze, the same fluttery sound that bedsheets made on the clothesline when Mom hung them out to dry in our backyard.

The tide is changing.

A girl with rich brown skin and eyes as dark as midnight pearls stood confidently at the helm. Ocean air played with her long braids like wind chimes as she rocked a giant wooden wheel back and forth to navigate through increasingly rocky seas. Across the empty bow, a thunderhead darkened the horizon. It was blue and purple, like the bruises under Liam's eyes.

"Don't be afraid," the girl said. "You're safe onboard my ship."

"Can my friends come too?" I asked.

Her smile was like sunlight breaking through the storm clouds and warming me from the inside. "Of course. Gamerz are always looking for good crew." She leaned in and dropped her voice to a whisper. "I'm Zelda. Come find me."

Mesmerized, my mouth moved on its own as I whispered my reply.

"Yes, Captain."

I didn't tell Liam or Yvette they were in my dream. Best to just forget it. There were more important things to focus on, and I'd slept in longer than I'd meant to.

The padlock on the gym doors had been undone for the morning, so I slung on my backpack and slipped out unnoticed on my way to the girls' locker rooms. My scalp had started to itch something fierce, and I couldn't stand my own stink. A few pumps of liquid soap from the sink made do as shampoo, and I used paper towels to wring the water from my hair. My heart ached for the feel of a fluffy towel on my skin and the smell of Mom's fabric softener. It was just one of the million wonderful things she'd done that I'd foolishly taken for granted. I don't think I thanked her for doing my laundry, not even one time in my whole life… If Denny's cure did work someday, I made a vow to make it up to her.

Laughter and bustling from the cafeteria warned me everyone else had already headed to breakfast. So, I snaked my way around the hallways until the chatter faded and I could be alone with my thoughts. Well, just one thought actually.

How was I going to find Carlos?

The squeak of rubber sneakers down the hall forced me to duck into the nearest classroom and ease the door shut behind me. What if it was Denny's henchman? Or worse, Xander? It'd be stupid to get caught alone with any of those jerks without some backup. At least I had my hammer in my backpack.

I held my breath and braced my shoulder to the door. Had they seen me?

A few seconds later, two older teens skipped past, flirting, giggling, and kissing. They apparently wanted to be alone too.

I wanted to gag.

The coast was clear, but I stopped short when I realized I hadn't wandered into a classroom at all. It was the teachers' lounge.

A giant coffee machine on an auto timer spit brown liquid into an overflowing cup. Judging by the puddle on the counter, it must have been running for days. A large color copier squatted in the corner, once used to pop out kid-torturing quizzes as teachers scarfed down their lunches.

Wait… a copy machine!

If the little note I'd posted on Carlos' bedroom door had gotten a response, imagine what neon flyers posted around the entire town could do? I knew just what to write to get his attention.

A sharpie on loose-leaf paper did the trick.

After pressing every button on the copier and pulling off the right combo after the zillionth try, I shoved the thick stack of flyers into my backpack along with a stapler and roll of tape. Leave it to teachers to always have extra supplies laying within arm's reach. With no time left to double back for breakfast, I raced toward the parking lot to report for my second day of scout duty.

Waldo was waiting to ambush me at the main entrance. My mood soured. The last thing I needed right now was this kid all up in my face. If he hadn't blabbed to Violet, Liam would still be working in the computer lab.

"You're late." Waldo folded his arms across his speech and debate t-shirt. "I've been waiting for you."

"Well, next time make an appointment," I sneered. "Let me by."

"We need to talk." He clutched a fuzzy yellow ball in his hands.

"Whatever it is, we're good." I moved to push past him, but he blocked my path.

"Xan told me about the baby stuff he made Tyrell leave at that truck," Waldo said. "I… wanted her to have this."

He shoved a tennis-ball-sized emoji plush toy into my hands. The stupid thing winked up at me with a pink tongue sticking out one side of a toothy grin.

"It used to be a keychain," Waldo said. "It's not a real toy, but it's the only thing I've got…"

"Um, thanks?" I fingered the stitching where he'd taken the time to remove a piece of hard plastic. "No, I mean it. This is really cool of you. Xander's a total jerk…"

"He's not. You don't even know him." Waldo pushed up his glasses though he didn't look me in the eye. "Xan has been protecting me… He's the only one who understands…"

"Did you see what he did to Liam's face?!" My blood pressure spiked. "He's a monster. A complete psycho…"

"He's my friend." Waldo blushed hard. "Xander's been through a lot and…"

"Whatever," I hissed. "Any friend of Xander is an enemy of mine. Keep your stupid toy. I'm outta here."

I drew back my arm to chuck it.

"My baby sister…" Waldo put his hand on my arm. "Toni is six months old, and I have no idea where she is…" He let go and turned away from me, but it was too late. I'd already seen the monsoon of tears pouring from his eyes. "If Mom worked late and Christie - the babysitter - was at our house that night, Toni may be safe somewhere. But if my Mom came home early…"

I braced myself against the wall, still clutching the smiley face in my fist. Toni. That was my mom's name… *Antonia*.

"In the computer lab two days ago… you knew Sara's age right away," I gasped. "That's because Sara Angelina's the same age as your baby sister, isn't she? Waldo… did you… look for her?"

He nodded.

"We got to my house, but I was too afraid to go in." He shuddered. "But Xan went for me. He said there was no sign of her."

No sign was as good as sign as we could hope for.

"I've only told one person." He swiped the glasses from his face and rubbed his sleeve across his watery eyes. "I don't know why I spilled all that to you just now… Xan says I'll never survive if I don't toughen up. I've got to get back to work. Denny's already ticked off at me. Just… give her the toy, ok? Please. Just do it."

"Wait!" I called to the back of his head, but Waldo didn't turn back. Across the parking lot, Xander honked the horn like a maniac. My butt was going to be in big trouble if I didn't get out there STAT.

"It wasn't your fault, Waldo," I whispered to myself, slipping the toy into my pack. "You can't save everyone."

Xander slouched in the driver's seat revving the engine and smoking a nasty, skunky cigarette that stunk up the truck. Liam was belted into the backseat looking as frightened as he was on the stairs the morning we escaped my attic. I squeezed his hand to let him know everything was going to be ok.

I hoped it was convincing because I sure as heck didn't believe it myself.

Xander's newly shaved head unsettled me. It made him the spitting image of a drill sergeant and uncovered a large, crescent shaped scar trailing from the back of his head all the way down his neck. I knew better than to ask how he got that and didn't let him catch me staring at it either.

"Didn't see you at breakfast, Girl Scout," Tyrell called over his headrest from the passenger side seat. "Today might be a long one by the mission we got."

He tossed me a granola bar.

"Are we going back to SuperMart?" I asked as Xander staked me out suspiciously in the rear view.

"Nah. The kids in the bio lab need some kind of special microscope to see the virus." Tyrell rolled down his window. "I guess they only got them at the college, so that's where we're headed."

I gulped.

If a geist could survive during the daytime in my garage, how many could be crawling in the darkened lecture halls of a college campus? If it were up to me, we wouldn't take such a stupid risk.

But it wasn't up to me.

Liam's eyes drooped and his head bobbed as the truck bounced over potholes and swerved around dead cars in the road. My stomach twisted like I was carsick, but it wasn't that. The thought of Liam going on this mission when he could barely keep his eyes open made me so worried I wanted to puke. So, instead, I focused on my rage and daydreamed about beating Xander to a pulp.

The college was completely across town, and none of us had ever been on campus before. How were two middle schoolers, one high school jock, and a bald, bad-tempered psycho going to find a super exotic microscope in a university science wing *by ourselves*? It's not like we could ask someone for directions... and any person we came across would probably use our bones for toothpicks.

"What do these microscopes look like?" I asked.

"Beats me." Tyrell shrugged. "When we get there, we're supposed to do a livestream with the biology team and have them guide us."

Ty tossed me a phone.

"But I thought we couldn't have phones?!" I said.

"Being a scout has its perks." Ty grinned at me. "But we're only allowed to call the numbers programmed into the favorites. Right now, that's just Denny and the bio team."

Liam and I exchanged glances. Was his beat down yesterday all for nothing? No. It was Liam's number that mystery person texted. His phone was still the only clue I had to finding my brother.

As we drove, Ty made notes on which streets were completely blocked so we could avoid those on the way back. The highways were still completely impassable, so we had to wind our way through side streets to get around. Each day, more and more cars seemed to be pushed to one side of the road or the other, as if someone was set on clearing a path for a single vehicle to move through.

Our truck pulled up to a stretch of large concrete buildings decorated with sweeping archways of concrete pillars and tall windows. The flag hung limply at half-staff, guarding the base of an expanse of stairs that opened into an outdoor courtyard.

It didn't look like any college I'd ever seen. Weren't colleges all red brick covered in ivy like in the movies? The architect who designed this place must have been from the future. The campus was eerily quiet except for the soft thumps of our own footfalls and rush of water from a fountain at the base of a huge clock tower. When it chimed, we all nearly jumped out of our skin.

"Fan out," Xander ordered. "Meet back here in 30. No one goes inside without my say so. Got it?"

We all nodded in agreement and split ways.

As soon as he was out of the bald-psycho's peripheral vision, Liam doubled back for me, never letting me out of his sight for a second. We peered in window after window of ground floor classrooms, pressing our faces against the glass to get a good look. These windows were floor to ceiling, so I didn't even have to stand on my tiptoes to look in. Just like that, I had a new appreciation for modern architecture.

"It's going to take hours to find the lab this way," Liam muttered.

"Right, which gives us enough time to post these." I whipped out a stack of fliers from my backpack.

Liam smiled for the first time since his nose got smashed. "You're amazing, you know that?"

Amazing? Nobody had ever called me amazing *before.*

Suddenly, my cheeks were inexplicably rosy and warm despite the chill in the air between us. Liam's smile had dimples on either side, how come I never noticed that before?

"I just wish we'd gone into town or back to SuperMart," I said. "What are the odds my brother would come to a place like this?"

"You never know," Liam said. "Weirder things have happened, right?"

I couldn't argue with that.

We set to work posting neon orange and green flyers everywhere we could find. Advertisements for student activities stapled to a campus bulletin board fluttered in the breeze. Two masks, one laughing and one crying, announced auditions for a play next week. It was something called an *adaptation* of a book, *Lord of the Flies*. I grimaced at the creepy title and imagined auditorium seats packed with ghosts cheering at the final curtain call as college students whizzed about the stage in fly costumes. Whatever that play was really supposed to be about, I'd probably never know. I stapled a flyer over it.

Liam had a knack for flyering. His stack was half spent in no time, having been taped up to pillars and windows at regular intervals. I'd peer into every building we passed, in case we got lucky enough to find the science lab too, but it was all just empty lecture halls, offices, and a library.

We made our way around the outer edge of the complex that faced a street running alongside campus. I figured my flyers would have more visibility on that side, so we focused the bulk of our remaining effort there.

Between the two of us, 50 flyers went up in no time. I wished I'd printed more, but we were out of tape anyway, and I tossed the empty dispenser in a garbage can out of habit. In my wildest dreams, I couldn't have imagined getting such a lucky break as having both Liam's help and Xander out of my hair at the same time. I felt sure we could've done double this amount and resolved to pack more flyers next time.

"Hey, look!" Liam's voice echoed through the external corridor. "I found a map."

The campus buildings were color coded like a mall directory with a thick red "X" and the words "You Are Here" indicating our place on the map. I snapped a picture with the phone Tyrell had given me in case we got lost.

"Hey! You slugs are supposed to be split up looking for the lab!" Xander bellowed from beneath a concrete archway. Liam hid the stapler behind his back.

"Liam found a map," I said. "But the science buildings are on the complete opposite side of campus. That way."

Xander's eyes narrowed, but he turned from me to study the map for himself. Liam took several steps backward toward a row of bushes and tossed the stapler in.

"Dammit," Xander said. "We parked in the *worst* spot. You idiots, get back to the truck. If Ty's late, we leave him."

Our irritable scout leader stomped off, cursing and spitting when he accidentally walked through a cloud of ash he hadn't noticed until it was too late. I sidestepped a few more noting that geists must have concentrated themselves around the fountain last night. We were nearly to the rendezvous point when Xander stopped dead in his tracks so abruptly I almost smashed into his back.

"What the hell is this?" He snatched a fluorescent green flyer off a window. "This wasn't here before."

I shrugged and put on my best innocent-little-girl face.

"You did this!" Xander thrust the paper an inch from my nose. I flinched.

"No, she didn't!" Liam did that twisty thing with his mouth. A dead giveaway.

We were doomed.

"Read it!" Xander demanded so he could scrutinize my expression as I read the flyer aloud.

"It says, 'J-o-d-o-n-a.' And it has a phone number. That's it."

Xander grabbed my shoulder and whipped me around, ripping open the backpack which still hung on my back. "There's nothing in here but a hammer and a flashlight!"

"Not true," I snapped. "There's a granola wrapper too."

"Wait." Xander clutched a fuzzy yellow ball in his fist. Sara's toy. "You steal this?"

"Give that back!" I spun to face him. "It was a gift."

"First Denny, then Ty, now *Waldo*? You worm your way into people's heads and wrap them around your little finger, don't you? Get them to give you whatever you want?" Xander took a step forward, slow and deliberate. The flyer crinkled in his grip. "You're a spy, aren't you?"

"Spy?" My mind stuttered before I quickly found my tongue again. "Why would I post a flyer with a phone number on it?! I don't even have a phone, remember?"

"Maybe it's a code word." Xander muttered to himself as he dialed the number on the flyer, a test to see if my pockets would start ringing. It went straight to an automated voicemail. I knew it would. Liam wasn't stupid enough to bring an illegal phone along on this trip.

"The Gamerz put you up to this." Xander tightened his jaw. "What are they paying you?"

"Paranoid, much?" I said. "In case you forgot, I'm the one who told Denny to rescue Jayden from the Gamerz!"

"Yeah. Isn't that convenient?" Xander stuffed the crumpled flyer into his back pocket and chucked the smiley face in the trash.

"Hey, guys!" Tyrell waved as he jogged toward us and called

out breathlessly, "I found a map! The science buildings are on the other side."

"We *know!*" Xander screeched so hard that white spit sprayed from his mouth and splattered on my cheek. "Everyone back to the truck!"

As our psycho scout leader stomped away, I caught Liam fishing Sara's toy out of the trash.

"We'd better wash it now," Liam said. "But Sara's gonna go crazy over this thing. It's so cool Waldo thought to get her this."

"Yeah," I muttered as he slipped the smilie back into my bag. "Yeah, it was."

We stopped at the gaping mouth of a broken window to the right of a plaque that read *Shaughnessy Science Building*. Glass shards as jagged and sharp as teeth of a T-Rex threatened to bite us in half if we dared to poke our heads in. Inside the classroom, a mountain of overturned desks and chairs had been used to barricade the doorway. So, at least some of these college students had brains. The middle of the classroom door was cut by a narrow pane of glass, offering the smallest glimpse of the darkened hallway beyond.

Scrawled across the whiteboard in red marker, hasty handwriting screamed at us like a warning from six days ago.

> *"Humanity has oft sought to live forever*
> *To unravel the strings of our mortal tether*
> *Seek ye not immortality, for ye shall find*
> *The eternal life thou seekest may not be so kind."*

Who would use their last moments to babble such nonsense? Some preppy rich-kid at this fancy school, that's who. I rolled my eyes.

Ty wrapped his jacket over his arm and used his elbow to

dislodge shards of broken window, shattering them into a gazillion pieces on the concrete.

Big mistake.

The door jolted. It was just a single tremor at first, but the next one came like a seizure. The furniture stacked in front of the door pulsed with each beat of the gnarled gray fists smashing it from the other side. Groans and snarls spit from the darkened bowls of the building, and the hallway beyond threatened to spew a horde of geists any second. We scrambled back into the sunlight. After a few moments, the demons were silent again.

"You, Girl Scout," Xander whispered. "Go check it out."

"Why me?"

"Because I said so!"

"'I'll go." Tyrell moved back into position and raised his leg over the broken sill.

"No!" Xander grasped Ty's shoulder and yanked him back. "The girl's the lightest one. I need her to climb up onto that pile of furniture and look through the window in the door. Get a count of how many geists are inside."

Sweat ran down my neck.

"We need to know what we're up against," Xander insisted. "That's an order."

"No."

"What do you mean *no*?"

"You heard me." I widened my stance.

Tyrell and Liam stepped up beside me, puffing out their chests.

"Fine." Xander's eye twitched. "I'll do it myself."

My mouth gaped open. Not even Xander could be crazy enough to pull this stunt, could he? Before this, I'd assumed he was just another coward bully, but Xander was something far more dangerous than that. At least a coward bully was predictable.

He went over the sill.

Behind the barricade of furniture shielding the door, creatures roiled in the dark, chittering. Xander froze mid-step, listening.

"Don't do this, man," Tyrell whispered. "We'll just tell Denny…"

"Shut it." Xander straightened himself, balled his hands into fists, and crept forward. He sidestepped an overturned chair and just nearly missed slipping on a fallen pen that rolled away when he nudged it with his toe. Step by step, he inched closer to the makeshift barrier of piled desks.

Fanned out face-down on the floor, a Biology 101 textbook stared up at me. This had been a classroom full of college freshman: each one eighteen or nineteen years old. Too young to turn into geists themselves, but something bad had definitely happened here. A man's button-down shirt and dress pants lay in a heap under the whiteboard. Their professor likely tried to give his science students first-hand instruction on the evolution of the food chain… and their new place at the bottom of it. But by the signs of the struggle, twenty students had apparently been able to overpower their flesh-eating teacher and barricaded themselves inside the classroom. It was my best guess anyway since there wasn't any dried blood or bones anywhere.

Eventually the students must have smashed the window and climbed out. After that, who knows what happened to them.

I climbed in.

"What are you doing?!" Liam swooped in after me.

"You guys are crazy," Ty shook his head and joined the rest of us.

Xander flicked the light switch. It was dead. The four of us meandered around the room looking for clues.

And there it was.

A loose sheet of paper printed with someone's class schedule caught my eye with the words *Microbiology Lab… Professor Liang… Room 211.*

"Room 211," Ty whispered as he read it over my shoulder. "That probably means the labs are on the second floor."

Xander climbed the heap of furniture, balanced on a desk, and braced his hands on the wall above the door to steady himself. My heart leapt in my throat the way it did when my family played Jenga, waiting for the whole darn thing to come crashing down.

"How many you see?" Ty whispered.

"It's too dark." Xander squinted and moved his face closer to the pane of glass in the center of the door. "I can't see anythi… ack!"

A gray fist exploded through the window and grabbed Xander by the throat. A flurry of geist arms wiggled through the opening like the tentacles of a sea monster getting ready to swallow him whole. Xander teetered backward, the desk toppling over beneath him. His legs kicked the air as the geists held him suspended four feet off the ground.

Liam froze in wide-eyed terror.

I bolted forward, wrapped my arms around Xander's waist, and yanked him back in an epic game of tug of war: me against an army from hell.

I wasn't winning.

"Amaia! Watch out!"

My body jerked back at Ty's warning, though I still held Xander tight. The geist's gnarly gray fingers reached for my hoodie but grabbed only air.

Tyrell punched the geist that had Xander by the throat, nailing it square in the face. It was a blow that would have K.O.'d a full-grown man, but the geist barely flinched.

Choking gasps leaked from Xander's mouth as his eyes rolled back in his head. His face was turning purple. He was going to die.

I hated Xander. I'd dreamed of nothing but revenge since he broke Liam's nose… I'd wanted him to suffer. But now that he was, I knew I had to stop it.

Xander was slipping out of my grasp…

There was only one way to save him.

I let go.

One strap of my backpack stayed hooked on my shoulder as I flung my pack around my chest… Geists pulled Xander toward the door, but the flashlight was already in my fist. I used it without mercy, burning their soulless faces. The monsters shrieked and retreated into the dark just long enough for Ty and me to pull Xander away from the overturned furniture. Our scout leader gasped and sputtered as his windpipe made a creaking sound. A few seconds longer, and his throat would've been crushed.

My puny flashlight wasn't strong enough to make the geists explode, but it sure as heck ticked them off. They hurled their bodies against the door with renewed hate.

"Go, go, go!" Ty screamed as he lifted Xander over his arm. The barricade finally gave way. Demons burst forth, flooding into the room, crawling over each other like insects. We raced toward the broken window. I pushed Liam out ahead of me with Tyrell and Xander just behind.

Once we made it into the sunlight, the snarls stopped, but we kept on running anyway and didn't stop until we were in the truck.

Not one of us looked back.

I didn't even have time to buckle up before Xander stomped on the gas and ran over the curb. Tyrell hit the power locks three times to make sure. A streak of gray ash coated the back of his jacket from the geist that exploded on his heels.

Ty had risked his life for Xander. We all did. But did we get a *thank you*?

No. Of course not.

"The lower hallway is jammed, there's too many of them." Xander's voice scratched like sandpaper as he rubbed his throat. "We need a ladder. We need to get up to the second floor."

"Are you insane?" Liam's voice squeaked. "You almost got us all killed!"

"Listen you piece of crap," Xander hissed. "We're all going to die in a few years. You. Your ditz girlfriend there. This meathead next to me. All of us. Before we do, I'm going to kill every single one of those things I get my hands on."

Xander's knuckles went white as he strangled the steering wheel again. Blood vessels had burst in his eyes, making him look like some demented demon himself. At the same time, I knew how he felt. Killing geists was the most sensible thing I'd ever heard Xander say.

"We'll need lights," I said. "Lots of them."

"That flashlight barely stunned them," Ty said.

Xander shook his head. "Flashlights aren't bright enough. We'll need to talk to the science team. Text Denny and let him know."

Tyrell sighed reluctantly as he bent his head over his phone.

"You can't really be serious about going back in there?" Liam flashed Xander a dirty look he caught in the mirror.

Xander turned the radio on full blast. Ugh, not *death metal* again. My head was already pounding.

Liam gave me a meaningful look, and we both buckled our seatbelts. Apparently, the rest of today's mission was a bust, because we were headed back already. Not that I minded. I wanted to crawl back in my sleeping bag, throw my pillow over my head, and forget today ever happened.

We were only a few blocks away from the school when I had a creepy feeling like someone was watching me. I twisted in my seat.

An ice cream truck wearing Christmas lights and a crown of barbed wire rode several car lengths behind us. A pack of motorcycles flanked it on either side and drove over sidewalks, expertly maneuvering through the debris on the streets.

The Gamerz were following us.

I slinked down below the headrest.

Xander was too lost in his thoughts under the blare of his music to hear the rumble of their engines. He didn't glance in the rearview, and I wasn't stupid enough to bring it up. Xander was already driving like a lunatic, taking tight gaps between dead vehicles way too fast, debris crunching under our wheels. If he knew Gamerz were on our tail, he might smash into a building or run off the road… Honestly, I didn't know who to be more worried about: the gang of kids stalking us or Xander behind the wheel of our getaway truck.

I held my breath until we crossed into the school parking lot. Tyrell tensed when he spotted the ice cream truck in the side view mirror. He smashed the radio dial. Xander shot him a look like he'd rip his throat out for turning the music off, until Ty said, "We got company."

The seatbelt cut into my shoulder as Xander slammed on the breaks, skidding to a stop two car lengths from the glass double doors. He threw the gear in park and leapt out of the truck without bothering to shut his door.

Ty reached over and laid on the horn several times.

He was sounding an alarm.

"Stay out of sight." Tyrell's eyes were full of fear, but he blinked and steeled himself behind the toughest mask he could muster. "Get back into the school quick as you can, you hear me? Get Denny."

Liam and I nodded.

Before he got out, Ty turned back for a moment, his mask cracking. "Listen, if this goes bad… just… Make sure Yvette's ok?"

With that, Ty slammed the door and marched down the walkway toward the invading battalion of enemies that awaited him. Xander balanced on the curb screaming obscenities I'd never even knew existed. What was he trying to do? Start a war?

We needed Denny.

I peeked my head around my headrest as the first wave of Gamerz took off their helmets and dismounted their motorcycles. One of the bikes looked like the exact same model my dad used to have. It was even the same color, though it was in desperate need of a new paint job to fix the scratches.

Two lookouts perched on top of the truck behind the barbed wire, but they weren't holding rifles like they'd been when I'd seen them before. They were unarmed. In fact, not a single gamer held a weapon of any kind. The doors to the ice cream truck burst open and a throng of Gamerz thundered out. How were there so many of them?

And why was I shaking? It's not like these kids were a horde of geists. But they inspired fear. Each one moved like a Navy Seal, lined up in formation, and snapped to attention.

Their captain climbed out of the driver's seat wearing a black sweater, army boots, and oversized men's jacket. Her braids were pulled back into a low ponytail away from her perfect face. Even though a pair of tinted aviator sunglasses shielded her eyes, I couldn't help but feel Zelda was staring past Xander and Tyrell, looking right at me. I shrank back and flattened myself down on the seat.

"Come on," Liam whispered as he opened his door and slid out onto the sidewalk.

We bolted straight for the gym.

Tyrell's blast of the truck horn hadn't gotten anyone's attention, kids were still messing around in the gym without a care in the world.

"Denny!" I panted with my hands on my knees. "Where's Denny?"

"Chill drama queen." Peggy rolled her eyes at me from the bleachers. "Your little crush is getting so annoying. You can't keep nagging him all the time. *Seriously.*"

I had no time or patience for petty insults. There were more important things than defending my pride.

"Gamerz are here!" I called over my shoulder as Liam and I

sprinted back down the hall. Before we'd made it halfway, Peg had already caught us. Apparently, cheerleaders are actual athletes or something because this girl was like some kind of champion sprinter.

"I know where Denny is," Peggy said. "Follow me!"

Kids dove out of our path as we stampeded through the school. Angry voices echoed from the cafeteria, and at first I didn't even recognize it was Denny yelling. Since when did he lose his cool?

"What happened to the rest of it?!" the president shrieked.

"I already said, we ate it!" A kid in a chef's hat cowered.

Peg didn't pause to eavesdrop but burst into the cafeteria full steam.

"Denny! Come quick!"

"Not now, Peg."

"But…"

"NOT NOW!" He threw one finger up to silence her.

A handful of brown boxes strewn across cafeteria tables told me the problem right away. Mom always said having teenagers would eat her out of house and home.

"At the rate we're going, this will last us two weeks." The chef twisted his fingers nervously. "We need the scouts to bring back food. We can't eat walkie talkies and toilet paper…"

"Denny!" I interrupted. "Gamerz are outside."

Denny's brow scrunched like he'd misheard me, but then his eyes lit on fire with understanding.

"They're early." He snapped into action. "Peg, round up the muscle and meet me out front. Girl Scout, you follow me."

"I'm going, too," Liam said.

"No." Denny drew himself up to his full height. "You've got two black eyes and a busted nose, not the face we want to show during negotiations. We need strength, not weakness. You'll stay out of sight, or so help me, I'll break the rest of your face."

I sucked in a breath. How dare he threaten Liam?! We almost died today on his wild goose chase for that stupid microscope!

"I'll stay out of sight." Liam held his chin high. "But I go where Amaia goes."

Denny ignored him. "Girl Scout, where's Xander?"

"Out front with Tyrell."

"Good," he muttered. "At least I can count on someone around here to do their job."

By the time we reached the glass double doors of the main entrance, half of Unity had already gathered to see what was going on. They parted to let us through.

Muscly boys in gray flanked us on either side as Peggy brought up the rear. She was rattled, like a bomb ready to explode. Her scowl made it clear that she was ready to beat down an army of Gamerz herself if they didn't give Jayden back pronto.

Maybe Peg was cooler than I thought.

The ice cream truck had been backed-in so that the large double doors faced us. Two Gamerz swung them open to reveal the cage with my brother's best friend still locked inside.

"Jay!" Peg cried as she rushed forward to break through the defensive line. "Jayden, baby, are you ok?"

"It's cool. I'm ok."

"Let him go, *now!*" Peggy railed at Jayden's captors. Tyrell had to hold her back as she kicked and growled as fierce as any geist I'd seen. She was a maniac. What Unity lacked in well-disciplined soldiers we made up for with a healthy dose of lunatics.

"I got your message." Zelda's eyes were locked on Denny. "You owe me, Red."

"You capture one of mine and think I owe *you*?" Denny replied.

"Captured?" Zelda laughed. "We *saved* your scout from the geist that nearly chewed his head off."

Denny snapped his gaze on me.

"You didn't tell me he'd been *bitten*," The president growled under his breath.

"I didn't think it mattered," I shot back.

Denny's face turned redder than his hair, and it reminded me of what Yvette said. *The biggest egos are the most fragile.*

But I was starting to think maybe this guy needed to be knocked down a peg.

A smile played on the corner of Zelda's lips.

"Name your price!" Peggy called to the Gamerz as she wiggled her way out of Tyrell's grasp. "We'll give you anything! Just let Jayden go!"

"Shut up!" Xander hissed.

"What's the matter Denny? You don't want your scout back now that he's *damaged*?" Zelda teased. The captain had made certain her voice was loud enough for everyone to hear, and its effect was instant. Unsettled murmurs rippled through the Unity kids crowded behind us.

Denny stood firm.

"No one divides Unity," he said. "Give me my scout back."

Zelda grinned. "What's he worth to you?"

Denny nodded to one of his henchmen who dragged up a five-gallon bucket of diesel. I frowned. It wasn't the same color as the bucket Ty helped me fill at SuperMart.

Zelda clicked her tongue.

"My spy tells me you've got twenty of those buckets stocked up. So, why don't you play nice and make it five for the scout?"

Denny sucked a sharp breath through his teeth. "Spy?"

Zelda pinched her lips.

"Why don't we just kick their faces in?" Xander pounded a fist into his open palm. His posture was oozing testosterone and adrenaline… he was even sweating despite the chill in the air. If the leaders didn't diffuse this soon… there was going to be a war.

"You win Zelda." Denny's voice had a hard edge. "Five buckets… and the name of the spy."

The captain's smile faded from her eyes. "I won't do that."

"Then no deal. Keep the scout. He's your problem now." Denny turned his back on her. "Everyone inside!"

The congregation of children shifted uneasily on their feet, though most of them ultimately shuffled back inside the school.

Peggy wailed in dismay.

"Ok!" Zelda said. "Three buckets."

"Give me the name of the spy," Denny spat through his teeth.

"We don't need the witch to tell us anything." Xander pulled a crumpled sheet of neon paper from his back pocket. "This is how we find the traitor!"

Denny snatched the flyer. His temper was so hot, he could've ignited the paper in his hands.

I focused all my energy on keeping my face impassive, but inside I was screaming my head off.

"Two buckets," Denny said.

"Done."

Zelda nodded and Gamerz unlocked Jayden's cage. He bolted out of the back of the truck and ran straight into Peggy's arms.

Whew. Glad that was over.

I spun around, desperate to find Liam. Where could he have disappeared to at a time like this? Tyrell tapped me on the shoulder.

"You're still needed up here, Girl Scout," he said. "Denny's orders."

Ugh.

Jayden's eyes were fixed on the funnel of kids pouring back into the school, and I didn't have to be a mind reader to know he was anxious to get inside and far away from the Gamerz. Despite being a prisoner for a few days, he seemed more rested and refreshed than the rest of us. His wounds from the geist bite had even been cleaned and bandaged. I wondered if whoever did that dressing could take a look at Liam's nose... but how could I possibly ask now without people thinking I was the spy?

Denny planted both fists on his hips, watching another

henchman drag a second diesel bucket up the walkway. I wasn't sure what I was supposed to be doing, so I just stood my ground and tried to look tough.

"It was impressive how you stood up to Denny like that," a low, velvety voice whispered over my shoulder. "You're the girl who discovered Jayden when we were outside of Food Eagle, aren't you?"

Zelda hovered beside me, twirling a set of silver keys around her finger.

"Maybe." I raised an eyebrow. "How would you know that?"

"Because I watched you sneak out from behind the tire." Zelda's eyes flashed with mischief. "I heard you promise Jayden you'd help free him. That was brave. And selfless. I really only agreed to meet Denny because I was hoping for the chance to meet you."

"Why?" was the only reply I could manage as I squirmed under her gaze.

"I've got my reasons." She shoved the keys in her pocket. "I hope you know I only put him in that cage for the safety of my crew. I want you of all people to understand that. No hard feelings between us?"

Me of all people? What was she talking about?

My mind whirled that the leader of the Gamerz had singled me out. What would the other Unity kids would think, seeing me talking to Zelda? Would they think I was the spy?

It was a chance I'd have to take. This opportunity wasn't coming around again, and I'd been itching to give the so-called *captain* a piece of my mind.

"If you didn't want hard feelings, Zelda, then you shouldn't go around throwing people in cages when they didn't do anything wrong!" I squared off my shoulders and puffed up my chest. "Besides, you don't have one shred of proof that getting bitten turns people into geists! Do you?"

A pained look flashed over Zelda's perfect features like I'd just slapped her across the face with my words. Had I imagined it? This girl didn't even know me. How could I possibly have hurt her feelings?

"One person's freedom isn't worth risking everyone else's life," the captain said. "If someone in my crew gets bitten, they'd stay locked up. Forever."

"What if *you* get bit?" I demanded. "Are you going to lock yourself in a cage for the rest of your life?"

Zelda appraised me, her dark eyes turning cold for the first time.

"Yes. I already gave the order."

Yikes. I wasn't expecting that. "You can't be serious," I said.

"Dead serious." Zelda's jaw tensed. "You can't win all wars with violence. Some require sacrifice. If keeping yourself locked in a cage could save the life of someone you love, wouldn't you do it? Even if that meant forever?"

I shifted my weight. "Of course, I would… but it's not that simple."

My parents' faces flashed in front of my eyes. And Carlos. Would I trade my freedom for their lives? In a heartbeat. But none of them would want me to throw my life away for nothing if it couldn't save them.

"It doesn't matter if it's simple or not, Amaia. It's a risk." Zelda sighed. "Bottom line is: I refuse to gamble with the lives of my crew. I hope you can understand that."

"Wait." My spine went rigid. "How do you know my name?"

"I could ask you the same question." Zelda flashed me a mischievous smile.

I pressed my mouth in a tight line.

"The things I know might surprise you." Zelda took a step forward, engulfing me in her shadow. "I know you've got a strong heart and a fighting spirit. I know you volunteered to save your friend. You'd make a great Gamer… If you wise up and decide to jump ship, we live in the old church on Excalibur boulevard. Do you know the place?"

"St. Mary's? Yeah, it's the one my family and I go to."

She patted me on the shoulder. "Maybe that's a sign you belong with us after all."

Despite Zelda's warm smile, an icy feeling settled in the pit of my stomach. As the captain slipped her hand off my arm, I turned my head in time to catch Denny glaring a hole right through me.

CHAPTER
TWENTY

Where the heck was Liam?! My breath hitched in my throat as I passed one of Denny's henchmen on my way to the gym. The brute was skulking around like he was up to no good. *What else was new?*

The president's warning to Liam echoed in my mind.

"You'll stay out of sight, or so help me, I'll break the rest of your face."

How could I not have seen Denny for the big jerk he really was? Ugh, what was I thinking? He's not even that cute anyway. His nose was way too big and his Adam's apple bounced weird when he talked. Had he ordered his "security" to round up Liam? The memory of those kids getting beat up in the kitchen shot goosebumps up my arms. What if that was happening to Liam right now in some classroom where no one could hear him screaming?

I was two seconds from charging up to that freckled faced bully, punching him in his stupid neck, and demanding he give Liam back to me, when my best friend decided to pop out of nowhere.

"Are you ok?" Liam's brow creased. "You look upset."

"No, I'm not ok!" I snapped. "You scared me to death disappearing like that. Where were you?"

"Shh!" Liam led me through the maze of boys' tents and pulled me into the shadows behind the bleachers. It was nasty under there. Some slobs used it as a garbage heap because they were too lazy to find a trash can. There were half eaten burgers, boogers, and… was that dog poop? Yuck, no. Regular poop.

"They're gonna think we're spies!" I whisper-screamed at him. "I never should've made that stupid flyer."

Liam's eyes darted a nervous glance back toward the boys' tents.

"Don't worry. I took care of it," he said. "But right now, we're going to need an alibi."

······))) ● (((······

We raced by the cafeteria, passed the nurse's office, and scoured classroom after classroom searching for Yvette and Sara. I was frantic by the time we burst into the engineering room, but my feet stuttered to a stop on the threshold.

The top-secret project the engineers had been building when we'd first arrived was finally finished. The shadow of a plexiglass box loomed over me. I'd seen an identical one once before. In a text message from Paris.

Jayden sat inside the plastic prison, his breath fogging up the clear walls around him.

"… and half of them are vegans!" Jay said. It must have been the punchline of some joke because everyone was holding their sides and shaking with laughter.

I wasn't smiling.

"Seriously, the Gamerz didn't feed me anything other than rice and beans," Jayden said. "Black beans, red beans, garbanzo beans…"

"That box's gonna stink up real quick." An engineer waved his hand in front of his nose and raucous laughter shook the classroom.

"What the heck is going on?" I demanded. "Why is Jay locked in there?!"

"It's cool, Amaia!" Jayden flashed me a grin. "It's only a precaution. I have to sit in here for a week to make sure I'm not going to turn into a geist. Then I can get out."

"And I can stay with him." Peggy's eyes glittered. "Denny said I don't need to go to the gym for curfew while Jay's in quarantine. Isn't that amazing?!"

I bit my lip. "Yeah, *amazing*."

"Amaia! Liam!" Yvette wheeled up behind me, Sara snuggled up safely on her lap. "Check this out."

From the supply closet, a figure sauntered out wearing a vest and helmet made of brilliant, white light. It was something out of a science fiction movie.

"Whoa!" I threw my hands up in front of my face, completely blinded.

"They're ring lights!" Yvette shielded the baby's eyes. "I use them when making beauty tutorials because I hate getting ugly shadows under my nose. Anyway, as you can see, they're wicked bright when you turn them up all the way. And better yet, they're battery operated!"

I tried squinting to get a better look, but it burned my eyes like looking at the sun.

"The amount of lumens emitted far exceeds the requirements for triggering geists' exploding mechanism," an engineer said. "And by concentrating on the back and front of the torso as well as the head - in this instance by affixing the ring lights to a paintball vest and a bike helmet - all the vital organs are protected."

"With this new advancement," another engineer chimed in. "You scouts could move around in total darkness. Geists wouldn't be able to touch you. You could go practically anywhere!"

"Wow." Liam let out a low whistle. "I think you guys just literally saved our lives."

"Uh…" The first engineer shifted awkwardly. "The design wasn't ours."

Yvette shrugged, "I was doing my makeup for Denny's propaganda video this morning when it just hit me. Fashion designers have been using LEDs to make ballgowns sparkle for years. Obviously, those aren't nearly as bright as these… but it's the same idea. Light as clothing."

Blinking hard, after-images from the glaring light stuck in my vision like ink blots in a Rorschach test. I hadn't even noticed the kid wearing the sci-fi getup was Tyrell.

"The sunglasses were Ty's idea." Yvette's cheeks turned rosy.

"Just so we can look at each other without getting blinded." Tyrell removed his shades, his massive, bulky frame twisting awkwardly in his fashion-forward getup. I tried to imagine him strutting down a catwalk. It made me smile.

"How many of those vests can you make with the equipment from photography club?" Denny leaned on the doorframe. Deep circles darkened his under-eyes. His meticulously gelled hair now just looked greasy. And he'd lost his cool with the chef from the cafeteria earlier… My dad once said the office of the president ages a person. Denny had the job for less than a week and already the stress was starting to show.

"These are the only ring lights they had." Yvette said.

"We need more." The president scratched his dirty scalp. "Enough for an army."

At dinner, I mindlessly pushed spaghetti loops around in my bowl. My stomach grumbled, but I couldn't make myself choke down this salty garbage. After what I'd overheard the kitchen-kids saying earlier, Denny should be having us scouts replenish the food supply, but that wasn't tomorrow's mission.

"If you don't contribute, you don't eat." Denny's henchman shoved a kid out the cafeteria doors.

"There's no more work for me!" The kid protested. "Come on, I haven't eaten since yesterday."

"Not my problem."

Liam and I exchanged a look.

Instead of re-upping on food, the president ordered us scouts to find more ring lights, vests, and helmets tomorrow. Denny said our top priority was getting Yvette and the engineers what they need to make us more suits so we'd be ready to storm the college lab to get those microscopes.

It was stupid. What good would a cure be if we all starved to death first?

But I couldn't waste any brain cells on that right now. There were more immediate dangers on my mind.

"Hey, what are we going to do about Xander?" I asked.

Liam leaned into me and made his voice so small I could barely hear it over the clamor of the cafeteria.

"I already told you. I took care of it," he said.

How could he *take care of it*?

Tables around us feasted on gossip. Apparently, nothing was juicer than a traitor in our midst. When he or she was caught, something horrible was going to happen. Even watermelon basketball hadn't gotten kids this excited.

We're dead meat.

Violet burst into the cafeteria like a banshee, shrieking and tearing the mousey, frizzy hair right out of her own head. Both eyes were bloodshot red. Her nose glistened as it ran down her top lip. Is that how I looked when I had my panic attacks? Yeesh.

A gaggle of girls flocked over in interrogation formation.

"What happened?"

"OMG, are you ok?"

"How… could… he… do… this… to… me?" Violet's bottom lip kept getting sucked in over her teeth, pushed and pulled with each hysterical breath. "The… spy…"

"What? They found the spy?"

"Oh my God, who is it?"

Violet wailed. "W… W…. Waldooooo!"

"What?"

"Did she say *Waldo*?"

"That nerd?"

"That *bastard*!"

"Waldo?" Liam leapt to his feet so fast his thighs smashed into the table. His bowl of spaghetti loops spun faster than a top and splattered red soup across the floor. Nobody else noticed, but I frowned at the mess. The overcooked noodles looked like a bunch of maggots swimming in a pool of blood. I vowed never to eat spaghetti loops again.

Liam pushed through the crowd and grabbed Violet by both shoulders.

"Why do you think the spy is Waldo?" he demanded.

"Because." She sniffled. "Denny found the phone in his tent!"

"Wait…" Liam hesitated. "Isn't that Xander's tent too? What if *Xander* is the spy?"

"Well, duh, they share a tent." Violet rolled her puffy eyes. "But Xander *couldn't* be the spy. He's the one who led the hunt for the spy in the first place. Besides, Waldo already betrayed Denny once when he blabbed everything to me about the Paris thing. He's *obviously* the spy."

"I was there!" Liam's voice cracked. "Waldo only spilled his guts because you threatened him! You *made* him tell you about the Paris thing, remember?"

Violet narrowed her eyes and shook out her curls. She looked like Medusa with a head full of rattlesnakes ready to rip his throat out. Liam backed up.

"Liam's right." Violet called over the murmurs of the crowd. "I did threaten Waldo. I never liked him. Deep down, I probably suspected he was a traitor all along!"

"I'll kill him!" A boy in gray punched the air with his fists. As he shot out of the cafeteria, a mob of dozen kids trailed behind him like the tail of a meteor, adding more force to the impending explosion. This was sizing up to be an extinction-level event.

"Let's get that jerk!"

"He'll wish he'd never been born!"

"How could he do this to me?" Violet wailed as girls pushed in to console her.

"Watch Sara!" Liam called to me. He was already bolting past the empty vending machines, chasing down the comet.

I nearly slipped on the puddle of spaghetti loops.

"Liam, wait! Where are you going?" I cried.

"To stop them from making a huge mistake!"

Liam confessed.

The truth poured out of him in frantic desperation, tears of shame streaking down his face. At first, he whispered his crime only to Denny. Then he screamed it at the top of his lungs to anyone who would hear him. Liam was the one who planted the phone in Xander's tent. Waldo was innocent.

Watching my best friend freak out in front of the entire school was cringey, but the worst part about it was…

Nobody cared.

The mob was certain Waldo was guilty, the president had verified it, and absolutely nothing would change their minds. Only the prisoner's humiliation and torture could satisfy their thirst for vengeance.

"That scout with the busted nose said Waldo was innocent!"

"Waldo? Innocent? That scout must have brain damage."

"I'm pretty sure I saw Waldo with that phone this morning."

"Well, I overheard him plotting with the Gamerz!"

"Me too!"

Denny's styrofoam throne had been placed to the side to make way for benches used in mock trials during history class, which gave me flashbacks of the time Mr. McCarthy had our class role-play judge and jury. Some Unity kids had even rolled out the podium the principal used when diplomas were given out at graduation. Violet stood behind it shouting "Order, order!"

Where that frizzy haired troll got the judge's robe and gavel she was banging, I couldn't be sure. They were probably more props from the theater department.

Violet wasn't a judge. She was just a kid in a costume, wasn't she?

Wasn't she?

Waldo hung his head in center court, his hands bound with duct tape.

"Denny, please." Liam begged. "You have to believe me! Amaia and I are looking for her brother. That's why we hung up those flyers. Xander was trying to frame us as spies. So, I forwarded my number to the scout phone and planted mine in what I *thought* was Xander's sleeping bag. Waldo is innocent!"

"I believe you." Denny tapped the side of his nose with a finger. "But betrayal has consequences. Waldo's being punished because I can't trust him to keep his mouth shut... and it looks like I can't trust you now either." He narrowed his eyes. "You'll have to watch Waldo stand trial for your crime. I think that's a fitting punishment for you, don't you agree?"

Liam's mouth gaped open.

"I didn't do it!" Waldo sobbed. "I'm not a spy! I'm not! I love Unity! You guys are my friends!" His voice softened as he reached for the sleeve of Xander's t-shirt. "Xan, please! Don't do this... You know me... You know I would never... Xan, I told you that I...."

A roll of duct tape squeaked as Xander ripped off a length and slapped it over the boy's whiny mouth before he could utter another word. Kids hurled garbage. Crumpled up papers. A dirty sock. A styrofoam container full of half-eaten french fries.

"Court is in session!" Violet hissed. "I get to be judge. Xander will be prosecutor."

"I'll be the defense!" Liam waved his hand in the air. "Waldo gets to have a lawyer!"

Violet looked to Denny, who nodded.

"Fine. Liam is defense," she said.

Xander scowled.

"Take Sara somewhere safe." Liam gently brushed aside the baby's hand when she reached up to poke the purple bruises under his eyes.

"No. I'm staying."

"Amaia… *Please.* Waldo's already being punished for what I did. What if Denny decides to punish you, too? Or Sara?"

The fear in Liam's eyes reminded me of Carlos prodding me up the attic ladder, begging me to hide in the one place he thought I might be safe. Sara grew heavier in my arms. I was finally starting to understand what it meant to be responsible for your little sister's life when the world was crumbling around you.

My throat felt like I'd swallowed a frog and it got stuck halfway down my windpipe.

"Liam!" I croaked as he disappeared into the crowd. "Be careful."

We barricaded ourselves in the nurse's office where Sara Angelina went into an epic meltdown for two excruciating hours. Waldo's toy distracted her for five minutes, but it didn't last. She kept biting her own fingers, and I kept yanking them back out of her mouth. Strings of spittle dripped down her chin and soaked the front of her onesie. Did the baby get this nasty finger-chewing habit from Liam?! It was bad enough I'd seen him bite his nails til they bled, but now he's got Sara chomping on her own knuckles too! How could he be such a bad influence on her?

That's when I saw it.

A white speck the size of half a Tic Tac had poked out from her lower gums.

"Ha! You have a tooth, you cranky baby!" I squealed with delight and tickled her under her armpits. She belly laughed for a moment along with me, until she remembered how much her mouth bothered her, and started fussing again.

Bee da bleep.

I froze.

Bee da bleep.

My left pocket was ringing. The scout's phone.

"Hello?"

"Amaia?" said a girl's voice on the other end.

My heart hammered in my chest. "Yeah. Who's this?"

"Knock it off with those flyers. You're gonna get us all in trouble."

Wait. I know that voice.

"Brit?"

Her reply was silence.

"Brit, is that you?"

A quiet sniffle. Uneven breaths. She was crying.

"Brit, where are you guys? I can come get you. I've got friends… Liam and Tyrell and Yvette. They'll help. Just tell me where you are."

She said nothing, but I could hear her breathing.

"Brit?"

"Carlos said stay in the school." Brit steadied her voice. "Stop being a pain in the butt and do what you're told."

Click.

Did she just hang up on me?!

My fingers pounded with my own heartbeat as I redialed the number. It rang twice then went to voicemail. I smashed the buttons over and over. No answer. I texted Brit a flurry of desperate, angry messages splattered with alternating crying and swearing emojis. No response. Somehow, I knew she'd never call me again.

My brain spun in my skull. What the heck was taking Liam so long?

I exploded into tears. How could Brit do that to me? How could Carlos? Sara Angelina was crying again too, so I scooped her up and rocked her in my arms. Without even thinking, I started singing a lullaby my mom used to sing to me.

> *Que linda niña*
> *Mi querida hija*
> *Te cantaré, Te cantaré*
> *Dulces sueños, mi bebé*

Sara seemed comforted by the melody, so I sang it on repeat. Eventually, I tweaked the lyrics. I decided to change *querida hija* to *hermanita*... after all, Sara Angelina wasn't my beloved daughter, but my little sister.

I smiled to myself and made a secret plan to teach her Spanish so the two of us could talk about Liam right in front of his face and he wouldn't know what we were saying. Sara wrapped her hand around my finger, and I shook it like we'd struck a bargain.

Liam should be back by now. Something's not right.

Maybe I'd just take a quick peek into the gym to make sure he was ok. I strapped Sara to my chest in her carrier and snuck back to check on him.

Boos and jeers echoed off the crimson lockers lining the hallway, and for a split second, I thought the trial was over and a basketball game had started. But when I rounded the door casing, the gym was just as I left it except Waldo's mouth wasn't duct taped anymore. Sweat poured down the front of the boy's speech and debate t-shirt, painting a dark stain under his neck in the same shape as the bib we'd found in Sara's diaper bag.

When I'd left him earlier, Waldo had looked terrified. Now, his brow was set low and creased with frustration. Despite perspiration misting his glasses, he glared at the audience in rage.

"The prisoner confesses!" Xander waggled his finger inches from Waldo's face.

"I didn't confess!" Waldo's vocal cords were hoarse. "I simply said that we should *all* have our phones back anyway!"

"So, you decided to disobey and keep an illegal phone for yourself!" Xander folded his arms triumphantly.

"That phone isn't mine!"

"It's mine!" Liam pounded his own chest. "I already said it's mine! Why won't any of you listen?"

Xander smirked. "We already determined the defense is confused because of a head injury."

"That YOU gave me!" Liam shot back.

Violet banged her gavel.

"Order! Order!"

"We have a right to know!" Waldo shouted. "If the bio team doesn't find a cure, none of us are going to live past nineteen. More than ever, we need to be sharing knowledge, putting our heads together! Us kids need to be smarter than all the adults that came before us. We have what our parents didn't have: time. Adults only had a few months from when the ashes first fell to when they all became geists, but we have *years* to find the cure. If we share information with the other teams from around the world, if all of us are dedicated to working together not only for Unity's survival, but for the survival of the entire human race, I know we can do this! We can survive! But we can't do it if we elect people who would censor everything we say and hear!"

Several faces in the crowd twisted in confusion. His words had left them unsettled, making far too much sense for comfort.

Denny stood from his throne and cracked his knuckles. His blazing red hair was a fire outmatched only by the spark in his eyes. As soon as the echo of Waldo's last words faded from the gymnasium walls, Denny spoke.

"Waldo's right."

Angry dissent erupted in reply, but Denny raised his hand and quieted them as he continued. "He's right that we cannot make our parents' mistakes. But some information is dangerous."

"Ignorance is more dangerous than the truth!" Waldo shot back.

"But how can we know the truth when so many people are spreading lies?" Denny addressed the crowd. "We've got our whole lives ahead of us, yet fear-mongers like this traitor would have you believe we're only going to live until we're nineteen. Where's his proof? Some spoof videos on the internet? He wants you to waste the best years of your life trying to find some cure that you're not even going to need!"

A wave of kids nodded in agreement.

"People have the right to listen to the information presented on both sides and decide for themselves!" Waldo said.

"Lies are poison!" Denny continued. "For our own safety, we need to silence anyone who would use their words to say things that would divide us!"

"Unity can't be safe unless people are free to speak up!" Waldo cried. "If something's wrong, we've got to be able to call it out without getting duct tape slapped over our mouths. We can't just put our fingers in our ears and pretend these things aren't happening. Those comments about Denny getting expelled from his old school are…"

"Lies!" Denny shrieked. "Lies are dangerous. Lies will tear us apart. We need to block out fear and doubt and live our lives in peace and happiness. I, for one, want to play paintball and swim in jellybeans! Waldo would have you doing homework for the rest of your life!"

A chorus of boos made the air in the gymnasium hum. Waldo cringed as his face twisted in more hurt and humiliation than when they'd been hurling garbage earlier. One hundred voices crescendoed, a symphony of deafening accusations. Spit flew through the air as kids curled back their lips and screamed in

Waldo's direction. All of the pain, anger, and grief they felt from losing the lives they had before the Plague of Ashes now had a face they could put to it. Waldo raised his bound wrists and pushed his foggy glasses up the bridge of his nose.

Bang, Bang, Bang

"Order, order!" Violet smashed her gavel on the podium. "It is time to pass down judgement!"

Denny strolled casually forward with his hands clasped loosely behind his back.

"I will not banish Waldo," Denny decreed. "If we can show him the error of his ways and make him see that thinking the way he does is dangerous and wrong, Waldo will be able to live with us in the safety of the school. We will show him mercy and forgiveness."

Kids howled like a pack of angry wolves at this proclamation, and this time, Denny's raised palm couldn't quiet them as they each held up two fingers in the air and chanted:

"Rule number two! Rule number two!"

The back of my neck prickled the same way it had back when the geist stalked me in my kitchen. What was rule number two? I had to turn the pages back in my mind to remember my initiation, even though it was only three days ago.

Rule number two: Obey or be punished.

"We will show him mercy, but first…" Denny's voice rose to a lion's roar. "He will be PUNISHED!"

All around me, fists pumped in the air as hyaena cackles and wild whoops pounded in my ears. Liam and I locked eyes from across the room.

"Get out of here." He mouthed the words to me.

Sara's fist was in her mouth completely covered in slobber. I backed away from the madness and carried her back to the safety of the nurse's office.

Another agonizing hour later, Liam knocked our secret knock, and I was quick to unbolt the door. The look on his face said it all: things had gone from bad to worse after I left. I didn't push him for information, but I also couldn't bring myself to immediately gush about my phone conversation with Brit either.

We had tons to say but no words to say it, so the two of us sat in silence watching Sara Angelina sleep.

"She got her first tooth," I said as I scooted back on the nurse's examination table. It wasn't particularly comfortable, but I was so tired it might as well have been a feather bed.

"Really?" Liam's face lit up. "Top or bottom?"

"Bottom." I smiled wearily. "And there's another thing… I got a phone call."

"Oh," Liam's eyes fell to the floor. Perhaps it was too soon for me to bring up the fact that Liam's plan to call forward the number from his old phone to the scout phone actually worked. He was wracked with guilt about what happened to Waldo, but I couldn't hold back my secret any longer.

"It was Brit," I blurted out. "My brother's girlfriend."

"The cheerleader on the motorcycle?"

"That's the one." I snapped my fingers. "Brit told me to stop putting up flyers. She said Carlos says I have to stay in the school."

Liam frowned. "I don't know if that's going to be possible for too much longer. It… it got pretty scary in there after you left. I don't know what they are going to do to Waldo, but they want to make an example out of him."

Liam buried his face in his hands.

"It's not your fault." My hand cupped his shoulder, but he shrugged it away.

"Of course it's my fault!"

"Maybe they'll calm down by morning." I yawned. "Everyone is just tired… and cranky… and…"

"You didn't see their faces when they handed out the guilty

verdict, Amaia." Liam shook his head. "These kids are more bloodthirsty than the geists!"

I rolled my eyes. I was in no mood for exaggerations.

"Maybe it's just that they've been cooped up so long in the school they've all gone stir-crazy," I said. "Tomorrow, everyone is going to come to their senses. They'll probably do something embarrassing to Waldo like make him parade around in a chicken suit and that will be the end of it."

"I don't think they'll let him off that easy," Liam warned. "Watching them turn on one of their own just because he disagreed with them… it was scary. And if they can turn on Waldo, what about either of us? What about Sara? It's not safe here anymore."

The words Sara had spoken in my dream echoed in my head. *It's not safe.*

"We can't leave," I said. "Where will we go?"

"I don't know," Liam muttered. "But even with the geists trying to break down the door, I'd take another night in your attic over what I'm afraid is about to happen here."

Bodies milled around aimlessly, too disturbed to sleep. It was almost curfew, but the air in the gym was so electrified, one wrong word could ignite a riot.

I'd had enough madness for today. I gave up. The only thing I wanted was to bury my face in my pillow and hope I didn't have one of my weird dreams again.

"Where are you going?" Yvette wheeled up to us in a panic. "Why aren't you guys on the roof?"

"Roof?" I rubbed my eye with the side of my fist. The room was wobbly, and I really wished Yvette hadn't intercepted me on the way to my sleeping bag.

"Yvette, what's going on?" Liam asked.

"Denny's going to carry out the sentence tonight to get it over with." Yvette glanced over her shoulder and lowered her voice. "He says tomorrow morning Waldo will be forgiven if he helps the biology team with some experiment... Denny said Waldo's banned from the computer lab from now on and needs a new way to *contribute*."

"But why does he have to go up to the roof?" Liam pressed.

A sour taste rose up my throat as a belch escaped my lips, the flavor of regurgitated spaghetti loops. They were even more gross the second time around.

All this stress was wrecking me. I needed to rest.

"It can't be for anything good," Yvette said. "I'll take Sara. You go make sure Waldo's ok."

"Right." Liam forked over the baby. "Amaia, you stay here with Yvette. I'll be right back."

Why does everyone keep saying that to me?!

"Wait up!" I was in no hurry to see whatever awful thing Denny had planned, but no way was I going to let Liam go alone this time. Liam spun on his toes and bolted out the door along with ten other kids who all had the same idea. Little did I know, we were sprinting toward something we should've run screaming from instead.

Kids packed in shoulder to shoulder like wiggling sardines in a fisherman's net, making the narrow stairwell to the roof impassable. With the demeanor of a pissy tabby cat, Xander blocked the doorway at the top and swatted back any mouse that tried to brush past him.

"Go to bed, maggots," he ordered. "It's past your bedtime!"

Xander was right. The sun was nearly down. I couldn't believe I was thinking this, but I wished for once everyone would listen to Xander. Why not get some shuteye and deal out Waldo's punishment in the morning?

Kids spat curses that would've got them detention for the rest of the year. They'd be waving pitchforks too if the theater department had any left over from their last production of *'Animal Farm: The Musical.'* But no one was getting onto the roof this way.

Liam and I tiptoed back from the stopgap and sped in the opposite direction, away from the tangle of kids.

Teachers always said I never paid close enough attention, but the obnoxious red door in the custodian's wing that warned

"Roof Access: Authorized Personnel Only" had been kind of hard to miss. Other than the generator, it was the highlight of the tour Denny gave us on the first day.

Liam looked over his shoulder several times to be sure we weren't followed. I didn't care. I'd feel sorry for the poor fool who wanted to mess with me in this minute. I'd taken a cue from Sara and was in full-on cranky baby mode.

Only, I had all my teeth and was ready to bite someone's head off if they crossed me.

My breath swirled in the early evening air as we cracked open the steel door at the top of the narrow staircase. A group of only ten kids - Denny's inner circle of henchmen, engineers, and scientists - were staring out over the low wall around the roof's perimeter. Their eyes were all fixed on a distant, reflective object planted in the middle of the football field.

A yellow spotlight, bright enough to put the bat signal to shame, cut a triangle of light to the 50-yard line. The school used this spotlight to light up the singer for the national anthem at night games, and Carlos would stand tall, his hand reverently pressed over his heart. The choir girl who used to sing the anthem wasn't one of the faces I'd seen around the school. I guess she didn't make it.

"Is that… Waldo?" Liam squinted into the twilight.

"It can't be…"

Center stage in the spotlight's beam, smack dab on the 50-yard line, stood an illuminated plexiglass box with a boy trapped inside.

"What are you two doing?" Tyrell grabbed us both by the scruffs of our collars and yanked us back from the ledge. "You shouldn't be up here!"

"You're up here!" I cocked my head to one side. "I'm not leaving until someone tells me what the heck is going on."

Tyrell furrowed his brow.

Thickening clouds condensed throughout the parking lot,

making me uneasy despite how high our perch was above them. The wind whipped up a flurry of ashes and snowflakes, and Liam pressed his shoulder against mine when our teeth started to chatter. Shadows moved under the football bleachers as the last bit of pink in the sky faded to black.

"Girl Scout!" Denny grinned. "How did you get up here?"

I didn't respond. I wasn't in the mood to put on a smile and play nice with this jerk. I had enough monsters to deal with already.

"There's a second stairwell. In the Janitor's wing," Liam said.

"You two look tense." Denny gave Liam an ironic smile. "Let's let the past be past, ok? You both are just in time to witness a historic moment. The engineering team has invented a way to trap a geist!"

"Trap a geist?" The words stuck in my throat.

"Yes, but we needed bait." Denny smirked. "Lucky for us, Waldo volunteered."

I swallowed hard. Liam was a shade of green I'd never seen him before.

"It's perfectly safe," an engineer assured us. "The spotlight is bright enough to trigger the geists' exploding mechanism on contact. We've tested it for the past three nights. That's why Waldo's been set up on the 50. Any farther than that and the geists don't explode right away. Once a geist gets in the box with Waldo, we'll shine the light on it and poof! Waldo is totally safe."

"It'll scare the tar outta him though." Xander snickered. "Waldo will probably piss his pants if he hasn't yet."

Peeing pants was something I knew something about. I squeezed my lips into a thin line and felt my face burning with embarrassment. To my relief, Liam didn't let on or even glance my way at all.

Xander swung the spotlight away from the plexiglass box and passed the beam over the bleachers. Geists lurking in the shadows squealed as it touched them, each one exploding into ash as soon as it hit.

Xander belted out a hearty laugh, his bald head bobbing in the moonlight.

"Denny's going to make history." Peggy's usual pigtails were twisted into a bun on top of her head. "The other teams will be experimenting on twenty-year-olds who are new geists. We'll be the first ones to capture a geist from the original infection!"

Jayden stood beside her and squeezed her hand.

"They let you out, Jay," I observed.

"They needed the box." Jayden shrugged. "Honestly, I know it's safe and everything... but I'm just happy it's not me out there. The Gamerz kept the ice cream truck parked under a streetlight at night when I was in that cage. The geists couldn't get me of course... but it was still scary as hell being out there with them."

"Sit back and enjoy the show you guys." Denny wandered off to congratulate the rest of the engineers.

"Those geists are already reforming under the bleachers," Liam said. "Look!"

The light was fixed again on Waldo in the box, but in the black depths of the stands, clouds of ash began to quickly reform in the shape of demons once again.

"Denny thought of that," Violet butted in. "Once a geist is in the box, we'll keep the light on Waldo for the rest of the night. We've also got the flood lights surrounding the field that we can turn on, so that kid is actually gonna be safer out there than we are up here. At sunrise, we'll be able to collect him."

"Then what?" Liam demanded. "You're gonna bring the box inside? You're actually going to bring a *geist* inside the school?"

Violet's smile twisted into a frown.

"Well, the engineering team says the geist can't get out once it's in there..."

"Why didn't you give Waldo the vest Yvette made with the ring lights on it?" I demanded of an engineer. "Just in case something goes wrong? He should have his own light out there!"

Xander rolled his eyes.

"That defeats the punishment," he said. "The point is to scare him straight. Worked for me at bootcamp. It'll be good for him. Kid needs to toughen up."

"And we get to trap a real geist for the biology team to experiment on." Violet's braces flashed as she bared her teeth in a smug smile. "If we can be the first team to find a cure, we'll be rich! The other teams would trade us *anything* to get it. I know what I want. I want a whole designer wardrobe straight from Paris!"

"And what plane are they going to fly it over on?" Ty raised an eyebrow.

Violet opened and shut her mouth like a goldfish, but no words came out. Overhead, the moon dipped behind a cloud. Even it was afraid to see what'd happen next.

"Denny!" I thrust up my chin and got right in his face. "You need to stop this."

"Stop what?" Denny smirked. "Stop us from saving the world? Because that's what we're doing, Girl Scout." He swept his arm out in a grand gesture. "Without a geist to experiment on, there's no way our scientists can find a cure."

In the distance, Waldo kicked and clawed the glass, frantic to get out. He was a kid. Not some lab rat.

I glared at Denny. Why couldn't people in power see people as people?

Panic rising, I frantically scanned for someone - anyone - who might see reason.

"Xander!" My voice rose to a hysterical pitch. "*Please.* Don't do this!"

"You heard the man." Xander cracked his knuckles and grinned. "We're *saving the world.*"

"I'm not asking you to save the world..." My eyes flooded with tears. "I'm asking you to save your friend!"

There was a flash, a moment's hesitation, as his eyes moved beyond me to the plexiglass box in the distance.

"Denny knows what he's doing," he muttered.

The president smirked triumphantly, moving close enough to whisper in my ear. "We're doing Waldo a favor," Denny said. "Like I told Xander, after this, Waldo will go from a sniveling, crying waste-of-space traitor to an actual hero. Maybe he'll even toughen up enough to be a scout."

"You want someone to be a hero?" I curled my lip in disgust. "Maybe it should be *you* out there!"

The way his eye twitched told me I'd gone too far.

Liam tugged at my elbow. "Amaia, come on. We shouldn't be here…"

I yanked my arm from his grasp. "I'm not leaving!"

"Ready, everyone?" Denny raised his arms like the start of a Nascar race. "Three. Two. One. Now!"

The spotlight made a deep metallic *thunk* as it switched off, leaving the field black as pitch. I inhaled a sharp breath. Liam pulled me closer, and this time, I let him.

A muffled scream sliced the night air.

"Is a geist in the box yet?" Violet called out. "I can't see anything."

"Do NOT turn on that light until we're sure we've captured one!" Denny ordered.

I pushed my palms over my ears as tight as they would go but couldn't block out the sound.

Screaming bloody murder…

Screaming bloody murder…

Without warning, my courage unraveled. I was the little girl in the toy box again, desperate to scream and hide and cry and be far away from that sound.

"Oh, relax you guys. The geists can't get at Waldo in the box," the engineer was saying. "We installed an extra barrier inside. So, he's in a box *inside* the box. It's like a mousetrap. Once the geist goes inside, the outside door will snap shut, but the geist still can't get Waldo. It's totally safe."

"Turn the light on!" I screeched. "Turn it on!"

The screams stopped.

Ten kids plus Liam and I stood in silent agony listening to growls and snarls from the field below. Maybe it was just in my head, but I could swear I heard the sound of teeth crunching on bone.

The warm hum of electricity sizzled through the night as the spotlight switched back on. Rippling explosions boomed like cannonballs underwater, and all at once, a massive thunderhead of ash swirled in the beam's rays. How many geists had been out there? There were too many to count.

The plexiglass box, torn open like a tin can, was missing the boy inside.

Shadows at the edge of the illuminated triangle disappeared under bleachers and melded into darkness as they escaped the threat of light.

In the end zone lay the only thing that remained of the kid from the computer lab. Waldo's speech and debate t-shirt had been ripped to shreds and soaked in blood.

"No!" Xander screamed and thrashed, bolting forward so fast that kids barely had time to pull him back before he would have hurled himself over the ledge. He was caught in the beam of the spotlight like a moth in a flame, casting a massive shadow over the football field. Tears cut lines down his face as several boys in gray t-shirts restrained him.

Air crushed out from my lungs as my knees buckled. Liam kept me from falling, though his skinny arms could barely support my weight. Memories flooded my foggy mind.

Waldo holding out the toy for Sara. The tears in his eyes as he told me how Xander searched for his baby sister when he was too afraid to go in the house himself. The tenderness in Waldo's voice as he called Xander by a nickname, *Xan,* and reached out his fingers to brush the sleeve of his friend's t-shirt during the trial. The squeak of duct tape had silenced Waldo from saying too much. The two of them shared a tent. Had they talked late into the night, whispering each other's deepest fears and darkest secrets? Had Waldo shared too much?

'Worked for me at bootcamp. It'll be good for him.' Xander had said. My eyes fixed on the crescent scar on the back of Xander's head. Tough love. It was the only way Xander had been taught how to. He'd been brainwashed to believe anything weak must be beaten until it had no choice but to be strong. But it didn't matter now.

Now, Waldo was dead.

There comes a time when we can't blame our parents anymore, when our crimes become our own.

Xander wailed, spit, and screamed. Tears splattered down his face as veins popped out of his forehead. He probably hadn't cried this much over his own parents. Maybe a dark corner of his heart had even felt relieved when they died and ended his torture.

Denny gripped the railing, looking like he was about to paint the side of the school in vomit.

I wasn't getting any air.

Don't fall apart. Don't fall apart.

"Breathe," Liam whispered. "I'm right here."

Anguish gave way to anger. Instead of hating himself for what he'd done, Xander furiously wiped his eyes and locked his gaze on his target.

"*You!*" Xander threw his whole bodyweight on an engineer, slamming him to the floor and wrapping his hands around the kid's throat. "You said it was safe! You told Waldo it was safe! You killed him!"

"Stop him!" Denny ordered as he snapped out of his own trance. Henchmen hurled themselves on top of Xander, tackling him like he'd been a quarterback.

"It wasn't my fault!" The engineer sputtered as he crawled out from under the tangle of bodies. "The scout with the black eyes! *He* was the one who planted the phone in Waldo's sleeping bag!"

Xander howled. He squirmed and kicked so hard that his boot flew off and nailed Peggy right in the face. Jayden leapt forward and held Xander down with the other guys.

"Help me..." I clutched Liam's hand so hard, a distant warning in the farthest corner of my mind feared I might break it. "Please."

My vision spun, the edges tinged with shadow as I began to collapse in the grip of my worst panic attack yet. Liam couldn't bear my weight and nearly went down with me. Someone scooped me up in solid, muscly arms and cradled me like a child.

"Carlos?" I buried my face in his chest, but the cologne was unfamiliar and my whole body went rigid again.

"It's ok. I've got you," Tyrell said.

I was vaguely aware of my feet dangling and my head bobbing as Ty followed Liam down the stairs, like a fireman carrying a dazed victim from the horror of a burning building. Somewhere far away, there was a porcelain doll locked in the darkness of an attic toy box. Tiny. Fragile. Cracked.

They're all dead. Everyone is dead.

I leaned against a book stack. How did I get into the library? In my mind, I was still frozen on the roof... waiting at the edge of darkness... helplessly listening to the sound of monsters eating pieces of a kid I once knew. A kid who tried to be my friend.

I crushed my hands over my ears, but the sound had burrowed itself deep in my brain like a parasite.

Screaming bloody murder.

No. We were safe now. The library was safe.

You! You said it was safe. You told Waldo it was safe!

"Of course I'll help. What about the baby?" Tyrell's voice

snapped me back into the present. "Yvette said she'd take care of her if you want her to stay here."

"No," Liam said. "Sara Angelina comes with us."

Tyrell peeked around the doorframe to be sure no one had followed. "I grabbed the truck keys, but he'll know they're missing in the morning. If Xander catches you…"

Liam cut him off. "He won't. We'll leave at sunrise."

"Not a minute later or he'll skin you alive. Did you see the look on his face? If those guys weren't holding Xander down…"

Liam shuddered.

"Hey." Tyrell paused. "It wasn't your fault, Liam. You tried…"

My heart beat itself against my ribs like a caged bird desperate to escape. The harder I struggled against the panic, the tighter it pinned me down. My legs and arms went numb, useless and weak. Like me. How was I going to make it through this? I wished my Mom and Dad were here.

"If you run, Liam, you know you guys can't come back," Ty said.

"We're not coming back."

"Is Amaia gonna be ok? She doesn't look so good."

"It's a panic attack. But I've never seen one last this long…"

"Can't you do something to help her? She's shaking…"

"We have to wait it out and remind her to keep breathing. It will pass. She's got to rest. Us talking probably isn't helping… but I promised I wouldn't leave her alone…"

I rocked myself back and forth. Waldo's face filled my mind. He was smiling… pushing up his glasses… taking a picture of the baby… stumbling out of his tent… tossing me the fuzzy yellow plush…

Liam squeezed me in his arms and kept me upright. "Ty, can you get our backpacks? And Sara's car seat?"

"Sure thing." Tyrell stuffed a set of keys into Liam's hand. "Just take care of Amaia. I've got the other stuff."

"Come with us," Liam said. "There's plenty of room for all five of us. We've got a place we can go… we can start over…"

Tyrell shook his head. "Can't do that."

Liam sighed. "Yvette won't leave the school, so you won't. Is that it?"

Tyrell nodded.

"I get it." Liam pressed his cheek to the top of my head. "I really do."

CHAPTER
TWENTY-THREE

News of Waldo's death sentence rocked Unity, and with all the commotion, Liam and I weren't missed in the gymnasium after curfew. We made camp for the night in the library and hid ourselves behind the last row of book stacks. After my panic attack subsided, exhaustion hit me like a ton of bricks. I must've fallen asleep sitting propped up with my back against the wall because that's the position I was in when Liam woke me up a few minutes before dawn.

"Where's Sara?" I jolted awake.

"She's here," Liam said. "Ty brought her up last night after you fell asleep. This was in her carrier. Yvette wanted you to have it."

Her turquoise and silver scarf.

The same one she'd lent me the night she did my makeup. I was too stunned to cry. Last time I wore this, I'd been dancing, twirling, and laughing. Crowd surfing. Now that we were running from this place, would I ever do those things again? Waldo never would.

"Isn't Yvette coming to say goodbye?" I caressed the soft material between my fingertips.

"No time." Liam shook his head. "The plan is for us to be out the main entrance before the gymnasium doors are unlocked. But we'll be cutting it close as it is."

"Liam…" my voice trailed off. "About last night… I'm sorry I fell apart. I thought I was stronger than that…"

Liam squeezed my hand. "You're the strongest, bravest kid I've ever met. You think strong people don't get panic attacks?"

"You don't."

"Maybe not, but at least you don't freeze." Liam sighed. "I've frozen every single time we've faced a geist."

"So?"

"So?! You're a fighter! I'd give anything to be like you. You're always the one swinging that hammer or pushing me and Sara out of danger. You think you're not strong? Without you, I'd never have made it out of your attic."

"I wish we never left." I pulled my hood up over my head to cover my eyes. "We never should have come here."

"The sun will be up in a few minutes," Liam said. "Last night, Ty gave me Xander's truck keys. As soon as the coast is clear, we'll make a run for it. But if that bald-headed psycho catches us…"

I cringed. "I get it."

It happened just moments later. The second the last geist was a cloud of floating ash, we were bolting through the hallways, flying down the stairs, and bursting out the main doors to the school. As Liam shoved the key in the ignition, I knew there was no turning back now. This time, we weren't just homeless. We were fugitives.

"Hey!" Xander screeched as he sprinted through the parking lot. Liam smashed the automatic locks. "Get out of my truck!" Xander punched his fist into the driver's side window and reeled in pain like he'd broken every bone in his right hand. The glass didn't break, but Liam flinched as he struggled to figure out how to put the truck in drive.

Beside me in the backseat, Sara screamed while I fumbled putting the seatbelt through the plastic slots in her car seat. She thrashed her head back and forth, making it impossible to get her buckled in.

"Why aren't we moving?" I shrieked. "We've got to go!"

"I can't concentrate!" Liam wailed as Xander slapped the glass. Wiper blades scraped over the dry windshield. The four-way flashers turned on. I clicked Sara's belt in place.

"It's that one! The stick thingy on the right!" I reached over the front seat and threw it in drive. Liam slammed down the pedal, but the truck only jerked forward and stopped. He pumped it hard, the vehicle bucked as it inched slowly forward.

"It's not working!" Liam screamed.

"You're dead! You hear me? DEAD!" Xander pounced, kicking the window next to Liam's head over and over with his thick black army boot. The glass vibrated with the effort but held strong.

"Liam, the other pedal! That one's the brake!"

"There are two pedals?"

"Are you being serious right now?!"

Liam stomped on the gas, which sent me flying into the backseat. The truck swerved. Xander staggered back, spitting and swearing at the top of his lungs. He sprinted after us down the main drive to the school and onto the first block. Liam ran straight over a tire in the road and narrowly missed careening into a lamppost.

"Slow down or we're gonna crash! He can't catch us, just slow down!"

I was right. After ten more blocks, Xander collapsed with his hands on his knees. Through the back window, he got smaller and smaller until he was gone for good.

We were getting close to Excalibur Boulevard, and even though Liam had never been to my church before, I could find my way to St. Mary's blindfolded. My family had gone every Sunday since I was born.

Until yesterday.

It was hard to believe that a whole week had passed since the Plague of Ashes took the life I loved from me. Tonight would be the one week anniversary of the end of the world. There was something else too. Something I couldn't bring myself to tell Liam.

Today was my fourteenth birthday. Mom had a costume party planned for me like every year… one of the cool things about being born on Halloween.

Normally, I'd be tearing open presents and stuffing my face with coconut cake. This year, I was running from a power-hungry tyrant, battling flesh eating monsters, taking care of a baby, and just plain lucky to be alive.

Growing up sucks.

"We're almost there, *hermanita*." I caressed Sara's foot. "Liam, turn left up ahead."

"What does that mean?" he asked. "That word you just called her."

"Hermanita? It means *little sister.*"

"*Hermanita.*" The word was awkward on Liam's lips, but I liked the sound. "Does Carlos call you that too?"

"Sometimes." I bit my lip. "But, he usually has a different nickname for me."

"The thing you wrote on the flyer? You never told me what it meant."

"It… uh…" I felt my cheeks warm. Why didn't I want Liam to know *jodóna* meant *pain in the butt*? "It doesn't really translate."

Liam stopped the car in the middle of the road when we were still several blocks away from the Gamerz hideout. Golding's Hardware waited a few buildings down on the right-hand side, a lock and chain still snaked around the door handles. I'd been right. No one else had thought to go there. The sign out front was covered in ash, as if someone took a giant eraser to it.

"The hardware store is on this street, right?" Liam asked. "Which building is it?"

"Liam…" I groaned. "We can't…"

"Why don't we just stay here?" he asked. "I mean, only the three of us? No Denny. No Gamerz. We could do what we said before. We could survive on our own."

I wavered.

"There's strength in numbers," I said. "Besides, I think it's a sign that the Gamerz chose St. Mary's. Maybe God wants me to go there."

Liam gnawed his thumbnail.

"We can't risk our lives based on what you think some imaginary god might or might not want you to do! That's crazy, Amaia!"

From my spot in the backseat, I reached around his headrest and ripped his hand away from his mouth.

"What's *crazy* is to get a sign and ignore it!" I said.

Liam slumped his forehead against the steering wheel in frustration.

"We might not get another chance to start over," he said. "We've got a whole day of light left to get ready for tonight. We have a truck. We'll never get a better shot than this!"

"I had a dream about the captain." I unbuckled myself. "I'm telling you, we need to team up with her! She's not the same kind of leader as Denny. She's good!"

"A dream? Now you want to risk our lives over a dream?!"

"I think it was a sign. Listen, Zelda was on a pirate ship, and I asked her if you and Sara could come too and she…"

"Just stop it. Stop it!" Liam's hands were shaking. "Stop it with God! Stop it with the dream! You don't know Zelda. You only met her for two seconds! And weren't you the one who was ticked off because she locked Jayden in that cage? You and me need to stay away from other kids. We can't trust anyone but ourselves."

"It didn't work out with Denny, but the Gamerz are different." I squirmed over the cupholder and climbed into the passenger seat. "The Gamerz have survived this long without the safety of the school. They're organized, which means they're not only our best chance but Sara's too. What if something happens to you or me? Huh? Who would look after her?"

Liam opened his mouth for a reply, but quickly shut it. I softened my voice the way Mom did when she was trying to convince Dad to do something he didn't want to.

"And one more thing." I got ready to score the winning point. "Sure, we can protect ourselves from geists with the lights from the hardware store. But who is going to protect us from Denny? Or Xander? Or those meatheads in the gray t-shirts? You think Denny's gonna just let us leave Unity without a fight? After what happened to Waldo? If he lets us leave, pretty soon, other people might leave too. He'd never let that happen."

Liam went very still, though I could tell his mind was racing a million miles a minute. Without another word, he put the truck back in drive and eased on the gas. The hardware store, and the life we could have had there, disappeared behind us in the rearview mirror.

St. Mary's was exactly like a gigantic version of the miniature porcelain cathedral figurine Mom set at the base of our Christmas tree each year.

Except for the barricade out front.

A pile of wooden pews had been stacked to form a barrier across the front of the building while swirls of thick ash lingered above the stone steps. Deep claw marks scarred the heavy wooden doors, the same sort of gashes we'd seen in the hallway the morning we escaped my attic. Why hadn't the Gamerz hadn't affixed motion lights outside to keep the geists off the stairs? Maybe I'd suggest it to the captain…

"Still want to go in?" Liam asked.

"Yep."

Liam didn't dare attempt parallel parking, so we left Xander's truck in the middle of the street, unpacked Sara and our bags, and headed for the door.

Would they let us in? I'd just assumed the captain's invitation was still good. What if it wasn't?

I raised my fist to knock when a voice called out from behind.

"I knew you'd come." Zelda said. "Nate, didn't I tell you she was a gamer at heart?"

"Yes, Captain."

"You must be Liam. And this is little Sara Angelina, am I right?"

"How would you know that?" Liam backed away and raised a suspicious eyebrow.

"Your reputations precede you." Zelda smiled.

"No, Liam." I shook my head. "Her spy told her who we are."

Liam's jaw tensed. "A kid *died* last night because people thought he was one of *your* Gamerz! If you didn't have a snitch at the school, Waldo would still be alive!"

"I heard about what happened. It's horrible." Zelda put a hand on his shoulder, but Liam slapped it away. Nate moved between them with a look like he'd re-break Liam's nose, but Zelda stopped her soldier by saying, "It's ok, Nate. He's just hurting."

"Who is the spy?" I demanded. "We deserve to know."

She didn't even hesitate.

"Xander."

My mouth snapped open to hurl some threat, to force her to confess the identity of the spy. I hadn't been prepared for her to actually *answer* my question. It couldn't be that easy.

"You're lying." My face got so hot, I felt like I was going to combust myself. "Tell me who it really is!"

"It's Xander. I swear to God." Zelda said. "If I had known they were going to punish that poor kid, I never would have kept silent. Human life is sacred and needs to be protected."

"But why would Xander be the spy?" Liam asked. "It doesn't make any sense."

"Sure it does," Zelda said. "Xander is a survivor, like you and me are, Amaia. Most people run away when they're afraid. But a few special people will stand and fight. There are three reactions you might have when you're staring Death in the face: Fight, Flight, and…"

"Freeze," I said, trying not to glance over at Liam.

Zelda nodded. "Xander's a fighter. He may be a hothead, but

he's not stupid. He knows that by siding with both Unity and Gamerz that he doubles his chances for survival. He's looking toward the future. Like we all should."

"Future?" Liam's eyes flitted between Zelda and her soldier. "Maybe we just focus on surviving tonight?"

"The captain's taught us there's a difference between surviving and living," said the soldier at her side. "The difference is having something to live for. A purpose. If you come inside, the captain can tell you all about it."

I folded my arms across my chest. "Before I can say if we're with you or not, I need to know the rules."

"Rules?" Zelda asked. "What rules?"

I shifted uneasily at her response. "I mean, what do we have to contribute to join the Gamerz? Like, do we have to play video games? Do we have to… you know… go out and shoot geists?"

Zelda gave me a rueful smile.

"We have one rule: don't get bitten. Other than that, we each do our part to help out around here, but we're not going to force you to do anything you don't want to."

"You're not going to make us be scouts again?" It came out of my mouth more like an accusation than a question. "Isn't that why you wanted me to join?"

"We've already got plenty of brave volunteers, like Nate here." Zelda's soldier clicked his heels to attention. "Besides, we don't have *scouts* the way Denny does. We have two teams that regularly leave the compound. The first team gets food and supplies. The second is search and rescue."

"Search and rescue?" asked Liam.

"The captain saved my life," Nate said. "Not just me, she saved every kid here, and we rescue more every day. We've got seventy-nine in total. Eighty-two now with you three joining. The music from the ice cream truck was Zelda's idea, and it works like a charm. We drive around neighborhoods and the survivors come running right to us. When we pick up a kid, we bring them back here and give them food, water, and shelter."

"Counseling too," Zelda said. "For those that need it. We've all been through a lot, and it helps to talk about it."

"Wow." I flashed a look at Liam who seemed equally, though begrudgingly, impressed.

"I'm sorry we didn't get off to a better start," the captain said apologetically. "But in time, I hope that you and I will be the best of friends, Amaia. It isn't much, but it's home, and you two are more than welcome here."

Zelda pushed open the heavy wooden doors.

"Feel free to take a look around," she said. "Make yourselves comfortable. Nate and I will go scrounge up some uniforms for you guys. I've got just the thing for this little one." Zelda tickled Sara's foot and was rewarded with a giggle.

That was comforting. At least Sara seemed to like her.

The captain and her foot soldier left Liam and me on the threshold of the church before marching off toward the adjacent rectory, a separate building next door with a giant parking lot sandwiched in between.

Liam paused on the steps. "Did something about that seem weird to you?"

"Ugh, you're not even going to give this a chance, are you?"

"Hey! I drove us here, didn't I?"

I dropped the argument because, well, Liam was right. Something did seem weird about how happy Zelda was that I switched sides. What's so special about me anyway? Like almost every answer on my math tests, it didn't add up.

The spice of incense sweetened the air the moment we stepped inside the church, whisps of smoke that normally carried my prayers to Heaven curled in finger-like tendrils, beckoning us deeper into the sanctuary. All at once, I was flooded with memories of all the Sundays I spent here with Mom, Dad, and Carlos. My first communion where I'd worn a frilly white dress and veil Mom picked out for me. The lace gloves itched, and I lied and said I forgot them at home, but really, I'd just stuffed them between the cushions in the back seat to get out of wearing them. I was certain my dad imagined he'd walk me down this exact aisle someday if I were to ever have gotten married. Dad never would've thought any boy was good enough for me, but maybe if I liked one enough, I could've convinced him. Now, I'd never get that chance.

Zelda said to look to the future, but how could she stand it? All I could think about were the happy days that I'd never see. My dad was stolen away before he could give me away.

I choked back tears as I took my first step down the aisle.

Most of the pews had been used for the barricade outside, but a few remained as benches. Instead of the dark, reverent gray walls I was used to, Christmas lights had been strung up on all sides and across the ceiling, creating a room of light within the cavernous space of the cathedral. Bathed in the soft, warm glow of twinkling fairy lights, I felt I'd wandered into an enchanted castle.

When I imagined the evil enemy's hideout, this wasn't what I pictured.

Plastic tables covered in red and white checkered tablecloths sat ringed with folding chairs, making a cozy dining area as inviting as an outdoor summer picnic. The sleeping quarters were marked with rolled up sleeping bags stacked neatly under statues of kindly saints who I imagined watched over these children while they slept.

"Beautiful." Liam murmured.

"What is?"

"Uh… nothing." He got all weird and turned beet red in the face. What was his deal?

I thought there might something on my nose and maybe he just didn't want to tell me, but then I noticed something strange.

The softness of the fairy lights had magically turned Liam's hair into spun gold. He wore a sleepy kind of smile I hadn't seen before as the twinkling bulbs all around us reflected a galaxy of stars in his crystal-clear eyes.

"What's with you?" I asked. "You've got a goofy look on your face."

"Oh... I...." Liam cleared his throat. "This place is cooler than I thought it would be."

Ugh. That twisty thing with his mouth again. Whatever secret Liam was keeping from me this time, I'd get it out of him later. I was ready to explore.

Gamerz mostly ignored us as we shuffled our way to the front. Two girls were having a heated intellectual debate about whether Batman or Spiderman would win in a death match. Several kids were lounging on bean bag chairs reading comic books and drinking hot chocolate. I grinned when we came to the group practicing Judo on exercise mats. Training in hand-to-hand combat? Count me in.

In the alcove where prayer candles were lit, a magnificent mask in the shape of a golden skull hung on the wall surrounded by dozens of lush pink roses. Soft candlelight reflected a twinkle in its eyes as if the skull were a loved one welcoming us home.

"Looks like a memorial," Liam whispered, though I wasn't sure why. This thing didn't belong here. It's not like this tribute was part of a church service... and yet... I had to admit there was something sacred about it.

"Yeah, I suppose it is..." My eyes traveled to the only three unlit prayer candles in a sea of flame. Sticks for lighting were thrust in a bin of soft white ash. I plucked one.

For you Dad. I lit the first candle.

For you Mom. My flame caught the wick of the second.

Carlos... My hand hovered over the third candle as fire crept closer to my fingers...

No. I won't light a candle for you yet.

I blew it out as the golden skull glowed even more fiercely in the firelight. The mask was probably crafted for some fancy Halloween masquerade party... and the flowers were almost certainly from the grocery store... but it was heartbreakingly beautiful. It represented all the loved ones we lost in a way that didn't grieve them but celebrated them.

Mortal tether.

I hadn't understood what those words meant when I read them on the blackboard, but now, I knew what they meant to me. A mortal tether is what binds us to this world. It's all the beautiful things in our life that make it worth living. It's the love my parents had for me that lives inside me even though they're gone and the knowledge deep in my soul that my Mom and Dad would want me to fight and live on and find a way to be happy again. It's the hope against impossible odds I'll see my brother one day and get crushed by one of his annoying bear hugs. It's the pitch of Sara Angelina laughs when I tickle her foot. It's the deep pink of Liam's blushes when he steals glances at me and thinks I can't see.

It's love, family, and friendship and the memories that make all those relationships possible.

Liam balanced Sara on his hip, moved beside me, and lit the last candle.

"I still don't believe," he whispered. "But this one's for my parents, just in case…"

Everything was perfect, until it wasn't. A racket ripped us away from the peaceful memorial to the very front of the church where the marble altar had been transformed into a gaming center.

Televisions perched on the sacred table as blue light flickered across the unblinking eyes of digital worshippers huddled before them. A kid belched as he tossed himself down on a couch littered with empty chip wrappers. A plush leather recliner, reserved for the captain, now blocked the way to the tabernacle.

My blood boiled as I stopped to genuflect.

"You suck!" A kid chucked his controller to the floor only for it to be scooped up by the pixie-haired girl at his side. My stomach turned when I realized what they were playing.

Zombie Slayer 3.

"Over there! Get it! Get it!"

"Damn!"

"Great shot."

Slaps of high fives were smacked all around.

Tiny hairs on the back of my neck stood on end. That pixie-haired girl blowing virtual zombies away with a CG rifle… she'd practiced in the real world on the geist that used to be my mom.

"Do you know what you did?" I nearly screamed it.

"Yeah." The girl grinned. "I just smashed this idiot's top score. Why, new girl? You wanna crack at it?"

"Amaia, don't." Liam whispered at my side. But I couldn't stop myself.

"Just so you know." I clenched my fists. "You shot my mom."

The girl's head snapped up. Confusion clouded her expression, but I didn't need a mirror to know what she saw when she looked at me. I could feel it on my own face. Rage. Hate. I loathed this girl with every blood cell in my veins. I spun on the balls of my feet so the girl wouldn't see the tears flooding my eyes.

Liam followed as I trudged as far away from them as possible, back to the plastic picnic tables. He was right to stop me. If I ripped a bald spot in the pixie-haired girl's head like I wanted to, Zelda would toss us out on our butts for sure. But I wouldn't have taken revenge. Mom wouldn't want it. Besides, I could never do violence here. Not in this holy place.

I knew that girl's bullet hadn't hurt my mother's geist, but it had hurt me.

We sat in silence for a long time, listening to the laughter and hollers over the sound of bullets flying and computer generated zombies snarling across multiple television sets.

Sara's lip quivered.

"This is crazy!" I raked my hands through my hair. "After everything we've all been through, how can those idiots think that game's fun? It's sick!"

Sara Angelina was on the edge of another meltdown. I knew how she felt.

"Shhh, it's ok Sara. It's not real." Liam lifted the baby out of her carrier and bounced her on his knee, waving Waldo's toy in front of her face.

"I can't stand it," I griped. "How? Just *how*?"

Liam gave up on the toy and swapped it for a bottle. "You know, my dad told me once that when people live through something traumatic, everyone expects them to react a certain way…"

"What are you even talking about?" I snapped.

"Remember me telling you about my aunt?"

That got my attention.

"You mean…" I lowered my voice. "About why she got the gun?"

"Yeah." Liam hesitated. "What I didn't tell you before was that my aunt didn't leave my uncle the first time. Or the second. Or the third. She went back to her ex-husband over and over even though he beat her up every time."

"Why would she go back? I don't understand…"

"Me either. And I think that's my dad's point." Liam leaned into me. "People react to bad things that happen to them in ways we might not always understand. That doesn't mean they don't deserve our compassion anyway. Maybe those kids are playing Zombie Slayer 3 because that's their way of dealing with what's happened. People are… complicated."

"Yeah, well, those *complicated people* over there didn't have to trash my church," I grumbled as I fished out a jar of baby food from my backpack.

"It's *our* church now." Zelda tossed a pile of clothes on the table in front of me, making me jump in my seat. "Sometimes you have to compromise. Besides, I was always taught that it's people who are God's church, not the building."

"What compromises have you made?" I demanded.

Zelda pulled up a chair.

"When we first started doing organized search and rescues, some of my crew got it in their heads they wanted to play Zombie Nights for real. It was stupid and dangerous, but I was also formulating a strategy to keep everyone alive. I needed to know if bullets could hurt geists."

"It's horrible." I uncapped the baby food, dipped in a spoon, and slid it over to Liam.

"It just lets them blow off a little steam." Zelda shrugged. "I am never going to apologize for putting my people's survival first. I've only lost one Gamer on my watch. I made a vow. Never again."

I knew I shouldn't ask... but my mouth loves blurting out the worst possible thing sometimes.

"What happened?"

"Amaia," Liam cautioned me. "Don't."

"No, it's ok. She has a right to know." Zelda's eyes moved far away. "The night the plague hit, just before dawn, we'd already saved a bunch of kids. I had no idea that geists would become ashes again at dawn. We didn't know anything at that point. Only minutes until sunrise, we found two stray kids getting attacked on the street. One of the kids made it... but the other..."

"Oh." I traced the outline of a red square on the tablecloth with my finger. "They died?"

Zelda shifted like she had a terrible weight on her shoulders. "He fought so hard. But in the end... it wasn't enough. I swore never again am I going to lose someone like that. Nothing is more important to me than protecting my Gamerz."

For a long moment, Zelda stared at Liam as he spoon-fed Sara.

"Anyway," she continued. "I convinced the others that playing Zombie Slayer for real was a waste of ammunition since it doesn't actually *hurt* the geists. Bastards are immortal apparently. What if we have to hunt animals for food in the future? Wasting bullets could mean starving in a year. So, three days ago, we set up gaming consoles so kids can play inside the church where it's safe. I thought they'd take it hard, but so far there have been no complaints... except yours."

I fidgeted with the hem of the camouflage shirt on the table.

"Don't get me wrong, I'm glad you stopped them from using geists for target practice. It's just that... this place is supposed to be a place to talk to God. To honor God."

"I'm sorry your church isn't what you expected anymore," Zelda said. "If it really bothers you, you can bunk away from the others in the back office for now. I was going to suggest it anyway, since Sara will probably cry in the middle of the night. That's where the last baby slept."

Liam sprang up in his seat. I nearly fell out of mine.

"What do you mean 'last baby'?" Liam asked.

I noticed for the first time, a camouflage onesie Sara's size on the pile of Gamer clothing Zelda had set out on the table for us.

"We gave shelter to a girl and her three brothers who came through the second night. I picked up some baby clothes in case they come back." Zelda sighed. " I begged them to stay, but Christie went to find the rest of their family in Vermont. She wouldn't leave the baby... said she hoped to reunite the little one with her brother if she could find him after they get back. As I said, they were only here one night, but I think the office worked out good. Better for everyone for the baby to have a private space. I really want you guys to be happy here. Just let me know what you need, and I'll see it done."

A cold feeling crept up in my chest. "The baby's name... it wasn't Toni, was it?"

Zelda's posture went rigid.

"How...?" She frowned, her eyes flicking to the group of Gamerz clustered around the television.

"Not a spy," I swiped a tear that slipped down my cheek. "Her brother was a friend."

Liam clutched my hand under the table.

"I'm so sorry," Zelda said. "But you're safe here. We're not losing anyone else to the geists, I swear it."

The captain patted my shoulder and turned to rejoin her crew still hovered around the gaming console. As I watched her go, all I could think was.

We didn't lose Waldo because of geists.

We lost him because of us.

The priest's office was more luxurious than I'd expected. I never had any reason to come in this room before, though it was right down the hall from where I used to have CCD and where Carlos had his confirmation classes.

A burgundy suede sofa stretched along one wall under a shelf recessed into the wall where a statue of the Virgin Mary stood watch. The porcelain figure cradled baby Jesus sweetly in her arms while crushing a green serpent beneath her bare feet. Can a person be beautiful, gentle, loving, and fragile but also strong enough to stomp out evil? I was beginning to think it might be possible.

People are complicated.

"Liam?" I asked. "Do you get the feeling Zelda is being extra nice to me?"

"She's better than Denny, at least." He yawned as he changed Sara's diaper. I didn't think Liam understood my question, but I let it drop. What I'd meant was, why would someone so important go out of her way to make an insignificant nobody like me want to be her friend? Why does Zelda care what I think?

I didn't trust it. Denny only tried to make me feel special so he could control me. Maybe the captain was doing the same thing? But she seemed so… so… *good.*

A girl missing one of her front teeth brought in two steaming bowls of rice and beans for Liam and me around dinnertime. The church's kitchen facilities that were used to feed the homeless must have been a real bonus for the Gamerz when they found out about it. That, and the diesel generator that powered the whole building off-grid made this the next best thing to the school. One of the Gamerz said this neighborhood hadn't been affected by the power outage, so they didn't even need to use the generator yet, but they'd been making a stockpile of diesel in the basement for if they did.

Liam was smiling at me funny again. What was up with him anyway?

"Remember when I found that chocolate at Food Eagle?" he asked.

"Ugh, how can I forget? Sucks that Denny confiscated it…"

"Well, I have a confession to make… I'd actually found two chocolates. I've been saving the other one for something special." Liam pulled a shiny silver and brown wrapper from his pack and tossed it to me. "Happy Birthday."

I actually gasped.

"How did you…"

"Your birthday's on Halloween, right?" Liam blushed. "I guess you probably don't remember… your Mom invited me and my parents to your birthday party once… but we weren't there very long because your brother pelted you with a water balloon, and it exploded right in your face and you had to go to the ER… I think someone said it scratched your eyeball or something…"

"Oh!" I clasped my hands over my mouth. "You were a slice of pizza!"

"Yeah," Liam grinned sheepishly. "Pepperoni. You were a unicorn, and I think your brother was supposed to be dressed up as Einstein?"

"Carlos was trying to pop the balloon on my horn." I groaned. "My brother is proof wearing a costume doesn't make a kid smart."

Liam threw back his head and laughed.

"They made me wear an eyepatch for three weeks!" I chuckled. "Oh man… I totally forgot you were at my party." I turned the present over in my hands. "But you remembered…"

Liam rubbed the back of his neck. "It was kind of hard to forget."

I unwrapped the chocolate bar, broke off a piece, and tossed it to my best friend.

Liam let me have the sofa for a bed while he took a sleeping bag on the floor next to Sara's bassinet. She'd chewed Waldo's toy until it was a disgusting, squishy wad of spit. We had to take it away, which she threw a fit over. Now that we had a more private space, I resolved to get the baby a proper crib. And toys. A mountain of toys.

Since we didn't need money anymore, I could get her the most fancy baby things that only rich people used to be able to have. My sleepy grin stretched all the way across my face.

Despite some of the bad omens, like those televisions set up on the altar, I was beginning to feel like the church really could be home. I checked the scout phone a dozen times. No messages from Brit. Though I guessed Denny could have un-forwarded the calls...

No. I couldn't regret my decision to leave the school after what happened. No matter what, I'd do whatever it would take to find Carlos. Maybe Zelda would help me? Yeah, that's it. If Zelda wanted me to be her friend, the least she could do is help me find my brother. She rescued kids every day. Maybe she'd order her whole army of Gamerz to go looking for him? With their help, we'd find Carlitos in no time!

I knitted my fingers behind my head and stared up at the statue of The Blessed Mother who looked down on me lovingly like I was her own child. For the first time in a long time, I was safe and warm in a comfy bed. My eyelashes knit themselves together. I said a silent prayer and fell fast asleep.

"Fire!"

Was I still dreaming? Liam's voice was far away, but then suddenly he was right beside me, shaking me awake.

"Five more minutes," I grumbled and turned over.

A bell pealed as rain poured from the ceiling and splashed onto my face.

No, not rain.

The sprinkler system.

"What's happening?" I bolted awake like I'd chugged ten pots of my parents' coffee.

"We're under attack," Liam said. "The front door's on fire."

"What?"

"Unity's thugs are throwing Molotov cocktails. They've all got light suits on like the one Yvette made." Liam shoved Sara's baby things in the travel bassinet he was struggling to fold back up into a backpack again. "Denny probably convinced everyone you and me were the spies. They're here for revenge!"

I slapped my forehead. How could we have been so stupid? Leaving Xander's stolen truck parked out front like that... We led them right to us!

"What time is it?" I asked.

"An hour to sunrise. Maybe more. The fire's out of control,

but geists have the church surrounded. If we stay, we'll burn to death. But if we try to run… we'll never make it."

"Stay here with Sara." I pulled on my sneakers. "There's an emergency exit down this hall. If the flames get too close, get her out and run for the streetlights."

"Amaia! No, you can't go!"

But I was already speeding down the hall, slipping on puddles of water as I went. By the time I got to the front of the church, orange flames had completely engulfed the heavy wooden doors and were now licking the stone archway and devouring the carpet runners.

Gamerz fought fire with bottles of water, juice boxes, and half drank mugs of leftover hot chocolate. It wasn't nearly enough. Thick black smoke enveloped the vaulted ceiling high above our heads. Through the flaming, gaping hole of the now wide-open entrance, a horde of geists writhed in hungry anticipation, looking in on us like we were pizzas in a wood-fired oven.

Liam was wrong. We weren't going to burn to death or be geist chow. It was going to be a bit of both.

"Keep fighting!" Zelda shouted as she whipped flames with her sleeping bag. Just then, the heart of St. Peter exploded as a bottle shattered through a stained-glass window and shot flames on seventy sleeping bags still spread out across the floor.

"Put it out! Put it out!" Zelda screeched as kids rushed to keep up.

Nate positioned heavy yellow work lights closer to the entrance to drive the geists back.

A girl screamed as her sleeve caught fire. The flesh on her forearm blistered pink then red then black as she tried to outrun the searing pain. Two Gamerz tackled her to the hard stone floor and smothered her arm with a jacket. My stomach did a loop-de-loop at the stench of her burning flesh, a smell strangely like barbecued pig.

Yeah, I was probably gonna die tonight, but if I didn't, I just officially became a vegetarian.

Focus Amaia!

The fairy light strands strewn about the walls and ceiling melted as twinkling bulbs burst in the heat like mini grenades. Toxic fumes seared my lungs, and my brain felt like it was being squished in my skull. I stumbled over my own two feet, dizzy from lack of air. In the chaos, kids fought valiantly, but it was no use. In minutes, our sanctuary would be lost.

Everything in me was screaming *fight*. My first instinct was to fall in line with the others and snuff out the flames with my bare hands if I needed to. My church was burning. I was desperate to save it.

But it was too far gone. This war was over before it started. And now… every single kid in this building was going to die unless someone stood up and said something. I had to speak up. To hell with the consequences.

"Zelda!" I gasped through a lungful of smoke. "We need to run!"

"No!" The captain shot back. "We can't give up the church! It's too valuable. The generator… the ammunition…"

"You told me the building was just a building!" I grabbed Zelda by the arm and forced her to face me. "You said the church was the people, remember?"

The captain scanned her scrambling troops like surveying the losing side of a bloody battlefield. Several of the smaller kids were cradling their heads in their hands and sobbing as flames inched closer. She held my gaze for a moment, her eyes pleading for it not to be true.

"They'd never listen to me," I insisted. "You have to lead them out. Why are you just standing here?"

Zelda stood frozen, and in the back of my mind I remembered Dad on our living room sofa watching one of those boring old war documentaries… something about *shell shock*?

"SNAP OUT OF IT!" I shook her shoulders as hard as I could. "You said you wouldn't lose a single Gamer again, remember?… LOOK AROUND! You're about to lose them all!"

Sweat dripped down our necks in the oppressive heat, both of our chests heaving against the lack of oxygen. Her eyes hardened like steel. For a moment, I was certain she'd throw me out the front door and feed me to the geists for disobeying. It's what Denny might've done. Instead, the captain blinked a few times and gave my shoulder a squeeze.

"Thank you." Zelda breathed before she cried out above the chaos. "EVERYONE FALL BACK! Grab the work lights. Follow me! We're going out the rear exit!"

Under their captain's rallying cry, Gamerz joined together, helping fallen friends to their feet. Those with the least injuries scooped up work lights, yanked extension cords from their sockets, grabbed battery powered LED panels, and raced toward the back of the church.

We held in tight formation and squeezed our way into the back hallway. Up ahead, Liam poked his head out of the office. He had a blanket draped over Sara Angelina's carrier to keep the smoke and sprinkler water out of her face. The now soaked carpet runner squished under my sneakers as I inched forward step by step while the evacuees shuffled toward the exit.

Our orderly line quickly descended into panic as kids behind me started pushing, scrambling, shoving. We were packed in too tight. Someone slammed me into the boy in front of me, burying my face in the back of his sweaty, soaked t-shirt. Like always, I was the runt of the litter. Everyone was taller than me. I couldn't see. Suddenly, keeping my feet was the only thing keeping me alive. Would these kids trample me to death? My heart pounded as bodies closed in on me.

"Stay calm!" Nate bellowed. "Nobody panic!"

Yeah, right. It's a little late for that.

"Bring the work lights to me!" Zelda ordered. "Everybody listen up! The other side of this door is crawling with geists."

Everyone froze.

"My plan is to get everyone under the streetlights, but they're too far from the door," Zelda said. "We'll need to drag the work lights out as far as the extension cords will let us and make a pathway of light! We'll go in small groups and ferry the lights back and forth to this door. Make sure you stay close to the lights! Now, where can we plug them in?"

"There's an outlet in the office here!" Liam said.

"Good!" Zelda replied. "Everyone look for more outlets! Hurry!"

"Amaia! Your backpack!" Liam tossed my bag to me, and I slung it over my shoulders.

"Battery powered lights go to the injured!" Nate commanded.

I remembered the flashlight in my bag and spun to take the pack off. She was right behind me.

At first, there was only confusion in her green eyes. Her mouth hung open as she reached for me, both of us uncertain if the other was a ghost.

"Brit?"

"Amaia! Come quick!" Brit motioned for me to follow and spun away, pushing through the crowd and darting down the stairwell leading to the church basement.

"Wait! Stop!" I lurched forward through the mass of bodies pressing the opposite way, like a minnow swimming upstream against the current. Zelda and the others were too distracted setting up the work lights to take any notice.

I broke free from the river of kids and bolted down the empty staircase.

The last time I'd been in the church basement was for the annual bake sale, but now instead of fresh baked cookies, the room was saturated with the odor of charred wood and burning carpet.

"I can't get him out," Brit cried as she reached her fingers into the cage. "We have to do something!"

The whole world moved in slow motion. The embers on the far side of the ceiling glowed as the floor above threatened to cave in. Stacks of automatic weapons and rifles were piled alongside ammunition in a haphazard armory. I recognized the five gallon buckets of diesel from Jayden's prisoner exchange, with a pyramid of at least twenty more beside them. Far away from all that, on our side of the room, were many things of little consequence. A portable TV. Two sleeping bags. A paper cup with two toothbrushes next to a comb laid out on a rickety table. But it wasn't any of those things that made my heart stop.

Waves of heat danced between us. He appeared as a mirage. A desert oasis. A miraculous living thing surrounded by death and heat.

My brother's dark brown eyes watched me in horror.

"Hermanita!" Carlos cried. "What are you doing here? Get out! Get out *now!*"

"I don't have the key!" Brit yanked the lock. "Please... help me!"

"Carlos, you stupid jerk!" Angry tears stormed down my face. "I thought you were dead!"

"Oh my God. Brit, what were you thinking?!" Carlos gripped the bars of his cage. "How could you bring Amaia here?! I told you to go!"

"But I can't leave you here, I can't..." Brit stifled a sob. "I love you. Amaia can help me look for something to break the lock. We've got to look for something..."

"Babe." His voice turned hard. "If you really love me, you won't let my little sister die here. Please Brit. You two gotta go."

"Knock it off Carlos!" I snapped. "Brit was right to get me. So, shut up you two and let me think before we all burn to death!" The ceiling above me crackled and hissed.

"Jodóna!" Carlos punched the iron bars with a fist. "Mom and Dad put me in charge. You have do do what I say! And I say, *get yourselves out!!!*"

I whipped off my backpack and tossed out the pacifier, diapers, and a can of formula until I found what I was looking for. When I pulled my fist out of the bag it held my father's hammer.

Carlos lept back in surprise and pressed himself against the rear of the cage.

A battle cry rose from my gut as the hammer fell.

Bang!

"How dare you leave me in that attic?" I smashed the lock again.

Bang!

"Do you have any idea how scared I was?"

Bang!

"45 minutes *in case you hit traffic*?! It's been a week!"

Bang!

"Then you don't even tell me where you are so I could come rescue you? Of all the stupid-machismo-fueled-idiotic decisions… and you dare call *me* jodóna?! Carajo! You're the one who is a pain in the butt! WHEN I GET YOU OUT OF THERE, I'M GOING TO KILL YOU!"

Bang!

Crack!

The lock popped open. I ripped it off the latch and chucked the mangled metal across the room as Carlos burst through the door, gathering me up in his powerful arms. My toes lightly brushed the ground as my brother carried me toward the stairwell with Brit two steps behind, the flaming roof groaning under its own weight behind us.

"Ok, fine." Carlos grinned. "Maybe Mom and Dad should've left you in charge."

The last group stood anxiously on the threshold of the emergency exit when Carlos, Brit, and I finally burst out from the basement. Liam had refused to leave without me and made them wait, clutching Sara's car seat to his chest with the baby strapped inside.

"Amaia! Where were… oh, wow!" Liam's mouth popped open then burst into a grin as the three of us barreled toward him.

A ground-shattering crash reverberated through the body of the church. Part of the floor had finally collapsed. How long until the flames would reach that stockpile of diesel and guns?

"Go, go, go, we gotta move!" a Gamer cried. He didn't have to tell us twice.

Work lights illuminated our path as a crowd of geists thrashed and foamed at the mouth on either side of us. Every instinct in me was screaming to run, but we could only inch our way forward, tethered to the work lights, gently pulling them with us as far as they'd go. Up ahead, nearly all Gamerz were already huddled safely under the glow of streetlights that illuminated the church's parking lot. Ten of us lingered in this last group.

The first extension cord pulled taught.

"Careful not to yank it out of the socket!" Liam cautioned the boy dragging the light. Geists weaved forward and backward, testing our reflexes.

Fifteen feet of shadow stood between us and the rest of the Gamerz.

Geists were already filling the gap.

"We need those handheld LEDs!" I shouted to the captain.

Zelda frowned at Carlos.

"I'll stay by these lights," my brother called out to her. "Just help the others get to safety!"

"No!" My voice broke. "Zelda, please! You can't leave him out here!"

The work lights flickered.

"Captain?" Nate turned expectant eyes on her.

Zelda pressed her lips in a tight line and nodded. "Do it."

In a flash, a small group of Gamerz advanced on us armed with LED lights. It was the digital worshippers, those same kids who'd been playing video games at the altar. They moved like an elite team of soldiers, a well-oiled machine that had spent countless hours training just for this moment.

"Three o'clock!"

A geist lunged. The stroke of my hammer missed. Just as its hand wrapped around my throat, the pixie-haired girl swooped in to my rescue, forcing the demon back with her handheld light. The monster squealed and raised its hands to shield its face. Its flesh sizzled, making me gag on the stench of grilled-geist.

She just risked her life to save mine.

"I missed the shot," she said breathlessly. "I need you to know that. I've never hit a female geist. Not ever."

My eyes were locked on hers in amazement, but I caught a low shadow reaching for her leg. "Behind you!" I pulled her forward as the head of my hammer came crashing down on a geist's claw, sending fragments of bone and nail clattering to the pavement. The geist hissed, but the girl drove it back again with her LED.

"Hang tight," she said. "Stay by the work light. I'll get you on the next pass."

Liam clutched Sara's car seat carrier tighter to his chest.

Only fifteen feet.

There weren't enough LEDs to cover everyone, so Gamerz ferried two kids at a time across the darkened abyss. Carlos, Brit, Liam, Me, and two boys were left stranded on a shrinking island, desperate to be rescued.

The Gamerz were heading back for me when a massive explosion shook the ground beneath us, flooding the air with a quick burst of light and heat and shrapnel. Everyone screamed, including the geists. I pressed my hands over my ears and ducked my head as bits of debris smashed across my back, leaving welts and bruises in their wake. A piercing ring echoed through my brain as I struggled to stand. When I opened my eyes, I could barely see.

Because the work lights had switched off.

"Run!"

We made a mad dash, but geists swooped in like vultures on roadkill. A gray hand grabbed Liam by his collar and swung him back as another monster began to wrestle the baby carrier from his arms. Sara was screaming. The two boys and Brit cried out and scattered as geists darted after them like a game of man hunt.

"Liam!" I nailed a geist in the face with my hammer and pushed forward, but Liam was swept out of my reach.

"Amaia!" he screeched as a geist yanked him into the shadows. "Help!"

I crouched, ready to sprint through hell to Liam's rescue, but Carlos put me in a bear hug and yanked me back. My hammer slipped out of my fingers, arms pinned to my sides. I kicked my legs with all my might, landing blow after blow to the geists that descended upon us. All the while, I whipped my head from side to side, trying to keep my eyes on Liam and Sara. My linebacker brother wrapped me in his embrace like I was a human football, and with a burst of strength, we barreled forward and rolled across the concrete into the safety of the streetlight.

"No!"

Sara's baby blanket flew through the air.

Liam screamed.

Under the terror in his voice, there was something else.

Something I knew well.

A battle cry.

The hairs on my neck prickled.

Through a wall of geists, I caught a glimpse of Liam head-butting the monster gripping Sara's carrier. He wrestled it free and drew his elbow back to nail another geist right in the throat, but his spaghetti noodle arms weren't strong enough to make the creature release its hold on him. Shadows roiled in the dark.

"Let go of me!" I thrashed and squirmed with all of my hamster-like upper body strength. My brother held firm. "I've got to help him!"

Geists poured in from all sides. Liam shrunk in the middle of an insurmountable ocean of death that couldn't be crossed by either of us. Another explosion rocked the church, this one more epic than before. A fireball shot high across the night sky like a meteor. Everyone cried out at the burst of light and sound and shrapnel. The geists closest to the church exploded into ash, but many more had only been stunned. In that split second while the geists were recovering, Liam broke free from their grasp and sprinted through the only opening he had.

The one that led farther into the darkness.

Geists reached for him, but he ducked and dodged their swiping claws. Liam disappeared around the front of the church, trailing half the horde after him.

"LET ME GO!" I screamed. "SOMEBODY DO SOMETHING!"

I bit Carlos' forearm to force him to release his grip. He gasped in pain but only held me tighter. Salty blood dripped off my lips and trickled down his arm.

"He's gone, hermanita," Carlitos whispered in my ear. "Let him go."

"No." My voice broke. "No. I've got to help him. I can save him… I can…"

Everyone stared. The look of pity in their eyes made me want to bash every one of their faces in with my fist. Brit wrapped her arms around my brother and me, hugging us both and stroking my hair as I sobbed violently. I didn't want to be comforted. I wanted to run after Liam and Sara and kill every single geist that got in my way… But Carlos wouldn't budge.

We all waited, listening. How many seconds had passed since Liam's footsteps faded in the distance? How many minutes?

It was quieter than a funeral in my head. The snarls of lurking geists faded into silence as I stared unblinking in the direction Liam had gone. This wasn't right. It wasn't supposed to end like this. Liam and me and Sara Angelina were a family. We were supposed to live happily ever after.

Kids started whispering condolences, but I refused to listen to their pathetic 'I'm so sorrys' and 'I'm sure it was over quick' or any of that other meaningless nonsense that wouldn't bring my Liam back to me.

Liam and Sara weren't dead. They couldn't be.

Please was the only word I had left. *Please. Please. Please.*

The garbled chimes didn't make sense to my brain at first, like a broken music box searching for a melody.

Music?

My eyes grew wide.

The Entertainer.

The ice cream truck peeled around the corner on two wheels, its engine growling like a lone wolf fighting for its life. A geist smashed into the windshield and rolled onto the roof, spitting and hissing as it got tangled in the barbed wire. Tires squealed as they swerved left and right in erratic jerks. Geists were crunchy road bumps under four thundering wheels as the ice cream truck plowed through them without slowing. Suddenly, the headlights blasted on, igniting a massive explosion of ash before our eyes. A waft of burnt rubber stung my nostrils as the vehicle skidded to a stop right in front of our streetlight.

Eighty children held their breaths.

Wipers scraped and squeaked over a dry windshield as the driver scooted across the bench seat and vaulted himself out the passenger side door.

"Liam!" I peeled Carlos' hands off me and flew over the concrete. I launched myself at my best friend, smashing us both into the side of the truck as I wrapped my arms around him.

Liam and I cried like maniacs, but neither of us cared who saw.

"I pushed all the buttons, but I couldn't figure out how to turn on the headlights." Liam sobbed into my hair.

"At least you found the gas pedal this time," I said.

"Ha!" He smiled and brushed tears from his cheeks. "Almost didn't. But I didn't freeze! Did you see me? I didn't freeze!"

"I saw! Is Sara ok?"

"Sara's fine. She's right here."

"Are you ok? Were you bitten?" I grabbed his face in my hands and twisted it from side to side, inspecting him.

"I don't think so." Liam rubbed his forehead where he'd head-butted it on the geist's face. "But I think I've got another bruise."

People really must be complicated after all, because for reasons I can't explain, Liam and I both burst into hysterics. I laughed so hard I nearly peed my pants, though I didn't, thank God. We hugged each other tight, but when our giggles subsided, our embrace didn't end. The melody of the ice cream truck's song must have put some spell on us because we were still in each other's arms, rocking and swaying to the music.

Wait. What?

Was this... was I... was I *slow dancing* with a boy? No. That's impossible. If I were slow dancing with a boy I'd be totally nervous. But this wasn't just a *boy*. This was Liam. My Liam.

And it's not like ice cream truck music really counted as slow-danceable music anyway.

Did it?

Sara Angelina scolded us from her carrier, demanding our attention like the little diva she was. I didn't mind. To my utter relief, she'd been strapped into her carrier, and other than being a bit jostled, Sara didn't have a scratch on her. Liam lifted the baby high into the air, spinning and twirling and turning this little corner of the parking lot into our own personal ballroom. Sara's laugh told me she loved dancing with Liam more than anything. I blushed hard and bit my lower lip because… well… I kinda knew how she felt.

Of course, I'd never tell *him* that.

"Did everybody make it?" Zelda was frantically doing a headcount. "Where's Carol? I don't see her…"

"Here!" A little blonde girl raised her hand.

"Miles? Owen? Delphine?" Zelda whipped her head from side to side, scanning the huddled groups of kids under the lights.

"All accounted for Captain. I triple checked." Nate raised an LED to force back geists that had ventured too close. "We're all here."

"We got everyone out…" Zelda took a wobbly step forward as her shoulders sagged under an unseen weight. Then this brilliant, strong, invincible leader did something I'd never have expected. She fell to her knees, buried her face in her hands, and cried as she said *Thank You God* over and over again.

To say we were all stunned would be the understatement of the century. One by one, Gamerz gathered around her in a circle and put their hands on her shoulders, comforting their captain as she wept.

That's when it hit me: the difference between Zelda and Denny. Unity feared and respected Denny. That's why they obeyed him. But he wasn't loved.

Zelda was loved.

As ticked off as I was that she'd locked my brother in that cage for getting bit by a geist, I couldn't bring myself to hate Zelda for it. She was just trying to protect her family. I understood that. Besides, she was just a kid too, after all. Somehow, God had given her the strength to deliver us all from flames and demons. Zelda wasn't perfect, but if anything called for sainthood, I'd say what she did tonight was pretty close.

Carlos and Brit held each other and did a lot more kissing than Mom would have felt was appropriate, but I let it slide. After all, Brit loved my idiot brother enough to risk her life to save him. Maybe the cheerleader wasn't so bad after all…

I turned my eyes up to the stars. The Milky Way stretched overhead like the rainbow after a storm. It was a promise that there was light everywhere, even far away in the darkest of places.

I searched for the big dipper, but my cup already felt full. I silently thanked God for letting me find my brother and for bringing Liam and Sara Angelina back to me. No matter what, now that we were together, I knew my life would be happy again. That was a future I really could look forward to.

As the church blazed before us, the brightness drove most of the geists away. Zelda turned on the LED panels covering the ice cream truck and Nate treated those who had been wounded in the fire with a first aid kit from the glove compartment.

We carefully moved farther and farther from the blaze until the sky turned from black to purple to pink. Now that the scary part was over, the golden sun was finally brave enough to peek over the horizon to see how our story would end. As the last geist exploded back into a glittering cloud, we left the shelter of the streetlights and ventured out into a brand-new day.

With the smoldering ruins disappearing in the distance, me and my familia broke off from the Gamerz to strike out on our own.

Zelda didn't argue. Instead, she generously handed an LED panel to Carlos as a parting gift. Though she didn't apologize for keeping my brother caged in the basement or for forgetting about him in the chaos when the fire started, I took her present as a sign the captain was having a change of heart.

Carlos kept a scowl on his face until the Gamerz were out of sight. Then his frown melted into a grin that lit up so bright, I thought his smile could explode a geist just by itself.

"Thanks for protecting my little sister!" Carlos pulled Liam into one of his colossal bear hugs. "I seriously owe you, kid."

Poor Liam, my brother was squeezing him so hard his face was nearly the same blue as his eyes. He squirmed like a captured chipmunk and was mortified by the time my burly brother finally set him down.

"I didn't." Liam blushed furiously. "Amaia's the one who saved me. I wouldn't have lasted one day without her."

My big brother rolled his eyes and shot me a disbelieving smirk. It was useless. Liam could never convince Carlos that his little sister was a hammer-wielding geist-fighter.

I smiled to myself because I knew the truth.

They were both wrong.

Liam and I saved each other.

EPILOGUE

Brit turned out to be way cooler than I thought.

Our first night away from the Gamerz, we had a heart-to-heart where she filled me in on the play-by-play of everything that happened after Carlos tried to take her to the hospital on Dad's motorcycle... and I finally understood why Zelda had been so desperate to make me like her.

Guilt.

The captain couldn't live with herself losing a Gamer under her watch... there was only one kid Zelda tried to save but couldn't...

It was Carlos.

It'd happened the night my brother left me in the attic. After saving Liam and wiping out on Dad's motorcycle, Carlos had become trapped under the safety of a porch light just as we'd suspected. But Zelda, Nate, and some other kids drove by just before dawn. Zelda pressured Carlos into making a run for their truck. In typical Carlos-trying-to-be-a-hero fashion, he used himself as a decoy so that the Gamerz could rescue Brit first. But my brother couldn't outrun the monsters. He bore the scars on his arms, legs, face, and neck. Miraculously, Carlos had fought his way out of a tangle of death and made it to the truck alive.

The Gamerz wished he hadn't.

Zelda and the other kids were violently convinced getting bit by a geist would turn a kid into one. Wasn't that the plot of nearly every single zombie movie and video game? When did we all stop believing movies were make-believe and start treating them like textbooks?

But the truth was far more terrifying than any RPG. The Plague of Ashes was a respiratory disease brought on by an alien virus, and every single one of us was infected already. And unless someone finds a cure… we'll all be geists in the end.

During his imprisonment, Carlos had been kicking the bars of his cage and screaming that he had to get out to save his little sister hiding in the attic. By this time, Zelda realized Carlos would've been safe if she'd just left him under the porch light instead of convincing him to get in her truck. To ease the guilt of her mistake, Zelda and her Gamerz went to my house on one of their search and rescue missions. Brit got there early and found the note I'd left for my brother, pocketing it before the others could see.

Because the geists had torn my house to shreds and the attic was empty, the Gamerz in the rescue party assumed I was a goner.

But Zelda discovered I was alive.

She had seen me earlier that morning when she'd spied me outside Food Eagle conspiring to help free Jayden. If she'd have known who I was, she wouldn't have let me go to Denny. Turns out, the house that Gamer kid mentioned they were going to after raiding the grocery store… was *my house*.

Even Zelda thought I was dead for a few minutes until she recognized me in the family portrait in my parents' room and knew not only that I was alive but that I was headed to Unity.

The captain tried to soften Carlos' anguish by offering that, instead of diesel, she could trade Jayden for me. But my brother didn't trust Zelda (for good reason) so he had Brit take a huge risk by stealing his phone back (which had been confiscated) and warning me to stay at the school.

Brit and Carlos had fought about it like crazy. She was desperate to tell me the truth, but my brother was afraid I'd do something extreme if I knew. He thought the only way I wouldn't risk my own safety was if I thought he was dead. He wasn't wrong. If I had known Zelda was keeping Carlos in a cage, I'd have burned down the church myself if that's what it took to get him back...

I decided to forgive Zelda for what she did to Carlitos. We expect the heroes to always be good and the villains to be straight-up evil. But that's not how life works. Sometimes the hero does something horrible they don't even understand is wrong. Sometimes the villain's agenda might actually end up curing a plague. There's light and dark inside each of us. From a distance, whether a person is good or bad really isn't black and white, but more like shades of gray.

The Gamerz found the perfect hideout, one that wasn't likely to burn down so easily this time around. The fire house came with a ton of new perks too, including sweet new rides. The twin set of shiny red fire engines were even more attention grabbing than the ice cream truck. The ladders would come in handy too, in case any kids needed to escape out of attic windows. More and more survivors were rescued every day, and within weeks, Zelda had saved hundreds.

Tensions escalated with Denny's crew. Several Gamerz demanded revenge for the attack on the church. The captain wouldn't allow it. Zelda had vowed not to lose another Gamer under her watch, and a war with Unity was the quickest way to break that promise. Zelda's calls for peace made their way into Unity, and Denny nearly had an uprising on his hands when his own people began protesting the violence done by their side. It turned out, once kids started speaking up, they had a whole lot to say... including demanding their phones back.

Zelda told me the protests were her spy's idea.

Xander said he did it for Waldo.

Weeks turned to months. My little familia had set up shop in Golding's Hardware and spent most of our time building new light rigs, setting up solar panels, and getting fuel for generators to keep the lights on. After we got our defenses set up, there was time for fun things too. Liam set up an indoor hydroponic garden. Carlos taught Brit how to salsa.

I went back home (wearing a suit modeled after Yvette's design) and got my dad's chess set out of the attic. Songbirds had made nests up there because of the smashed window I'd broken to toss out unbreakables the day we'd left.

The toy box seemed so much smaller than I'd remembered it. A nest of brown twigs filled with blue speckled eggs was perched on top of the lid, and I smiled at the new family who'd moved into my old house. The mother bird flew in and chirped angrily at me, evicting me from her property. My footsteps creaked softly as I made my way down the ladder for the last time.

There were two other treasures I decided to take: a pocket-sized family photo of the four of us and Abuela's recipe book she had passed down to Mom. I'd never get to have my Mom's cooking again, but maybe with enough practice, my *arroz con gandules* could get close.

I stopped to cry for a while, sitting at the foot of my parents' bed. A memory ran through my vision. I'd once lost a tooth and ran in here first thing in the morning, proudly showing off my four dollars from the tooth fairy. Dad said I could use it to buy ice cream when the truck came around, but only if I shared with my brother.

I wiped my eyes and caught a glimpse of myself in Mom's mirror.

Something in my face had changed these past months, and now I looked more like her than ever before. My reflection wavered through my tears as the corners of my mouth curled.

I even had her smile.

Defectors from both sides sought us out, and though it wasn't always easy to accommodate so many new mouths to feed, we never turned any kid away. If we were going to build a new world, we couldn't leave anyone behind. Each individual was precious. Who knows how one person could tip the scales?

If you were to have told me the things I would've been capable of the night I stuffed myself in the toy box, I'd have thought you were talking about some other Amaia. I'd never have believed I could be that brave. But faced with nearly losing the last people left in the world who I loved more than my own life, I found my courage.

If you truly love someone, you'll fight for them.

Fighting doesn't always mean wielding a hammer. Sometimes it means taking a hard job and doing something you don't want to do. And sometimes fighting for someone means holding them when they cry and helping them remember how to breathe.

In other news, Sara Angelina finally started talking.

It was utterly ridiculous that the first word out of her mouth was my name.

"Ah muh muh!" her voice squeaked like a mouse. We'd all assumed she was just babbling nonsense until finally one day she blurted out, "Ah muh yah!"

We all gasped, unsure we'd heard her correctly. But once she learned how to say it, I couldn't get her to stop. Sara insisted on my undivided attention whenever I was in the room and would nag me until she got it. Maybe I was just getting soft, but it made me happy Sara finally decided to like me. Of course, I rubbed it in Liam's face to no end.

He was crushed.

"Lee-yam," he shouted at Sara in slow motion. "Say 'lee-yam'! Come on Sara, you can do it! It's easier than *Amaia*. Lee-yam!"

"AH-MY-YAH!" She giggled and flung fistfuls of smashed peas at his face. "AH-MY-YAH!"

Sara Angelina was a tough little cookie. Stubborn. She also got a kick out of torturing the boys. Reminded me of myself. I guess the baby and me were destined to get along after all.

But more than that… me, Liam, Carlos, and Brit… we're her family now. Not the one she was born into, but the one she found and made her own.

There are so many things I can't wait to teach my little sister as she grows. Not how to tie her shoelaces now that she's also starting to walk, I'll let Liam handle that. But other things I only learned recently myself…

I want her to grow up knowing that a person can be both sweet and tough, fragile and strong… and just because a girl's in distress doesn't mean she's a damsel in distress. It's ok to need help. It's ok to break down and have to be rescued. In fact, sometimes asking for help is the bravest thing we can possibly do.

Eleven months after the church burned, Gamerz and Unity finally called an official truce. My familia stocked up a big stash of chocolates and diesel before sending messages to arrange a meeting between the three leaders for a barter exchange. It was easy to contact the Gamerz, just follow the sounds of the ice cream truck and fire engines. And luckily, we still had the old scout phone programmed with Denny's number.

Being leader of our group was not in my game plan, but somehow, I got stuck with the job. Carlos and Liam both agreed I'd get along with Denny and Zelda better than either of them could. There was no arguing with that. Carlos would probably knock Denny's teeth out if he met him in person. He still hadn't forgiven him for nearly blowing us all up.

A shopping bag full of chocolates was for Unity, and we siphoned three buckets of diesel for the Gamerz. In turn, we requested to fully charge all our dead batteries at the school and trade Zelda's crew for bottled water, rice, and beans.

Zelda requested the meeting take place on neutral ground, but I insisted it take place at my old school. I missed my friends Yvette and Tyrell and was anxious for the scoop on what was going on behind the walls of that brick fortress. I'd heard the kids in the biology lab had finally gotten those special microscopes they needed, and I was eager to know their progress.

Even though Denny was a cut-throat jerk who almost got us all killed, he was also the only one with the ambition and resources to try to find a cure. Denny would be working Unity around the clock til it happened. Sooner or later, some young brainiac somewhere in the world would find a way to stop the spread of the Plague of Ashes. I just hoped they figured it out before Carlos' twentieth birthday.

We still had three years to go.

No matter what happened, I knew that life is short. Who knows how much time we have left, plague or no plague? All we can do is cherish the people we love, dance every time there's music, and walk in the light as much as we can.

DISCUSSION QUESTIONS
BOOK CLUBS & CLASSROOMS

1. What are the major themes in Mortal Tether?
2. Does Amaia's faith impact her decision making? Why or why not?
3. Liam freezes when faced with paralyzing fear. What events lead to him finally being able to overcome this?
4. Both Zelda and Denny try to save the world in their own ways. Compare and contrast the two leaders. Which one do you believe actually has the potential to save the most people?
5. Who was the character in Mortal Tether you identify with most?
6. Xander is a loner who will do anything to survive. Why do you believe he tried so hard to toughen Waldo up?
7. After everything he'd done, why do you think Amaia acted to save Xander when he was being attacked by geists on the microscope mission?
8. Why do you think Yvette agreed to do propaganda videos for Denny? Do you think being the face of those videos would make her more or less powerful in the future?
9. Why do you think it was important to Denny to

confiscate everyone's phones? Was there a flaw in this plan?

10. Do you think Zelda was right to take the precaution of locking up Carlos? If not, what should she have done instead?

11. Do you believe a cure for the Plague of Ashes will be found? Why or Why not?

12. The children believe the plague was started by an alien virus that came down on a meteor. Do you agree with this theory?

13. In your opinion, was the most memorable scene in the story?

14. Amaia makes references to Lord of the Flies and Animal Farm. Do you see any parallels between this story and those?

15. How did Amaia change throughout the course of the novel? How did Liam?

16. What does the poem written on the blackboard in chapter 19 mean to you?

17. Amaia says, "Liam and I saved each other." In what ways is this true?

18. What qualities does Liam possess that make him a better caregiver for Sara than Amaia is?

19. When she returns to the toy box, Amaia notices it seems much smaller than it did when she was last there. Why do you think she feels this way?

20. Where do you see the cast of characters 3 years in the future?

DEAR READER

Thank you so much for taking the time
to read my novel. It means the world to me!

If you are interested in the upcoming Mortal Tether sequel,
please make sure you are subscribed to my free newsletter
to be the first to know when it's available.
Sign up at candicejarrett.substack.com.

If you enjoyed this book, please consider leaving a review
(or even just taking a few seconds to leave a star rating)
on Amazon, Goodreads, or BookBub.
Reviews & ratings help me get higher up in search results
so more readers can discover my book!

If you're on social media, drop me a line to say hello!
I'd love to hear from you.

Candice Jarrett

At its heart, Mortal Tether is a coming of age story about the bonds that make a family. Sometimes those bonds are DNA and shared childhoods. Other times, they are friendships so deep and soul-changing that your friend becomes part of your fam.

So, I'll start off my epic list of people I need to thank with my family and friends. First, my husband Chris, Mom, and my Aunt Carol P. who were the first people to read it and all let me talk their ears off about this book incessantly for the last five years while offering support and encouragement in return. That's love right there. And especially Dad and Liv for celebrating every milestone, always lifting me up, and for being proud of me. Love you all so much.

I want to especially thank my Great Aunt Dolores who - at 93 years old - has been the biggest cheerleader of me writing this book and encouraged me to shoot as high as I could designing an awesome cover. She keeps telling me I'm going to be a famous author one day, and the fact she believes that so wholeheartedly makes me smile.*

Special shoutout as well to my stellar team of beta readers (none of whom I'm married or related to) Luke, Cynthia, and Katy for giving me powerful and unbiased feedback, for asking tough questions, and for being so excited for this book to be published.

In my journey to publish this book, I spent a considerable amount of time querying the novel. Therefore, I want to thank Janet Reid who helped me craft a solid pitch for my story as part of that process. Thanks also to authors Rachel R., Karen Neary Smithson, Emma Lombard, and D. Dalton for their support and feedback on my query and pitch. Thanks again to Karen and D. Dalton and also to authors David Buzan, Michael Fletcher, and Elizabeth Hutchison Bernard for agreeing to write peer reviews as fellow authors. Appreciate you all!

After seven complete redesigns and endless hours of obsessing over it, I must thank my amazing nephews, cousin Jessica, and goddaughter Del for their invaluable feedback on the cover design. Thank you to my Grandma Joan and my Great Aunt Carol for being in the most wonderful book club ever and broadening the scope of the books I'm introduced to. Thanks also to my incredible in-laws (my MIL was the first person to sign up for my newsletter when I made the announcement!), Nick, Nadia (+1), Matthew Kreiner, John Keller, Courtney Nacco, Dr. Liang and Ayi for all your love and support over the years. And to all my family & friends whose names aren't written here: please know your names are written in my heart. Thank you all.

To my Gold and Silver Supporters: thank you for helping me fund my book launch! Appreciate you Sean Loftus, DonMega, Victor Rivera, AverageAndy, Rich Armstrong (AKA TapTapKaboom), Greg & Kate Treece, Kenny Nash, Lawrence Lowe, Jerry Smith and FigurativelyT, Jonah Lambo, ieatpngs.avax, 0xbayo.avax, ieatjpegs.avax, Mr. Wonderland, and Wrathtank (also for the amazing first ever artwork of a geist!). Doing this without a publisher has been tough, and your support has helped me get navigate some big early hurdles. Thank you all so much for believing in me.

Thank you to my Grandfather who was and remains the greatest storyteller I have ever known. I cherished every word. And thank you to my Grandma Marie. Her powerful influence in my own childhood shaped the course of these pages. (Que Dios Te Bendiga.) Thank you to Wally and Elsie for encouraging me to write with the gift of a diary when I was still a small child. You are all loved and remembered.

Last but certainly not least, I want to thank you dear reader. You could have spent these last several hours doing literally anything else, but instead you took a chance and dove into this world I created. It means so much to me.

Though I originally wrote Mortal Tether to be a standalone, I have fallen in love with this world and characters so much that I'm not quite ready to leave them. That being the case, I have begun work on the sequel to Mortal Tether. If you would like to be notified of it, please sign up for my newsletter at candicejarrett.substack.com. I very rarely send email, only for big announcements like this. ♥

Thank you from the bottom of my heart for sharing this journey with me.

I wrote this acknowledgement about my Aunt Dolores before she passed away and decided to dedicate the book to her.

ABOUT THE AUTHOR

Before embarking on her career as an author, Candice Jarrett has been known as an award-winning songwriter who performed on stages and television shows around the world. In addition to songwriting, Candice also wrote a play which was produced Off-Off Broadway in New York City.

Mortal Tether is the second novel Candice has written, but the first she has published.

Candice adores looking for seashells at the beach, eavesdropping on the conversations of songbirds, swimming with sea-turtles, Scrabble, and mint chocolate chip ice cream. She lives in a motorhome with her husband (and puppy!) and goes where the road and her heart takes her.

For more information, visit Candice's website at CandiceJarrett.com.

twitter.com/candijarrett

amazon.com/author/candicejarrett

goodreads.com/candicejarrett

bookbub.com/profile/candice-jarrett

tiktok.com/@bookvideo

youtube.com/@bookvideos

instagram.com/candice_jarrett

facebook.com/candicejarrettofficial

www.ingramcontent.com/pod-product-compliance
Lightning Source LLC
Chambersburg PA
CBHW020134310726

48970CB00006B/1860